LONE RIDER

Center Point
Large Print

Also by B. J. Daniels and available from Center Point Large Print:

The Montana Hamiltons
  Wild Horses

LONE RIDER

B. J. Daniels

CENTER POINT LARGE PRINT
THORNDIKE, MAINE

The text of this Large Print edition is unabridged.
In other aspects, this book may vary
from the original edition.
Printed in the United States of America
on permanent paper.
Set in 16-point Times New Roman type.

ISBN: 978-1-68324-089-1

Library of Congress Cataloging-in-Publication Data

Names: Daniels, B. J., author.
Title: Lone rider / B. J. Daniels.
Description: Center Point Large Print edition. | Thorndike, Maine : Center Point Large Print, 2016.
Identifiers: LCCN 2016024193 | ISBN 9781683240891
   (hardcover : alk. paper)
Subjects: LCSH: Large type books. | GSAFD: Western stories.
Classification: LCC PS3554.A56165 L66 2016 | DDC 813/.54—dc23
LC record available at https://lccn.loc.gov/2016024193

This book is dedicated to my cousins,
Sandy Olinger and Jackie Bowers.
Thanks so much for being my first audience.
When we were kids, they would sit quietly
in the tent at the lake and listen to my stories.
Thanks for believing in me.

Chapter
ONE

The moment Jace Calder saw his sister's face, he feared the worst. His heart sank. Emily, his troubled little sister, had been doing so well since she'd gotten the job at the Sarah Hamilton Foundation in Big Timber, Montana.

"What's wrong?" he asked as he removed his Stetson, pulled up a chair at the Big Timber Java coffee shop and sat down across from her. Tossing his hat on the seat of an adjacent chair, he braced himself for bad news.

Emily blinked her big blue eyes. Even though she was closing in on twenty-five, he often caught glimpses of the girl she'd been. Her pixie cut, once a dark brown like his own hair, was dyed black. From thirteen on, she'd been piercing anything she could. At sixteen she'd begun getting tattoos and drinking. It wasn't until she'd turned seven-teen that she'd run away, taken up with a thirty-year-old biker drug-dealer thief and ended up in jail for the first time.

But while Emily still had the tattoos and the piercings, she'd changed after the birth of her daughter, and after snagging this job with Bo Hamilton.

"What's wrong is Bo," his sister said. Bo had insisted her employees at the foundation call her by her first name. "Pretty cool for a boss, huh?" his sister had said at the time. He'd been surprised. That didn't sound like the woman he knew.

But who knew what was in Bo's head lately. Four months ago her mother, Sarah, who everyone believed dead the past twenty-two years, had suddenly shown up out of nowhere. According to what he'd read in the papers, Sarah had no memory of the past twenty-two years.

He'd been worried it would hurt the foundation named for her. Not to mention what a shock it must have been for Bo.

Emily leaned toward him and whispered, "Bo's . . . She's gone."

"Gone?"

"Before she left Friday, she told me that she would be back by ten this morning. She hasn't shown up, and no one knows where she is."

That *did* sound like the Bo Hamilton he knew. The thought of her kicked up that old ache inside him. He'd been glad when Emily had found a job in town and moved back to town with her baby girl. But he'd often wished her employer had been anyone but Bo Hamilton—the woman he'd once asked to marry him.

He'd spent the past five years avoiding Bo, which wasn't easy in a county as small as Sweet Grass. Crossing paths with her, even after five years, still hurt. It riled him in a way that only made him mad at himself for letting her get to him after all this time.

"What do you mean, *gone?*" he asked now.

Emily looked pained. "I probably shouldn't be telling you this—"

"Em," he said impatiently. She'd been doing so well at this job, and she'd really turned her life around. He couldn't bear the thought that Bo's disappearance might derail her second chance. Em's three-year-old daughter, Jodie, desperately needed her mom to stay on track.

Leaning closer again, she whispered, "Apparently there are funds missing from the foundation. An auditor's been going over all the records since Friday."

He sat back in surprise. No matter what he thought of Bo, he'd never imagined this. The woman was already rich. She wouldn't need to divert funds . . .

"And that's not the worst of it," Emily said. "I was told she's on a camping trip in the mountains."

"So, she isn't really gone."

Em waved a hand. "She took her camping gear, saddled up and left Saturday afternoon. Apparently she's the one who called the auditor, so she knew he would be finished and wanting to talk to her this morning!"

Jace considered this news. If Bo really were on the run with the money, wouldn't she take her passport and her SUV as far as the nearest airport? But why would she run at all? He doubted Bo had ever had a problem that her daddy, the senator, hadn't fixed for her. She'd always had a safety net. Unlike him.

He'd been on his own since eighteen. He'd been a senior in high school, struggling to pay the bills, hang on to the ranch and raise his wild kid sister after his parents had been killed in a small plane crash. He'd managed to save the ranch, but he hadn't been equipped to raise Emily and had made his share of mistakes.

A few months ago, his sister had gotten out of jail and gone to work for Bo. He'd been surprised she'd given Emily a chance. He'd had to readjust his opinion of Bo—but only a little. Now this.

"There has to be an explanation," he said, even though he knew firsthand that Bo often acted impulsively. She did whatever she wanted, damn the world. But now his little sister was part of that world. How could she leave Emily and the rest of the staff at the foundation to face this alone?

"I sure hope everything is all right," his sister said. "Bo is so sweet."

Sweet wasn't a word he would have used to describe her. Sexy in a cowgirl way, yes, since most of the time she dressed in jeans, boots and a Western shirt—all of which accented her very nice curves. Her long, sandy-blond hair was often pulled up in a ponytail or wrestled into a braid that hung over one shoulder. Since her wide green eyes didn't need makeup to give her that girl-next-door look, she seldom wore it.

"I can't believe she wouldn't show up. Something must have happened," Emily said loyally.

He couldn't help being skeptical based on Bo's history. But given Em's concern, he didn't want to add his own kindling to the fire.

"Jace, I just have this bad feeling. You're the best tracker in these parts. I know it's a lot to ask, but would you go find her?"

He almost laughed. Given the bad blood between him and Bo? "I'm the last person—"

"I'm really worried about her. I know she wouldn't run off."

Jace wished *he* knew that. "Look, if you're really that concerned, maybe you should call the sheriff. He can get search and rescue—"

"No," Emily cried. "No one knows what's going on over at the foundation. We have to keep this quiet. That's why you have to go."

He'd never been able to deny his little sister anything, but this was asking too much.

"Please, Jace."

He swore silently. Maybe he'd get lucky and Bo would return before he even got saddled up. "If you're that worried . . ." He got to his feet and reached for his hat, telling himself it shouldn't take him long to find Bo if she'd gone up into the Crazies, as the Crazy Mountains were known locally. He'd grown up in those mountains. His father had been an avid hunter who'd taught him everything about mountain survival.

If Bo had gone rogue with the foundation's funds . . . He hated to think what that would do not only to Emily's job but also to her recovery. She idolized her boss. So did Jodie, who was allowed the run of the foundation office.

But finding Bo was one thing. Bringing her back to face the music might be another. He started to say as much to Emily, but she cut him off.

"Oh, Jace, thank you so much. If anyone can find her, it's you."

He smiled at his sister as he set his Stetson firmly on his head and made her a promise. "I'll find Bo Hamilton and bring her back." One way or the other.

Chapter
TWO

Bo Hamilton rose with the sun, packed up camp and saddled up as a squirrel chattered at her from a nearby pine tree. Overhead, high in the Crazy Mountains, Montana's big, cloudless early summer sky had turned a brilliant blue. The day was already warm. Before she'd left, she'd heard a storm was coming in, but she'd known she'd be out of the mountains long before it hit.

She'd had a devil of a time getting to sleep last night, and after tossing and turning for hours in her sleeping bag, she had finally fallen into a death-like sleep.

But this morning, she'd awakened ready to face whatever would be awaiting her back at the office in town. Coming up here in the mountains had been the best thing she could have done. For months she'd been worried and confused as small amounts of money kept disappearing from the foundation.

Then last week, she'd realized that more than a hundred thousand dollars was gone. She'd been so shocked that she hadn't been able to breathe, let alone think. That's when she'd called in an independent auditor. She just hoped she could find out what had happened to the money before anyone got wind of it—especially her father, Senator Buckmaster Hamilton.

Her stomach roiled at the thought. He'd always been so proud of her for taking over the reins of the foundation that bore her mother's name. All her father needed was another scandal. He was running for the presidency of the United States, something he'd dreamed of for years. Now his daughter was about to go to jail for embezzlement. She could only imagine his disappointment in her—not to mention what it might do to the foundation.

She loved the work the foundation did, helping small businesses in their community. Her father had been worried that she couldn't handle the responsibility. She'd been determined to show him he was wrong. And show herself, as well. She'd grown up a lot in the past five years, and running the foundation had given her a sense of purpose she'd badly needed.

That's why she was anxious to find out the results of the audit now that her head was clear. The mountains always did that for her. Breathing in the fresh air now, she swung up in the saddle, spurred her horse and headed down the trail toward the ranch. She'd camped only a couple of hours back into the mountain, so she still had plenty of time, she thought as she rode. The last thing she wanted was to be late to meet with the auditor.

She'd known for some time that there were . . . *discrepancies* in foundation funds. A part of her had hoped that it was merely a mistake—that someone would realize he or she had made an error—so she wouldn't have to confront anyone about the slip.

Bo knew how naive that was, but she couldn't bear to think that one of her employees was behind the theft. Yes, her employees were a ragtag bunch. There was Albert Drum, a seventy-two-year-young former banker who worked with the recipients of the foundation loans. Emily Calder, twenty-four, took care of the website, research, communication and marketing. The only other employee was forty-eight-year-old widower Norma Branstetter, who was in charge of fund-raising.

Employees and board members reviewed the applications that came in for financial help. But Bo was the one responsible for the money that came and went through the foundation.

Unfortunately, she trusted her employees so much that she often let them run the place, including dealing with the financial end of things. She hadn't been paying close enough attention. How else could there be unexplained expenditures?

Her father had warned her about the people she hired, saying she had to be careful. But she loved giving jobs to those who desperately needed another chance. Her employees had become a second family to her.

Just the thought that one of her employees might be responsible made her sick to her stomach. True, she was a sucker for a hard-luck story. But she trusted the people she'd hired. The thought brought tears to her eyes. They all tried so hard and were so appreciative of their jobs. She refused to believe any one of them would steal from the foundation.

So what had happened to the missing funds?

She hadn't ridden far when her horse nickered and raised his head as if sniffing the wind. Spurring him forward, she continued through the dense trees. The pine boughs sighed in the breeze, releasing the smells of early summer in the mountains she'd grown up with. She loved the Crazy Mountains. She loved them especially at this time of year. They rose from the valley into high snowcapped peaks, the awe-inspiring range running for miles to the north like a mountainous island in a sea of grassy plains.

What she appreciated most about the Crazies was that a person could get lost in them, she thought. A hunter had done just that last year.

She'd ridden down the ridge some distance, the sun moving across the sky over her head, before she caught the strong smell of smoke. This morning she'd put her campfire out using the creek water nearby. Too much of Montana burned every summer because of lightning storms and careless people, so she'd made sure her fire was extinguished before she'd left.

Now reining in, she spotted the source of the smoke. A small campfire burned below her in the dense trees of a protected gully. She stared down into the camp as smoke curled up. While it wasn't that unusual to stumble across a backpacker this deep in the Crazies, it *was* strange for a camp to be so far off the trail. Also, she didn't see anyone below her on the mountain near the fire. Had whoever had camped there failed to put out the fire before leaving?

Bo hesitated, feeling torn because she didn't want to take the time to ride all the way down the mountain to the out-of-the-way camp. Nor did she want to ride into anyone's camp unless necessary.

But if the camper had failed to put out the fire, that was another story.

"Hello?" she called down the mountainside.

A hawk let out a cry overhead, momentarily startling her.

"Hello?" she called again, louder.

No answer. No sign of anyone in the camp.

Bo let out an aggravated sigh and spurred her horse. She had a long ride back and didn't need a detour. But she still had plenty of time if she hurried. As she made her way down into the ravine, she caught glimpses of the camp and the smoking campfire, but nothing else.

The hidden-away camp finally came into view below her. She could see that whoever had camped there hadn't made any effort at all to put out the fire. She looked for horseshoe tracks but saw only boot prints in the dust that led down to the camp.

A quiet seemed to fall over the mountainside. No hawk called out again from high above the trees. No squirrel chattered at her from a pine bough. Even the breeze seemed to have gone silent.

Bo felt a sudden chill as if the sun had gone down—an instant before the man appeared so suddenly from out of the dense darkness of the trees. He grabbed her, yanked her down from the saddle and clamped an arm around her as he shoved the dirty blade of a knife in her face.

"Well, look at you," he said hoarsely against her ear. "Ain't you a sight for sore eyes? Guess it's my lucky day."

Chapter
THREE

Senator Buckmaster Hamilton stood at the front window of his ranch house, stewing. He'd been either in Washington or on the road off and on since January with the presidential campaign, surrounded by staff, volunteers, donors and reporters with cameras in his face. When he'd finally escaped and come home to the ranch, he'd hoped for a little privacy.

But once the news of his first wife's miraculous return from the dead had hit the local newspaper, the story had gone viral. Reporters had begun calling the house and then showing up on the ranch with cameras and news vans.

He'd thought it would have died down after almost four months. But if anything, with his campaign going well, the media seemed even more bloodthirsty for dirt on his family—let alone photographs of Sarah. Everyone wanted to know where she'd been and if her alleged memory loss was real.

No one wanted to know more than he did. His "dead" wife's return had turned his life upside down since he'd remarried fifteen years ago. He was just thankful that of his six daughters, five of them were away from the ranch and doing their best to keep out of the limelight.

"You really should eat some breakfast," Angelina Broadwater Hamilton said as she came into the living room with two cups of coffee. His wife handed one to him and sat down with hers.

Sarah's return had brought out the worst in Angelina. But everything else that had gone on didn't seem to bother her in the least. It amazed him how she could apparently push all the unpleasantness of her brother's arrest and suicide away and not give it another thought. He wondered if it was an act. The same way she pretended nothing had changed in their marriage since Sarah had come back.

Angelina hadn't mentioned her brother's name since his arrest and suicide. Nor had she seemed to mourn his death, shedding only a few photo-op tears at his funeral. Lane Broadwater had been Buckmaster's campaign manager when he'd run for the Senate. When Lane was arrested for killing the man who'd been blackmailing Angelina for years, all Angelina had said was— "There's more to the story than you know."

There always was with Angelina. Buckmaster had married her after spending seven years mourning his first wife's death. Sarah's car had gone into the Yellowstone River one winter night twenty-two years ago, her body never found.

He'd married Angelina for her name and her society upbringing to help him with his political career. She and her brother had been a godsend in so many ways. Not only had they helped him win the Senate race, but also they'd put him in a position where the presidency was his if he wanted it.

And he wanted it.

Or at least, he had until his first wife had come back from the dead.

Sarah swore that she didn't remember anything about the past twenty-two years or her attempted suicide before she'd disappeared. Her last memory, according to her, was giving birth to the twins. Harper and Cassidy were now both recent college graduates.

Sarah's untimely return—right after he had thrown his hat in the presidential ring—had changed everything, especially between him and Angelina. For months they'd argued about him staying in the running for president. It had been his daughters who had talked him into continuing.

He'd thought for sure that Sarah's return and the story of her suicide attempt would have ruined any chances he had to get elected. But in a surprising turn of events, just the opposite had happened. The voting public were sympathetic to his dilemma. Even the press had cut him some slack.

Angelina took a sip of her coffee, studying him

over the rim of her cup. "I suppose you're going to see Sarah now that we're back."

"I'm not going anywhere right now," he said. "And I don't want to argue."

"It would just be nice if you would tell me when you were going to see her," Angelina said.

Nice? Who was she kidding? She didn't understand that even if Sarah was no longer legally his wife, he still felt responsible for her. She was the mother of his six daughters.

He stepped to the window. Several news vans and one older-model black pickup were parked out by the gate. Every time he left the house, they followed him. The cowboy in the older-model black truck had tailed him several times when he'd gone to meet Sarah, but he'd managed to lose the guy.

"I assume Sarah is still hiding out from the press?" Angelina asked.

"They are determined to find out why she came back now, where she's been and what happens next."

Angelina raised a brow as if those were questions she wanted answered, as well. "Why don't you leak it to the press where she is and get it over with?"

"Because I don't know where she is," he snapped, and saw her satisfied look.

It galled him that Sarah was staying with the rancher who'd found her the day she'd reappeared in nearby Beartooth. Russell Murdock had been driving along one of the narrow dirt roads just past the cemetery in the middle of nowhere when Sarah had apparently stepped out of the trees. She'd been scraped up and disoriented with no idea how she'd gotten there or where she'd been.

At least, that was her story. Angelina didn't buy it for a minute. She argued that Sarah was faking it and had only returned to ruin his chances of becoming president. He didn't know what he believed. Sarah had been the love of his life. He'd had six beautiful daughters with her. It had almost killed him when he thought she'd taken her life that night in the river. Then she'd come back from the dead, proving that she could break his heart all over again.

"I'm sure that once they find out where Sarah is staying, they *will* talk to her," Angelina said. "Maybe she'll start saying something that makes sense." She didn't sound the least bit sympathetic. She didn't seem to understand that Sarah's return had made him question everything about his life, maybe especially his marriage to Angelina and his run for president.

For him, a whole lot of things had changed. What was strange was that he'd sensed it coming. Worse, the darkness he'd felt on the horizon hadn't dissipated with Sarah's return from the grave. He couldn't shake the feeling that something even darker loomed over them all.

"Now more than ever, we need a show of solidarity," he said, not for the first time. Angelina's jealousy had brought out a nasty side of her personality that he'd never known existed.

"Where does Sarah fit in all that harmony?" she asked snidely.

He wished he knew.

As he started to close the drapes so he didn't have to see the reporters hanging around out by the gate, he noticed a pickup pulling a horse trailer up the road toward the house. He had hired armed guards at the gate to keep the reporters out, but someone was now roaring toward the house in a truck he didn't recognize.

"Now what?" he asked under his breath.

Jace had just knocked at the door when another truck drove up from the direction of the corrals. As Senator Buckmaster Hamilton himself opened the door, he was looking past Jace's shoulder. Jace glanced back to see Cooper Barnett climb out of his truck and walk toward them.

Jace turned back around. "I'm Jace Calder," he said, holding out his hand as the senator's gaze shifted to him.

The senator frowned but shook his hand. "I know who you are. I'm just wondering what's got you on my doorstep so early in the morning."

"I'm here about your daughter Bo."

Buckmaster looked to Cooper. "Tell me you aren't here about my daughter Olivia."

Cooper laughed. "My pregnant bride is just fine, thanks."

The senator let out an exaggerated breath and turned his attention back to Jace. "What's this about—" But before he could finish, a tall, elegant blonde woman appeared at his side. Jace recognized Angelina Broadwater Hamilton, the senator's second wife. The rumors about her being kicked out of the house to make way for Buckmaster's first wife weren't true, it seemed.

She put a hand on Buckmaster's arm. "It's the auditor calling from the foundation office. He's looking for Bo. She didn't show up for work today, and there seems to be a problem."

"That's why I'm here," Jace said.

"Me, too," Cooper said, sounding surprised.

"Come in, then," Buckmaster said, waving both men inside. Once he'd closed the big door behind them, he asked, "Now what's this about Bo?"

"I was just talking to one of the wranglers," Cooper said, jumping in ahead of Jace. "Bo apparently left Saturday afternoon on horseback, saying she'd be back this morning, but she hasn't returned."

"That's what I heard, as well," Jace said, taking the opening. "I need to know where she might have gone."

Both Buckmaster and Cooper looked to him.

"You sound as if you're planning to go after her," the senator said.

"I am."

"Why would you do that? I didn't think you two were seeing each other?" Cooper asked like the protective brother-in-law he was.

"We're not," Jace said.

"Wait a minute," the senator said. "You're the one who stood her up for the senior prom. I'll never forget it. My baby cried for weeks."

Jace nodded. "That would be me."

"But you've dated Bo more recently than senior prom," Buckmaster was saying.

"Five years ago," he said. "But that doesn't have anything to do with this. I have my reasons for wanting to see Bo come back. My sister works at the foundation."

"Why wouldn't Bo come back?" the senator demanded.

Behind him, Angelina made a disparaging sound. "Because there's money missing from the foundation along with your daughter." She looked at Jace. "You said your sister works down there?"

He smiled, seeing that she was clearly judgmental of the "kind of people" Bo had hired to work at the foundation. "My sister doesn't have access to any of the money, if that's what you're worried about." He turned to the senator again. "The auditor is down at the foundation office, trying to sort it out. Bo needs to be there. I thought you might have some idea where she might have gone in the mountains. I thought I'd go find her."

The senator looked to his son-in-law. Cooper shrugged.

"Cooper, you were told she planned to be back today?" her father said. "She probably changed her mind or went too far, not realizing how long it would take her to get back. If she had an appointment today with an auditor, I'm sure she's on her way as we speak."

"Or she's hiding up there and doesn't want to be found," Angelina quipped from the couch. "If she took that money, she could be miles from here by now." She groaned. "It's always something with your girls, isn't it?"

"I highly doubt Bo has taken off with any foundation money," the senator said and shot his wife a disgruntled look. "Every minor problem isn't a major scandal," he said and sighed, clearly irritated with his wife.

When he and Bo had dated, she'd told him that her stepmother was always quick to blame her and her sisters no matter the situation. As far as Jace could tell, there was no love lost on either side.

"Maybe we should call the sheriff," Cooper said.

Angelina let out a cry. "That's all we need— more negative publicity. It will be bad enough when this gets out. But if search and rescue is called in and the sheriff has to go up there . . . For all we know, Bo could be meeting someone in those mountains."

Jace hadn't considered she might have an accomplice. "That's why I'm the best person to go after her."

"How do you figure that?" Cooper demanded, giving him a hard look.

"She already doesn't like me, and the feeling is mutual. Maybe you're right and she's hightailing it home as we speak," Jace said. "But whatever's going on with her, I'm going to find her and make sure she gets back."

"You sound pretty confident of that," the senator said, sounding almost amused.

"I know these mountains, and I'm not a bad tracker. I'll find her. But that's big country. My search would go faster if I have some idea where she was headed when she left."

"There's a trail to the west of the ranch that connects with the Sweet Grass Creek trail," her father said.

Jace rubbed a hand over his jaw. "That trail forks not far up."

"She usually goes to the first camping spot before the fork," the senator said. "It's only a couple of hours back in. I'm sure she wouldn't go any farther than that. It's along Loco Creek."

"I know that spot," Jace said.

Cooper looked to his father-in-law. "You want

me to get some men together and go search for her? That makes more sense than sending—"

Buckmaster shook his head and turned to Jace. "I remember your father. The two of you were volunteers on a search years ago. I was impressed with both of you. I'm putting my money on you finding her if she doesn't turn up on her own. I'll give you 'til sundown."

"Make it twenty-four hours. There's a storm coming so I plan to be back before it hits. If we're both not back by then, send in the cavalry," he said and with a tip of his hat, headed for the door.

Behind him, he heard Cooper say, "Sending him could be a mistake."

"The cowboy's mistake," Buckmaster said. "I know my daughter. She's on her way back, and she isn't going to like that young man tracking her down. Jace Calder is the one she almost married."

Sarah Hamilton leaned into the porch railing of the old cabin and looked out at the Sweet Grass Valley. It stretched to the horizon, a gleaming array of summer colors. Closer a breeze stirred the pines, the sun making the boughs glisten.

Despite the beauty, this place made her anxious. She didn't like the quiet or the isolation or the fact that she'd been forced to hide out here for her own safety.

At the sound of a vehicle, she moved closer to

29

the railing so she could see the narrow dirt road that wound up through the trees. She held her breath, afraid someone had found her—and not a reporter.

The past twenty-two years were a dark hole that haunted her. While she couldn't remember anything from those years, she had vague, disturbing flashes of the past that came without warning at all hours of the day and night. While they made no sense, their dark ominous feel scared her. She was afraid to find out who she'd been the past twenty-two years. Or why she'd tried to kill herself all those years ago.

As Russell Murdock's pickup came into view, she leaned against the railing, weak with relief. He had been her sanctuary from the storm since her return. Russell, a soft-spoken sixtysomething rancher with a heart as big as Montana, had saved her when he'd found her in an isolated spot outside Beartooth. She been confused, not sure how she'd gotten there or where she'd been.

Her last memory was of giving birth to twin daughters. Was it really possible that they had both now graduated from college? She'd hoped they would come home for the summer so she could spend some time with them, but both had taken off to Europe to allegedly continue their studies abroad.

Their prolonged absence was Buck's doing. She hadn't even gotten to see them since she'd been back. While she'd met with her other four daughters, Cassidy and Harper hadn't been allowed to return home.

"If they come back here, they will be bombarded by the media asking if they've seen their mother, where she's been, why she's back, what she said, what she looks like, and on and on," Buckmaster had said irritably.

She couldn't argue with his logic. But she ached to see her twins all grown up. She remembered the sweet identical babies she'd given birth to and felt sick inside to think that they wouldn't even remember her. It was bad enough that her other four children barely remembered her.

Russell, understanding how upset she'd been about not seeing Harper and Cassidy, had offered to take her to visit them in Europe. But she'd declined. All she needed was to get the media circus going again by leading the press right to her twins. It had died down somewhat, even though she knew reporters were still looking for her. If Russell hadn't hidden her away in this cabin . . .

"The cabin is part of some land that my former employer W. T. Grant owned," he'd told her when it became clear that she would have to hide out for a while from the press. "It's my daughter's now, but no one uses the place. No one will think to look for you there."

"The media frenzy isn't going to die down,"

she'd told him. "Not as long as Buck is still running for president. Maybe it would be better if I just disappeared again."

"Where would you go? No, you need to stay here," Russell had said with a decisive shake of his head. "The cabin will be safe, and I'll come see you every chance I get. Don't worry about me being followed." He'd smiled, making him even more handsome. "I know how to lose them on these back roads."

She watched him drive up and park out front. As he got out of his truck, he stopped to meet her eyes. His expression instantly softened as if he knew what she'd been going through. He sensed things about her, things that would have turned another man away and yet if anything made him even more protective.

Her heart went out to him, but she didn't move. Didn't dare. She couldn't let him think she was falling in love with him. She'd given her heart away at twenty-four to Buckmaster Hamilton, and it was still his. Maybe would always be his.

Unless there'd been another man in her life during the past twenty-two years that she couldn't remember. That thought made her hug herself against the chill that raced up her spine. Had there been a man? She shuddered to think what kind of man he would have been, given her flashes of memory.

"I brought you strawberries," Russell called,

making her smile as he reached into the back of the truck and brought out a cooler. "I wanted to bring ice cream, but I knew it would melt before I got here."

He started toward her. She waited, anxious to know if he'd heard from Buck, but not wanting it to be the first thing out of her mouth.

Russell didn't ask how she'd been doing, because he already knew, as she led him into the small but modern cabin.

She felt guilty for involving him in her messy life. He'd been so kind. "I'm so sorry I—"

"Stop," he said, putting down the cooler and stepping to her. His big hands cupping her shoulders felt warm, reassuring. "I couldn't be happier helping you. Wasn't it obvious that I was at loose ends when you came into my life? I desperately needed a diversion."

Was that what she was? She feared he wanted more than that from her and needed to warn him what a mistake that would be. It wasn't just that she was still in love with Buck. No, her reasons, along with her fears, ran much deeper.

"Ready for your doctor's appointment?" he asked.

He hoped the neurologist would be able to determine what had caused her memory loss. She feared he might be right. "What if he tells me . . ."

"We'll face whatever he tells you together," Russell said quickly and reached for her hand.

"Still, I'm afraid that I will bring something dangerous into your—"

"I can handle whatever you bring." His gaze locked with hers. "I will protect you no matter what. Believe that."

She could see that he meant every word. Russell would protect her to his dying breath, and that scared her even more. She hated that she'd put him in that position. Like her, he sensed that something scary from her past would ultimately find its way to Beartooth. His fear for her safety made her all the more frightened that it was only a matter of time before her past found her.

Jace had hoped Buckmaster Hamilton was right and Bo was headed back to the ranch. But by the time he'd saddled up that afternoon, leaving his pickup and horse trailer at the Hamilton Ranch, there was still no sign of Bo. Even as he rode through the foothills and into the tall pines, winding his way up into the formidable Crazy Mountains, he still hoped to run across her.

It didn't take him long to pick up her tracks. The trail into the mountains was on Hamilton Ranch property, so no one else had ridden this way recently.

He knew there could be a good excuse why she hadn't shown up. She could have gotten injured. Or her horse could have. Either would have kept her in the mountains longer than she'd planned.

But the fact that she'd gone camping knowing that she had a meeting with the auditor first thing Monday morning made him suspicious that neither of those was the case.

Bo Hamilton grew up rich and insulated. This was probably the first real adversity she'd ever had in her life—and her way of handling it had been to run. That didn't surprise him at all given their past. As he rode, he became more angry with her. How could she leave her employees to face the mess at the foundation? It would be all he could do not to turn her over his knee when he found her. Instead he would take her back to face the consequences.

He hated to think what this might do to his sister. Em had a problem with trusting the wrong people. Hadn't he feared that Bo Hamilton would let her down, just as she had him? Worse, when he'd heard about the work Bo had been doing at the foundation, he'd wanted to believe she might really have changed, grown up, no longer acted on impulse. But if she'd ridden up into the mountains to hide . . . He'd wring her neck when he found her. And he *would* find her.

"Are you crazy?" his best friend Brody McTavish had exclaimed a few hours earlier when Jace visited to tell him where he was going. Brody had shoved back his Western straw hat to gaze at him with amused blue eyes. "You're doing this for your *sister?*" He'd laughed good-naturedly and with a shake of his head had turned back to mucking out his barn.

"This has nothing to do with Bo Hamilton other than the fact that I have to find her and make this right."

"Make this right? Or rewrite the past? Jace—" Brody turned to look at him, his face suddenly serious. "What if she took the money? What if she rode up into those mountains to meet some-one, and they are miles from here by now?"

"There is only one way to find out. Would you mind watering and feeding my animals while I'm away? I should be back by tomorrow afternoon at the latest."

"You know you can count on me," Brody had said. "But be careful. That family seems to attract trouble like bald tires pick up nails."

Jace had chuckled and given his friend a slap on the back. "Thanks for your help and your advice."

"Went in one ear and out the other, didn't it?" Brody sighed. "You just can't seem to get over her, can you? But I'm not going to tell you this is a fool's errand if there ever was one. Just don't make me have to come looking for you, too. There's a storm coming and we both know what that means in the Crazies."

Now, as Jace rode higher up into the mountains following the trail Bo Hamilton had left behind, he breathed in the fresh smell of the pine trees and told himself he knew what he was doing. It was the same thing he'd been doing since his parents had died, leaving a teenager with an already wild and out-of-control kid sister to raise. He was trying to save Emily.

A breeze groaned high in the treetops. Nearby he could hear the rush of water in a small creek. He tried to concentrate on the wildness of the country, the beauty and the incredible views. He loved riding into the Crazies, loved the cool air under the heavy pine boughs, the quiet broken only by the sounds of nature, the isolation. The mountains released a calm in him that he could find in no other place.

That had been something he and Bo shared.

He shoved that thought away, anxious to hear the sound of another horse. Another person. Today he was the hunter. He wondered how Bo Hamilton would react when she realized she was his prey.

Mostly he hoped to hell he wasn't making a huge mistake, since he really had no idea what he was going to find up here.

Chapter
FOUR

Alex Ross couldn't help worrying about the young woman who'd come into Big Timber Java coffee shop this afternoon. Normally she had a smile for him, her blue eyes bright as stars and her laugh . . . well, he'd fallen for her laugh the first time he'd heard it—even before he'd connected the laugh with the tattooed, pierced young woman.

Not that he hadn't been surprised when he'd finally put the laugh with the face of the young woman now mulling over her coffee. She was nothing like he'd expected and certainly not his type. That's why he'd never talked to her, even though he'd wanted to since the first day he'd heard her laugh.

Now, though, unable to stop himself, he quickly picked up a dishrag from behind the counter and headed for her table.

"Usually all it takes is coffee to put a smile on your face," he said as he pretended to clean her table. "It looks as if you've barely touched yours today, so maybe that's the problem." He wondered if he could sound any more lame.

She looked up at him, startled as if she'd been

deep in thought. He wondered what she'd been thinking about. Probably a man—maybe the same one who often came in with her on her coffee break. Or maybe the one he'd seen sitting across the street in his car watching her the past couple of days. A jealous boyfriend?

As she blinked those big blue eyes at him, she gave him a wan smile instead of her usual dazzling pierced lip grin, the one that made his day the few times she'd turned it on him. Not that she'd ever really seen him, he suspected. To her, he was just the barista behind the counter.

"You work here," she said as if finally realizing who he was.

"The apron was the dead giveaway, right?"

She looked embarrassed. "Sorry. My mind was a million miles away. I recognize you now. I haven't seen you that much behind the counter. You must work here part-time."

He smiled at that. Actually he owned the place and another five like them across the state. "Alex Ross. Part-time barista. That's me."

"Emily Calder."

"Pleased to meet you, Ms. Calder. How about I get you another coffee?" He took the disposable cup of cold coffee in front of her. "The usual?"

She quirked one pierced dark eyebrow. "You know what I drink?" Her smile was brighter and the worry in her eyes a little less noticeable.

He rattled off her usual. "One Montana Mocha

Grande with an extra shot of espresso, topped with whipped cream, a drizzle of caramel and a little shaved chocolate."

She laughed. "Do you know all your customers' favorites?"

Only the ones who made his day. He grinned. "I just happened to remember yours."

Bo's scream echoed across the narrow ravine, the dense pines seeming to smother the sound.

The man laughed as he held her tighter. "Ain't no one around gonna hear ya so you might as well shut your trap."

She screamed again as his fingers dug into her side.

"Keep that up, though, and I'm gonna cut ya good," he said next to her ear.

She felt the dull blade press into her throat, the scream dying on her lips. She could smell his rank unwashed body, his breath nasty. He slowly turned her as if to get a good look at her. His fingers bit into the flesh of her arm as he held her with one hand and brandished the knife with the other.

"I'll be damned. Yer a fine one. Where'd ya come from?"

When she didn't speak, couldn't with her heart lodged in her throat, he gave her arm a rough shake.

"I asked ya where ya come from."

Her mind, like her body, had frozen in astonishment when he'd first grabbed her. Panicked, her thoughts whizzed from one to the next too quickly. The only one she could catch and hold on to was *This isn't happening.*

She swallowed. "Down in the valley." From the time she was a young child, she had known that she was a Hamilton and what that meant. When your family was wealthy—especially if your father was a senator—there were apparently people who could hurt you, kidnap you and demand ransom. But growing up in Montana not far from the ranch, she and her five sisters had always felt safe. Their father had seen to that.

"Down in the valley," he mocked her. "I gathered that. You got a name?"

She hesitated. "Bo."

"Bo?" He let out another harsh laugh. "Like Bo-Peep?"

She'd been told that her older sisters had been allowed to name her and that it had been three-year-old Kat who'd come up with the name. Who let a three-year-old name the latest child? Her mother, apparently.

"Bo what?" the man asked when she didn't respond to the tired joke.

"Calder." The name popped into her head. With it came a stab of pain. Her name really would have been Calder if she had married Jace five years ago. Why hadn't she said Smith or Jones or anything except Calder?

Instinctively she'd known she couldn't give the man her real name. Something told her that would have been a mistake. But thinking of Jace made her remember his sister, Emily, and her daughter, Jodie, and why she desperately needed to get off this mountain.

It was almost as if he'd seen what she was thinking. "You ain't goin' nowhere, Bo-Peep, 'cept with me." He smiled. "I been up in these woods for weeks. It's damned lonely, but not no more."

"If I don't get back, they'll come looking for me," she blurted.

"That right?" He studied her for a full minute before he turned her arm so he could get a good look at her left hand. "You ain't married. So who's gonna be lookin' for ya?"

It was a good question. Did anyone even know that she'd left? One of the wranglers had seen her leave Saturday, but he might have no reason to mention it to anyone. Surely someone would eventually notice her SUV parked over by the "bunkhouses" her father had built for his daughters as they got older. They weren't really bunkhouses. That's just what he called them. They were actually condos, six of them with a connected large communal area. Her father had hoped it would keep his daughters on the ranch. It hadn't. Bo rented an apartment twenty miles away in downtown Big Timber near the Sarah Hamilton Foundation office. It was easier than driving in from the ranch five days a week.

"My family," she said with more assurance than she felt. "They'll be looking for me. They expected me back this morning. If I don't show up . . ." She let the rest hang, hoping he would loosen his steely grip on her arm and put away the knife.

The look in his eyes said that wasn't going to happen. "Then we best get movin'," he said. "Nice of ya to provide me with a horse. I about wore out my boots in this damned rugged country."

She looked down and saw he was right. His boots had definitely seen better days. He'd been living up here for weeks? That's when she noticed the metal bracelet-like loops on his wrists. Realization hit her like a horseshoe to the head.

Her gaze shot up to his face. He was much dirtier, his hair longer, his beard fuller, but in an instant she knew she'd seen his mug shot on television. This was the escaped fugitive from Livingston. The one believed to have killed a man during the robbery of a local convenience store. She'd seen it on the news but hadn't paid much attention, and yet she now recalled the name because law enforcement had been looking for him for weeks.

Spencer. Raymond Spencer. Her pulse thundered in her ears. There was no doubt. She'd ridden into the camp of a violent criminal, and now she was his captive.

•••

Sarah couldn't help being nervous as the doctor came into the room. What was she afraid he was going to tell her? That there was a physical reason for her memory loss? Or was her greatest fear that whatever had caused it was psychological?

Dr. Turner introduced himself before taking a chair across from her, but it was clear that he knew who she was. Anyone with a television would have heard about her.

He was a small man with such a neat appearance that she wondered if he suffered from OCD. Even his movements felt too precise, too careful.

She looked away. He made her feel uncomfortable. Had she always been this sensitive to other people's . . . idiosyncrasies? Or was she overly observant because she'd lived too long not knowing whom she could trust? That thought did nothing to relieve her anxiety.

"You've experienced some memory loss?" he asked as he looked at what his nurse had written on the chart, seemingly unaware of her discomfort.

She glanced around his office rather than at him. Like him, it, too, was compulsively neat. She fought the urge to move something just to see what he would do. "I can't remember the past twenty-two years."

His head came up with a start. "But you remember before then?"

She nodded. "I remember giving birth to my twin daughters. They recently graduated from college."

He leaned back in his chair for a moment to study her. "When and where did you come to?"

"Four months ago I woke up on a dirt road just outside of Beartooth. I was confused. My only thought was that I had to see my daughters. I have six. The twins are the youngest."

The doctor picked up his pen and turned it slowly in his fingers as if inspecting it for even the slightest of smudges before asking, "Why did you wait four months to come see me?"

"I'm not sure I want to know why I can't remember."

He frowned. "Were you involved in any trauma that you know of such as an assault or car accident or violent collision in, say, a sporting event?"

"I'm told I crashed my car into the Yellowstone River in the middle of winter before I . . . disappeared."

He studied her again for a long moment before jotting down the information in her chart. "Does anything help improve your memory?"

She hesitated. "I get flashes like shadows that fade in and out sometimes, but they make no sense, so I can't be sure they're even memories."

"You don't have any short-term memory loss?"

"No." She watched him write.

"So you don't know why or how the memory loss began?"

"No." She answered questions about her medical history—at least the years she recalled.

"Drugs? Alcohol?"

She shook her head. "Not that I know of," she said, remembering the taste of vodka even though she couldn't recall ever drinking it.

"I'm going to do a physical exam along with some cognitive testing. Then we'll see about a CT scan to rule out damage or abnormalities to the brain. We'll take blood to check for an infection . . ."

Sarah felt like a sleepwalker as she went through the process. Later she found herself back in the doctor's office. She moved several things on his desk before he joined her.

When he came back into the room, he stopped before sitting down and asking, "Did you move something on my desk?"

"Why would I?"

He nodded. "Good question." He quickly replaced both items she'd moved to their original locations before he sat. "Yours is a very interesting case," he said once behind his desk again. "I can see no medical reason for your memory loss, no damage to the brain, no infection . . ." He closed the chart and steepled his fingers as he peered at her. "That leaves another possibility."

"That my memory loss might be psychological," she said, voicing her worst fear.

He nodded slowly. "I can give you the name of a psychiatrist . . ." She said nothing as he scribbled the name on a prescription pad he pulled from his top drawer. She took the sheet from him, folded it and put it into her pocket.

As she stood to leave, he said, "I would be interested to see how it turns out." His gaze locked with hers, and she saw that he'd made up his mind about her.

The moment he'd realized that she'd moved items on his desk, he'd known she'd done it to mess with his mind. Just as he'd known she was lying when she'd denied it. Now he was probably wondering why a woman would lie about losing twenty-two years of her memory.

Curious, Emily watched Alex Ross head behind the counter to get her another coffee. He'd been *flirting* with her! The thought surprised her. He was not the kind of man who normally gave her a second glance.

He wore an apron with Big Timber Java printed on it over his button-down shirt and chinos. His sleeves were rolled up, exposing surprisingly muscled tanned arms. She wondered what he did when he wasn't working here in the coffee shop. Then she shook her head as she imagined what her ex Harrison would have thought of the guy.

She instantly felt defensive on Alex's behalf. While he wasn't her usual type—not in the least—he was nice and kind of cute in his way-too-straightlaced clothes. He'd been so sweet when he'd come over to the table. He wanted her to feel better. Harrison had never cared how she was feeling one way or the other.

Just the thought of the man who'd gotten her arrested made her go cold inside. He'd been mean, taking out his temper on her with hard words and fists. But that was all behind her, she told herself as the barista returned with another cup of coffee. She reached for her purse.

"It's on the house. Your smile was payment enough," he said. "I was worried about you. You looked so serious. Can't have one of my favorite customers looking so sad."

Yep, he was definitely hitting on her. She grinned, more amused than anything. She certainly wasn't taking any of this seriously as she accepted the coffee. "Thanks." She took a sip. "Nice job."

He shrugged. "I try. I've seen you in here with Jace Calder. Any relation?"

"My brother."

He looked pleased to hear that. Had he thought Jace was her husband? "So . . ." His gaze went to her ring finger as if he was double-checking to make sure there wasn't a wedding ring.

"I'm not married," she said, even more amused.

He raised his gaze, his grin broadening into an embarrassed smile. "But you do have a boyfriend."

"Nope." She joked that she couldn't have a boyfriend until she could keep a houseplant alive. In truth, her priority was her daughter and had been for the past four years.

"Really? No boyfriend, huh?" One eyebrow shot up. "I thought . . . Never mind."

"I have a three-year-old daughter," she blurted out. If he was thinking of asking her out, which he probably wasn't, she wanted him to know up front. So many men weren't interested in a woman with someone else's kid.

"I've seen you with her. She's adorable."

"Thanks." She took a sip of the coffee, surprised how nervous she was. Alex was so not like the men she'd known. He had a job! True, it apparently was only part-time, but still . . .

She debated telling him she'd done jail time, but she reminded herself he hadn't asked for her life history. Or for a date. And yet, if her daughter hadn't scared him off . . .

"Would you like to go to a movie this weekend?"

"Really?" She hadn't meant to sound so shocked. The word had just slipped out. But she couldn't believe he was actually asking her out.

"You do go to movies, don't you?"

She laughed nervously. "Sure. I mean, yeah, I'd like to."

"Great. We can go to Bozeman and see one that's rated for kids if you don't want to get a sitter."

Who was this man? "You'd be all right with Jodie coming along?"

"Sure. Or we can see something else if you'd rather. I'm new at this, but I'd be happy to pay for the sitter." He sounded as nervous as she felt.

She laughed, and he seemed to relax. When he smiled, his brown eyes shone. "Maybe it should be you and me the first time." The words were out of her mouth before she realized what she'd said. She felt her face flush with embarrassment. "I mean—"

"Then it's a date." He smiled broadly and asked for her number. She watched him type it into his phone. A moment later she heard her phone ping, alerting her to a text. "I just sent you my phone number. Text me with what night would work best for you, and we'll come up with a time. Might as well have dinner before the show. Do you like Italian, Asian, Mexican or all-American?"

"All of the above," she said. Then, looking at her phone, she realized what time it was and shot to her feet. "I need to get back to work." Even with Bo gone and things in a panic at the office, she didn't like taking more time than she should have for her coffee break.

"Talk to you soon," he said as she rushed out the door, smiling to herself.

• • •

Raymond Jay Spencer Jr. couldn't take his eyes off the woman for more reasons than one. He hadn't believed it when he'd first seen her. It was as if his prayers had been answered—if he'd prayed. Praying had gotten him nothing as a kid when his old man was beating the crap out of him. He'd known then that there was no God. No teacher or neighbor or anyone had saved him from his father. He'd come to realize that all he had was the old man. Maybe he really did deserve what he got, like his father kept telling him.

"Bo-Peep," he said, trying the name and tuning out her pleas and reasons she needed to get back to town. The first time he'd crossed her tracks, he'd stared at the fresh horseshoe prints in the trail for a long moment. He'd spent the past three weeks making sure his path hadn't crossed another soul's.

This morning, though, his feet hurting, hungry and ill-tempered after all this time hiding out in the mountains, he couldn't help himself. Mostly he was sick of walking after he'd lost the horse he'd stolen. The damned animal had gotten spooked by a grizzly, thrown him and taken off, never to be seen again. The fall could have killed him, so he'd promised himself that if he ever did see that nag again, he would shoot the horse on sight.

He'd been on foot ever since. If his old man

wasn't going to be bringing him supplies and horses soon, he would have headed off these mountains in a heartbeat. But he'd learned the hard way over the years not to cross his father, Raymond Jay Spencer Sr., or RayJay, as he was known.

The prints in the dirt had looked like one horse, one rider. Damned tired of walking, he'd told himself maybe he would get lucky and could steal the horse without killing the rider. Or maybe not. He'd been in one of his moods, aching to hurt something or someone. So when he'd seen the horseshoe tracks, he'd looked at his worn-thin boots and told himself he would be riding soon.

But what was he going to do with the woman? He had some ideas. He gripped her soft flesh and let his imagination run wild as she went on again about how he really needed to let her go.

He didn't give a rat's ass about what she was saying. The problem was that his daddy wasn't going to like this.

Then again, maybe by the time the old man arrived, there wouldn't be any trace of little Bo-Peep.

The sun made its slow arc over the top of the pines, sinking behind the peaks as Jace rode into the mountains. As he felt the day waning, he grew more anxious. He'd thought he would meet her on the trail. The fact that he hadn't made him even more convinced that Bo was on the run.

A magpie landed in a pine limb high over his head in a flurry of black-and-white wings. It called down to him, breaking the silence of the forest. He stopped to rub the back of his neck, his hair damp against his skin. Ahead he could see a band of rocks that formed a steep cliff.

Where are you, Bo Hamilton? Are you watching me right now? Do you have the crosshairs of a rifle trained on my heart at this very moment?

He spurred his horse, worried that just might be the case. If she was on the run with the money and she had a male accomplice, anything was possible. He'd picked up only one recent horse trail, but that didn't mean she hadn't been planning to meet someone here, someone who'd been waiting for her. It was the reason he'd brought his rifle as well as a pistol, a knife and a length of rope.

Bo was going back with him even if he had to tie her to her horse. But what would he do if she wasn't alone?

Jace told himself he'd cross that bridge when he came to it. Right now his thoughts were with his kid sister. He worried about Emily all the time as it was and had for years. She'd been a rebellious little thing after their parents were killed. He'd been eighteen and didn't know squat about raising a kid, so he probably hadn't made things easier for Em.

When she'd gotten older, he'd hoped for a long time that she might meet some nice man. But most nice men were put off by a woman who looked and dressed the way Em did. She didn't seem to realize the image she projected.

"Sorry, but this is me," she'd said defensively when he'd broached the subject. "If a man can't see beyond the tattoos and the piercings, he isn't the man for me."

But her looks had also made it hard for her to get a job. He'd been surprised that Bo had seen beyond the image and hired her. Emily was smart and talented and a good mom. He'd seen the change in her since she'd come back here. She appeared tired of being that defiant, angry, wild girl she'd been. He saw that the job was responsible for the change in his sister. She loved her job and Bo. She looked up to Bo, wanted to be more like her.

The only shadow on the horizon was her criminal ex-boyfriend, Harrison Ames. Fortunately he was still locked up in prison. Jace dreaded the day the man got out. Ideally Em would have her life together and wouldn't even be tempted to get involved with the man again. Jace had never understood the attraction to begin with. Some women thought they didn't deserve any better. But his baby sister sure as hell did.

That was why he couldn't allow Bo to let Emily down any more than she already had.

Alex watched Emily hurry across the street, smiling to himself. He'd wanted to ask her out for weeks but hadn't gotten up the nerve.

His cousin Jeff, who worked for him, had tried to talk him out of it.

"You're not her type," Jeff had said.

"What do you think her type is?" Alex had wanted to know.

"Someone cool like a musician, an artist, a gang member—maybe a known criminal."

"Very funny. You're judging her by her looks."

His cousin had stopped working to stare at him. "Not just that. I heard she's done time."

"So she's turning her life around."

Jeff had shaken his head. "Also, she has a kid."

"I know. I've seen her with Jodie."

"*Jodie?* You know the kid's name?"

"I happened to hear her call her daughter by name. You're making too much out of this."

"Am I? I know you, remember? When was the last time you went out on a date?" Jeff had lifted a brow. "Exactly. You haven't dated since Carmen."

"Cathy. You know her name was Cathy."

Jeff had laughed. "How could I forget? All I heard for months was Cathy this, Cathy that. The woman broke your heart—just as I predicted. Didn't I try to warn you about her?"

"Yes."

"Did you listen? No."

"This woman is different."

"Boy howdy!" His cousin had laughed. Then, sobering, he'd shaken his head. "If you want to take a ride on the wild side, go ahead. But don't be surprised if this girl isn't interested."

"Why wouldn't she be interested?"

His cousin had laughed again. "Seriously? Because you're so boringly . . . normal. You're a computer geek who owns coffee shops and wears khakis and button-down shirts with loafers."

"You're that convinced that she'll turn me down if I ask her out?"

"Aren't you? Isn't that why you haven't asked her?"

He *had* been afraid she'd turn him down. But he hadn't let that stop him today, had he?

"So you finally did it," his cousin said now as Alex joined him behind the counter. Business had slowed enough that they could talk. "Did she let you down easy?"

"We're going to a movie this weekend."

His cousin raised an eyebrow. "Good luck."

"I like her."

"It worked for Beauty and the Beast. I suppose it could work for Goth girl and the geek. Maybe they'll make a movie."

Jeff was a cowboy, born and raised on the ranch. He liked women who wore Wrangler jeans and rode bareback.

While Alex had grown up with his share of girls like that, he found himself more intrigued by Emily Calder. She'd been raised here on a ranch just as he had. But she hadn't become a cowgirl or a cowboy's wife. Like him, she'd escaped to experience life beyond the state of Montana. But also like him, she'd come home.

She'd made her share of mistakes, from what Alex had heard. Now she was trying to do better for her daughter. He admired that about her. He found her interesting, and he was looking forward to getting to know her better.

If he could get past the first date, he thought as he watched her disappear into the Sarah Hamilton Foundation office across the street.

He caught movement out of the corner of his eye and saw the now familiar car that was parked down the block. The car was a beater, and the man behind the wheel didn't look much better than the car.

Alex had gotten only glimpses of him. Long, dark hair, tattoos on his neck and arms, a battered black cowboy hat.

The man waited until Emily left the coffee shop and returned to the foundation office before he drove off—just as he had done the other day when Alex had noticed him.

As he watched the man now, he was left with no doubt about the man's interest in Emily Calder.

Chapter
FIVE

As the day slipped away, all Buckmaster could think about was that Bo should have been back by now. He looked toward the mountains, imagining her riding out of the pines, back straight and head high, just as he'd taught her to ride. She would come back to face whatever problem she had at the foundation. She wouldn't run.

Misappropriation of funds . . . Those were the words that kept circling in his brain, thanks to his lawyer.

As he entered the living room, he saw the television was on one of the news stations. Angelina had taken to watching the news non-stop from the time she awoke to when she finally went to bed.

"He looks like a hardened criminal, doesn't he?" she asked, her gaze on the television screen.

He glanced at the mug shot of the man on the screen. Raymond Spencer looked still wet behind the ears. He had freckles, for hell's sake, and baby blue eyes. He also looked as though he wanted to cry.

Another mug shot flashed on the screen. In this one, he looked older and doped up. He'd shaved off all of his blond hair. Something in his eyes had changed, as well.

"Turn that off," Buckmaster snapped as the anchor said the man's escape was blamed on a communication gap between Livingston, Montana, law officers.

"The manhunt continues for Spencer, who is wanted in the armed robbery and death of a convenience store attendant. Spencer escaped three weeks ago after—" The television screen went black as Buckmaster turned it off with the remote.

Angelina stared at the blank screen. "He escaped in handcuffs. He would have to go somewhere to get those off, right?"

What was this obsession she had with crime? The moment Buckmaster thought it, he knew this was her reaction to what her brother had done.

"Do you think you could kill someone?" she asked, turning to look at him for the first time since he'd entered the room.

He sighed. "If I had to." He didn't have to ask her the same question. He knew. When her blackmailer had been murdered, her brother had been arrested. But Buckmaster had suspected Angelina had given him the gun.

She'd denied it. But he'd come to know his wife. Angelina could be merciless. Understanding that had changed the way he looked at her, which in turn made him feel guilty. He loved this woman as much as he was capable of loving her, since Sarah had always been his true love.

But with Angelina came a debt. He owed her. He knew he wouldn't have achieved his political standing without her. Also, he knew he should be glad that she was sticking with him, given what they'd been through lately. Better to have her on his side. She would make one brutal enemy.

"We should make sure the doors are locked," she said, getting to her feet. "Livingston isn't that far away. Who knows where that escaped killer is?"

"I'm sure they will catch him," Buckmaster said. "I thought I read in the paper this morning that they had tracked him through a bus ticket."

"To Reno, Nevada," she said. "They think he bought a car down there and might have returned to Montana. There is concern he's still in the area since he was raised on the other side of the Crazies in Wilsall. They're calling him a violent criminal."

"Angelina—"

"I just don't understand what makes someone do something like that," she said as if she hadn't heard him speak.

That was the problem. He suspected she did know what made a person do horrible things. He stepped to her and took her in his arms. Her back was ramrod straight, her body stiff and unresponsive. They hadn't made love in months. Not since Sarah had returned.

After a moment, she stepped from his arms, and he let her go.

After Sarah's appointment with the doctor, Russell brought her back to the cabin. He'd questioned her on the way home about what the doctor had said, but she'd been evasive.

"The tests were inconclusive. He just doesn't know."

Now Sarah picked up one of the strawberries Russell had brought her earlier and took a bite. She closed her eyes as her teeth sank into it, a smile coming to her lips as she savored the fresh berry. Russell watched her, entranced. Since the moment she'd stumbled out of the woods in front of his pickup, she'd captivated him.

At first he'd thought she was an apparition, because he'd attended her funeral twenty-two years ago. This Sarah seemed so utterly vulnerable, lost and helpless. Since the day he'd found her, though, he'd glimpsed a strength and determination in her that astounded him. This woman was someone to be reckoned with.

As he watched her relish the strawberry and sigh with contentment, he wanted to wrap her in his arms and protect her from the world outside this cabin. But she wasn't his. Fate might have brought them together and made him feel responsible, but ultimately, the woman was still in love with Buckmaster Hamilton. Because of that, Russell wasn't sure where he fit into her life—if at all.

She'd made a point of not asking about Buckmaster. Did she think mentioning the man would upset Russell? Admittedly, it did. He knew what she was waiting to hear. "Buckmaster has been calling."

Sarah looked up, her contented expression disappearing at just the mention of her ex-husband's — scratch that—husband's name. Buckmaster might have had Sarah declared dead after her body wasn't recovered from the icy Yellowstone River, then remarried seven years later, but in Sarah's mind and heart, Buckmaster was still her husband. Russell knew Buckmaster still thought of Sarah as his wife, as well.

"What does he want?" she asked as she pushed the small empty basket of strawberries aside.

He wants you, Russell thought. The senator, now with one too many wives, couldn't stand that this was one part of his life he couldn't control. At least in Russell's humble opinion.

"He says he's worried about you. He likes knowing where you are and if you're all right."

She smiled at that. "What did you tell him?"

"That you were safe and that he should worry more about his current wife."

For the first time since he'd stumbled across

this woman he'd thought dead for the past twenty-two years, she laughed a real laugh. It was rich, musical and delightful. He wanted to make her laugh for the rest of her life.

Quickly he quelled that thought, chalking it up to mere loneliness. His wife of more than forty years had died recently, leaving a hole that nothing had filled—until Sarah.

"None of this is Buck's fault."

Russell raised a brow. They'd had this discussion before. He thought *all* of this was Buckmaster's fault and had said as much. "You tried to commit suicide twenty-two years ago," he'd argued. "What happily married woman with six beautiful daughters, the twins only months old, drives her car into the Yellowstone River in the middle of winter in an attempt to kill herself?"

"Maybe one with postpartum depression or a houseful of young children and a husband who . . ."

"Who was distracted with his political career?" Russell suggested.

She shook her head. "He was involved only in local politics back then, and ranching."

"Something was wrong, and even if he didn't drive you into that river, he wasn't around enough to notice that you needed help."

Sarah sighed. "Unfortunately, I can't remember, so I have no idea why I would do such a thing."

Russell suspected something had happened to trigger her suicide attempt other than post-partum depression. He was betting Senator Buckmaster Hamilton was behind it. But Sarah didn't believe it. Or didn't want to believe it.

Russell didn't want to fight with her, though, so he said, "He wants you to come stay on the ranch. He suggested I bring you late at night to avoid the press."

"He can't be serious," she said, meeting his gaze.

Russell had said the same thing to the senator. "Apparently he is very serious. But you wouldn't be staying in the big house with his other wife. You'd be living in the bunkhouse complex he built for the girls. He said it's like a condo, and you would be comfortable and safe there."

"*Safe?* Does he know the woman he's married to at all?" She shook her head, looking miserable. "That's the most ridiculous thing I've ever heard. Moving onto the ranch with him married to another woman? Can you imagine what the press would make of it?"

Russell couldn't help his relief. "Are you going to tell Buckmaster about your visit to the neurologist?"

"What would be the point? Buck wants answers. The doctor didn't give me any." She let out a small, bitter laugh. "Buck won't accept that I might never recall the past twenty-two years. That those years might be gone forever."

Russell wondered if Buck might surprise her and be just as glad she couldn't remember. He could see that a part of her *hoped* she wouldn't remember the past. But he knew those years weren't entirely gone. He'd seen her look startled on occasion, her eyes growing dark and cloudy, her hands balling into fists. But it was her expression that told him she *was* remembering. Wherever she'd been, *whatever* she'd been, the memories terrified her. Who she might have been terrified her.

"For Buck's sake, I need to disappear again so I'm not such an issue with him running for president. But I want to have a relationship with my children. They already expect me to desert them again. The media has already made me out to be some flighty airhead who abandoned her husband and children, returning only because of my husband's political success."

"You could remarry," Russell said and then bit down hard on his tongue.

Her heart thudding against her ribs, Bo looked at the knife in the man's right hand. Her arm ached from the grip of his fingers digging into her skin. She could feel his dirty fingernails biting into her flesh. Her attempts to talk him into letting her go had fallen on deaf ears.

Now his gaze followed hers to the knife and back to her face. "That's right, sweetheart.

Unless ya want this blade plunged into yer belly, ya do what I say."

His words sent terror shooting through her. She fought to breathe as she met his eyes. Instantly she recoiled at the cold hatred she saw there. She didn't need a reminder of who this man was and what he was capable of. A man who'd already killed once. A violent criminal.

"We're goin' to walk down to my camp," he said and tugged on her arm.

All her instincts told her she had to think of a way to get away from this man. But he was big, a good six foot four or more, and solid as a new barn. Even if she could break free and avoid the knife, she doubted she could outrun him.

Looking around, she saw that her horse had stayed where the man had dragged her from it. If she could reach her horse—

"Ain't going to happen, so ya might as well put it out of yer pretty little head. You ain't goin' nowhere. Yer mine now."

She swallowed, terrified at the thought. "They'll be looking for me. You would have a better chance without me. If you took my horse—"

He jerked her arm, dragging her over to a tree where he had hidden an oily green pack. She watched him lay down the knife and lean over to reach into the pack with his free hand. Her whole body was trembling with fear, but she had to at least try to get away.

She spun to the side, his fingers losing their grip on her arm as she flung herself in the direction of her horse. She took a step, then another, longer one, trying to run on her quaking legs. If she could just reach her horse—

The blow to her back flung her to the ground. She sprawled in the dirt, the fall knocking the air from her lungs. Gasping like a trout tossed up on the bank, she struggled for breath as she tried to get to her feet.

His knee landed in her back, the weight of him crushing her to the ground again. She let out a scream of pain. He wound his hand into the hair of her ponytail and jerked her head back.

"Maybe I weren't clear. Yer with *me* now. Anybody comes lookin' for ya? I'll kill 'em. Ya want me to hurt ya bad? I will and I'll have fun doin' it. Try to get away agin? And ya will wish ya was never born."

He rose and she was able to take a breath, then another. Her back ached. So did her arm and the roots of her hair as he dragged her to her feet by her ponytail.

"Me and Bo-Peep. Ain't we a handsome couple?"

Bo felt sick to her stomach as he pulled her back over to his pack. He dug out a roll of duct tape, ripped a piece off with his teeth and, still holding on to her hair, one-handedly bound her wrists. She had the horrifying feeling that this wasn't the first time he'd bound a woman with duct tape.

Chapter
SIX

The senator glanced at the clock on the wall and swore. It had been hours, and no sign of his daughter or the cowboy who'd gone after her.

"Maybe I should call the sheriff," he said more to himself than to his wife.

"I thought you promised to wait twenty-four hours before you did anything," Angelina reminded him.

"Bo didn't take the money," he said, sounding as if he was trying to convince himself more than her. "It's just . . . *missing*." He realized it must have been missing for some time. He recalled his daughter Olivia's engagement party. Bo had been throwing down the champagne. He'd been concerned then. Why hadn't he talked to her about it?

"Even if she didn't take the money, Bo's responsible for it," Angelina said.

Bo would know that, as the president of the foundation it was her job to make sure nothing was amiss. If word got out . . . He realized he was starting to sound like Angelina. She constantly worried about even the breath of scandal hurting his chances of being elected president.

Angelina lived in fear of what his daughters might do to embarrass them all. Now that he had thrown his hat into the presidential ring, he felt as if he was on a runaway train. He needed all his attention on the race. But there had been one problem after another on the home front.

Problem? Hell, a tornado had torn through their lives. He found himself second-guessing the decisions he'd made from the age of twenty-five when he'd met and married Sarah, not to mention what he'd done after her presumed death.

Friends kept saying the worst was behind him and Angelina. Really? So why did he feel as if he was merely waiting for the other shoe to drop?

"Stop pacing! You're driving me crazy." Angelina moved past him to pour herself a drink.

Buckmaster watched his wife in surprise. Angelina had never been a drinker other than an occasional glass to be social. "Pour me one, too."

She turned to look at him but said nothing before turning back to make them both a drink. "I've been thinking about our future."

Their future? "If this discussion is going to be about Sarah again—"

"It's not." She handed him his drink and took hers to the couch. She didn't speak again until she'd sat down, run a hand down the length of her skirt and taken a sip of her cocktail. Her gaze was clear and steady as she looked up at him. "Are you going to withdraw from the campaign?"

It was the last thing he'd expected her to ask. He'd thought everything that had happened would have made the decision for him. Of course, it had come out that Sarah hadn't braked before she drove into the river twenty-two years ago. He'd thought for sure his poll numbers would have plummeted to the point that it would be ridiculous for him to stay in the race.

But people actually felt sorry for him. They admired him for trying to do the right thing in a difficult situation.

"Your numbers are good, better than good," Angelina said. "Even my brother's actions only strengthened your platform."

He shook his head, wondering how she could go on as if nothing earth-shattering had happened. What he hadn't known—and the press still didn't —was that Angelina wasn't the only one being blackmailed by the now dead Drake Connors. Her brother, Lane, had tried to hide his affair with the man. Realizing Drake planned to expose both him and his sister, he'd agreed to pay the blackmail, only to meet the man along a deserted road nearby and shoot him twice in the back. To avoid a trial and likely a lifetime in prison, Lane hung himself in his jail cell.

"I don't understand why we're having this discussion now. I'm in the race. Angelina, what is it you're so afraid of?" Buckmaster demanded.

Tears filled her eyes. "Other than you leaving me for Sarah?"

He opened his mouth to assure her but closed it. He cared too much about her to lie to her. He had no idea what the future held for the three of them.

"My other fear? That you'll be like your father and back out of the presidential race at the last minute. Like you, he was in a position where he could have taken the presidency. And then he just up and quit without any real explanation."

Buckmaster didn't know any more than anyone else about his father's sudden decision. "When my mother died, he must have felt as if he'd lost everything."

"I've often wondered if Sarah didn't get the idea to drive into the river from your father."

"He didn't try to kill himself. He'd been drinking, grieving, he was—"

"Brokenhearted over your mother's death."

Buckmaster sighed. The last place he wanted to go was down this particular trail. "Angelina, why do you keep digging up the past?"

"Why do *you?*" she shot back. "Oh, that's right, Sarah dug herself out of her grave to force us all back into the past."

"I thought this wasn't going to be about Sarah," he chided her.

"The past seems to have a way of repeating itself. There was a rumor that your father had another woman in his life, and that's what killed your mother."

He groaned. "A *rumor*. As far as I know, there was nothing to it. You know how these things get started. But I still don't see what any of this has to do with us."

"You don't see the similarities? You are primed to become the next president. There is another woman in your life. Who says you won't bail at the last minute like he did?"

"I'm not going to bail. You're not going to die. I'm not going to get drunk and roll my pickup and end up in the Yellowstone River." He stepped to her to place his hands on her shoulders. "Have a little faith that things are going to turn out fine."

"I'm scared something terrible is going to happen," she whispered as she looked up at him.

He hated that he'd felt the same way for some time now. "Like what?"

Angelina shook her head. "I just have this feeling . . ."

He wished he could alleviate her fears and his own.

She stepped away from him, finished off her cocktail and straightened. "You are still in a position where you can have everything you've dreamed of."

Not everything, he thought as he took a sip of his drink. The liquor burned all the way down.

The only way he could have the presidency now was if he stayed with Angelina, and she knew that. He couldn't win without her. He especially couldn't win if he left Angelina for Sarah.

He felt as if he had made a deal with the devil.

"The FBI doesn't seem to think there's a problem with Sarah Hamilton," Undersheriff Dillon Lawson said as he came into his boss's office and closed the door.

Sheriff Frank Curry waved him into a chair. "So that's it?"

Dillon shrugged. "They seem to agree with the media that she had an unfortunate accident and may have some mental issues, and they don't really feel it's necessary to put any manpower into finding out where she's been for the past twenty-two years. The general feeling is that she might have had postpartum depression, and that's what drove her attempted suicide. Her failure to end it all made her take off, possibly with help, and start her life over."

"And how was she supposed to start her life over without any money or a place to stay?" Frank demanded. "She couldn't even get a job without a Social Security number."

"She could have gotten a false identity. You know it isn't that hard. Maybe whoever helped her leave Beartooth also helped her obtain the documents," Dillon said. "As for money . . . she must have had some help there, too. She doesn't appear to have been cleaning motel toilets all these years."

Frank knew he had a point. There were ways to get by, especially for a woman. "So why come back now? And why drop in the way she did?" When he'd investigated the spot where Russell Murdock had found Sarah, he'd walked back into the woods. The area was isolated—only one road, no houses, not even a nearby ranch or farm. What he discovered was a paratrooper-type parachute caught in the trees. Sarah's DNA had been on the chute's harness.

"Why now? That's the million-dollar question and the one that has you worried, I suspect," his undersheriff agreed.

Frank shook his head. "Not just anyone gets dropped out of a plane in the middle of nowhere without any memory of the past twenty-two years."

"I'm sure you've considered that she might be lying about her . . . amnesia."

Frank let out a laugh. "The press definitely has. As you said, they consider her an unhappy wife with mental issues. Women especially have turned against her because she left six young children behind, including two almost newborns. But Sarah Hamilton isn't just *anyone*. She's the first wife of Senator Buckmaster Hamilton, the man who, according to the polls, is going to be our next president."

Dillon shrugged. "But if the FBI doesn't think she's a threat . . ."

"Then I shouldn't, either." Frank wished he could quell his concerns as easily. "Did they run an extensive background check on her?"

His undersheriff nodded. "Just like us, they couldn't find anything. No arrests, not even a speeding ticket. They have no idea where she's been."

Frank considered what Dillon had said. He hadn't been able to find any trace of Sarah in the past twenty-two years. She hadn't had a job—at least, not one that didn't pay under the table. Nor had she gotten another driver's license in another state. And she hadn't been arrested or had any reason that her fingerprints would have been on file.

Dillon hesitated at the door. "Once he's president, he'll have an army of secret service to protect him," he said as if to reassure them both. "There's a chance he might not even win. A lot of women out there could decide he drove his wife to suicide. No pun intended. Sarah might even disappear again, this time for good."

Anything was possible. So why couldn't Frank let it go? "An innocent woman would have gladly given us her DNA and fingerprints," he said for the sake of argument. When he'd asked her, she'd declined.

"But we got both from the parachute harness and that coffee cup she had been drinking from," Dillon pointed out.

Sarah had broken the cup. Frank was positive she'd done it on purpose, realizing that her prints would be on it. She'd been afraid that something would turn up.

"But neither her DNA or her prints came up on any criminal databases," Dillon said. "Your gut instincts are still telling you something is wrong, though." The undersheriff seemed to think for a moment. "We could put a missing persons out on her and see if it turns up anything."

It was a long shot. If she'd been arrested, something would have come up when they'd run her prints and DNA. But cops somewhere across the country could have run across her and might remember that face. "Let me think about it," Frank said.

For years, the Hamiltons had been the county's most upstanding family. Sarah's return had triggered something. Since she'd been back, there'd been blackmail, murder and a suicide in the family. While she couldn't be blamed for any of that, it still seemed odd to him.

His wife, Lynette, Nettie as everyone called her but him, had put it best. "There is a dark cloud over the Hamilton family." She'd shuddered when she'd said it. "I hate to think what will happen next."

76

"Still no word on Bo Hamilton?" Dillon asked as if thinking the same thing.

"No," Frank said, "and I'm starting to worry. The Crazies are such a large area to search. I hope it doesn't come down to that."

Ray turned in the saddle to look back at the woman. He was having misgivings about capturing her. His old man was going to kill him. Maybe he should end this now. The one thing he couldn't do was let her go. His only other option was to kill her and her horse and make sure no one found either body.

Not that it would keep people from searching these mountains for her. Better to shove her and her horse off a cliff.

She sure was pretty, though. Classy, too. He'd never had a woman like that. There was one other option, he told himself. He could keep her.

But fer how long afore she takes an ax handle to yer head and takes off? His father's mocking voice demanded. *Or are ya plannin' to keep her tied up the whole time like some mutt ya ain't able to trust?*

He scowled and turned back around, knowing his father was right. A woman like her would never want a man like him. She was so small and delicate, so different from him. He was lumbering and awkward.

When he was younger, he was always taller and

bigger than the rest of his classmates. He used to hate the way they gave him a wide berth as if afraid of him when he did nothing to scare them. They made him feel even bigger and clumsier.

He hated them for it, because he would have given anything to fit in. Once he realized he could use his intimidating size, he started taking whatever he wanted.

He heard the woman stumble and almost fall again. The rope he had her tied up with grew taut and slowed the horse. Even so, he would drag her if he had to.

As he reined in, he wondered what she saw when she looked at him and scowled at the thought. He told himself he didn't give a damn, but for the first time he did. It made him furious with himself.

His daddy always said that if you gave a woman any power over you, she'd destroy you. Bo made him feel inferior. Even if he forced himself on her, he knew he wouldn't feel that he'd had her.

Bo didn't know how long she'd been walking. Her legs and feet ached. Her clothing was torn, her skin scraped and bleeding from the times she'd fallen down and Ray Spencer had dragged her screaming behind her horse until she'd found her feet again.

"Please," she said now. "Can't we stop? Just for

a few minutes?" He'd given her a drink of water back down the mountain, but her throat was dry again, her mouth dusty, lips cracked. "I need more water."

"Ya need to keep walkin'. Ya said people'll be comin' lookin' for ya. If ya don't want 'em dead . . ."

Was someone looking for her yet? She couldn't bear to think about spending days up here with this man. Nor could she stand the thought of what would happen once they stopped and made camp.

She'd pleaded with him to let her go. "I won't tell anyone."

He'd laughed at that. "That's what they all say."

Her blood had curdled at his words. "I have money."

He'd seemed interested until he'd realized she meant back at her father's house.

"I'm worth money," she'd heard herself say. "My father will pay for my return unharmed." She had known what she was suggesting was more than a little dangerous. But it was the only thing she could think of that might keep this man from killing her. If he knew that she was worth more alive than dead . . .

"Oh, yeah?" Ray had seemed only mildly interested. "How much do you think you're worth?"

She had no idea. "A million?"

He'd laughed again, harder this time. "Sure ya

are. Anyway, I don't need no money up here in the mountains. A woman, though, I been hankerin' for one for weeks. And now I got you."

Those words had sent a shudder through her, and she'd shut up. There was no negotiating with this man. She had nothing to negotiate with.

Even as the sun set and twilight turned the mountainside to silver gray, Ray kept going, urging her horse on from high in her saddle, jerking at the rope he'd bound her with and half dragging her deeper into the mountains.

She could barely see where to step as daylight vanished and the trail filled with deep shadows. She stumbled and almost fell again.

"Ain't far now," Ray said. "Got jest the spot."

Darkness came quickly in the dense pines of the mountains. Once the sun set, a cool breeze had moved through the trees. The shadows grew longer and blacker.

Jace had been following Bo's trail for hours. The going was slow because he'd often lose it in the thick bed of dried pine needles and have to find it again. He'd seen the remains of other campsites. Telltale blackened rock rings with the remains of a campfire marking the sites. None of those had been used in the past twenty-four hours, though.

Which meant Bo hadn't wanted just a night of camping. She'd been set on total isolation farther back in the mountains. Knowing that gave him no peace of mind. More and more, he thought Bo Hamilton had looked to get away from civilization. But was it because of a guilty conscience and saddlebags full of loot? Or was there more to it?

He could understand wanting to escape a situation. Many times he hadn't been able to deal with his sister. He'd wanted to turn his back, run away from the problem. But he hadn't, and neither would Bo Hamilton when he found her.

Jace realized he wouldn't be able to track Bo much longer. He needed to make camp before it was too dark to see.

But just as he started to look for a spot to spend the night, he saw the footprints in the dirt. The tracks were man-size, large, moving in a scraping manner that dislodged a lot of dirt.

What caught his eye, though, was the fact that the tracks *crossed* Bo's horseshoe prints. Someone had walked past after she'd ridden up into the mountains.

Swinging out of the saddle, he studied them in the waning light. Seeing the man's boot prints in the dirt, he decided he wouldn't build a fire tonight. He staked his horse some distance away from where he'd rolled out his sleeping bag.

The last thing he wanted was to become the hunted, because if he was right, Bo Hamilton was on the run—and she wasn't alone.

When Ray finally quit dragging Bo up the mountainside in the dark, she collapsed on the ground in tears. Her wrists were rubbed raw from the rope cutting through the duct tape he'd bound her with. The fabric of her shirt was torn at both elbows, the skin beneath it scraped and bleeding.

"Get up," Ray ordered as he swung down from her horse. "And stop yer blubberin' or I'll give ya somethin' to cry about."

She couldn't move, couldn't walk another step. Nor could she stop crying. The sobs racked her body, generated by fear and exhaustion and the bitter taste of defeat. She was at this man's mercy, and he had proven he was merciless.

He took an intimidating step toward her. She closed her eyes and curled into a tight ball, bracing herself for the kick. To her surprise, he bent down close to her.

"Ya done good," he said, his voice sounding both surprised and pleased. "Yer tougher than ya look."

She didn't feel tough as he dragged her to her feet. As he untied the rope from her wrists and peeled off what was left of the duct tape, she flinched at the damage that had been done.

"There's water in that creek over there. It'll make ya feel better if ya clean up." The tenderness in his voice suddenly frightened her more than the gruff ruthlessness she had come to associate with him.

Before she could protest, he swept her up in his arms and carried her over to the water. It was full dark now, the sky overhead lit with stars and the gleam of a full moon as it rose up behind the pines to the east. The creek's surface shimmered in the silken light.

Easing her down on the creek bank, he pulled off her boots and her socks. When he reached for the buttons on her jeans, she tried to pull away.

He slapped her hard enough to snap her head back. "Don't fight me. Don't ever fight me."

She swallowed, her skin stinging from the slap. Closing her eyes, she felt him fumble with the buttons of her jeans before he jerked them down to her ankles, then off. She pressed her eyes closed more tightly, expecting him to remove her panties, as well. Tears leaked from beneath her lashes, but she was sobbed out.

Instead, she felt his fingers on her shirt. The snaps loudly *clacked* as he jerked her shirt open then eased it off one shoulder, then the other. She hugged herself, praying he wouldn't try to remove her bra.

"I'll help ya into the water," he said next to her ear a moment before he lifted her into his arms again. Wading out into the creek, he lowered her slowly into the icy water.

The cold took her breath away as she balanced

precariously on the smooth silken surface of the rocks beneath her, the water up to her thighs. He let go of her. She wobbled there in the middle of the stream, water rushing around her. The freezing water made her lower body ache.

"Wash yerself," he ordered, taking a step back, but not so far that he couldn't reach her if she tried to scramble out of the creek and up the adjacent bank.

Ray felt desire curl in his belly as he watched her. He didn't know how much longer he could contain himself. He wanted her, and it didn't help that he could take her so easily. There was no one around to hear her screams. No one around to be the wiser. Once he disposed of her body . . .

And what a body it was. His ache had a choke hold on him, and yet something inside him wanted more from her. He'd had women, but none like this one. He wanted this to be different from the others, most of them women he hadn't even had to force himself on. But they'd all left him feeling empty. This one, he thought, would be different. But only if she came to him willingly.

The thought almost made him laugh. Women didn't find him . . . attractive. Especially one like this. He wasn't bad looking for such a big, hulking guy. That was usually what reeled in the desperate women he'd known. It was when they'd seen his temper or got a glimpse of the darkness inside him—that's when they wanted nothing to do with him.

He couldn't hide that part of himself. At least not for long. He would end up hurting this woman. He always did. He would see the change in her eyes—just like he had the others. One minute they were fine with him. The next all they wanted was to put as much distance as possible between him and them.

But they never got away easily. He was too big, too strong, too fast for that. Even hurting them, though, hadn't given him the satisfaction he so desperately wanted, needed. Ultimately, they all left him, and he ended up feeling empty and alone.

For once, he wanted a woman to want him—with all his faults.

He stared at little Bo-Peep. She was different. She was the kind of woman he would never have stood a chance with off this mountain. Hell, she dressed like she had money. Even her horse looked expensive. Didn't she say her daddy would pay a million dollars for her?

He'd laughed at the time, but now he wondered if she hadn't been telling the truth. What had she said her name was? Bo Calder. The name didn't ring any bells. She'd probably been lying about the money as well as her name. Not that it mattered. For all his dreaming of her coming to him willingly, he doubted she would last the night.

Chapter
SEVEN

Bo cupped some of the water in her hands and brought it to her face. The icy cold had a numbing effect. She let it run down her arms, washing away the last of the blood but making her scrapes and cuts burn.

"I been thinkin'," Ray said, his tone softer, deadlier. "Ya and me . . ." He let his words trail off.

She looked over at him. He'd taken off his shirt and now splashed water up on him, under his arms, across his stomach. She hadn't realized how big he was, but standing in the creek he looked like a giant.

He saw her staring at his scars and quickly looked away. She did the same. Her legs were numb from the snow-fed stream by the time he waded out to her. He lifted her into his arms again and carried her back to a large flat rock on the creek bank.

She wished her entire body were as numb as her hands and legs. She tried not to flinch at his touch, sensing that anything might set him off.

His sudden kindness filled her with both hope —and terror. Did he feel sorry for her because he knew what was coming next? She watched him out of the corner of her eye. What was he thinking? She could well imagine given how he looked at her.

"You ain't married," he said. "I ain't never been married, not really. I've shacked up with my share. None like you." He stopped.

The almost full moon had reached the tops of the pines, sending an eerie light over the landscape. A hush had fallen over the mountainside. All of it felt surreal as if she was caught in a never-ending nightmare.

No breeze stirred the pines. Even the faint murmur of the creek beside her seemed far away. She wrapped her arms around herself, trembling from the cold and the terror of what would happen next as she watched him retrieve her clothes.

"Put these on," he said and looked away.

She swallowed, trembling with both fear and relief. She felt as if she'd dodged a bullet. But only momentarily, she reminded herself. She'd seen the naked lust that had lit his eyes brighter than even the rising moon.

Her heart pummeled her ribs. She pulled on her jeans and shirt, her fingers shaking uncontrollably as she tried to button her jeans. He'd put his shirt back on, covering the array of scars she'd seen across his chest and back.

"I'm just sayin' we could be good fer each other

up here. I'd take care of ya." There was something pitiful about the way he said it.

Her head jerked up as she realized he was asking her to be his mate up here in the mountains. The insanity of it couldn't have made any of this seem more terrifyingly real. She said nothing, couldn't have spoken if she'd wanted to.

"Ya must be hungry," he said, quickly changing the subject. "Come on." Picking up her boots and socks, he motioned for her to follow him back to the open spot where he'd left her horse. He'd opened himself up to her. Something in his look warned her that if she tried to run, things would go very badly for her.

She followed him, walking barefoot on painfully sore feet. He looked back at her once over his shoulder, and even in the light of the rising moon, she could tell he was pleased she hadn't tried to get away.

Bo took a breath, then another as she fought to understand this change in him. He wanted her to like him, and yet at the same time there was a heartlessness about him that would make him hurt her without flinching if things didn't go as he wanted.

This change in him seemed so incongruous that she felt as if she were walking a tightrope across a deep canyon. One wrong step . . . She took another deep breath. He'd said she was tough. Well, she would have to be. He wanted her to like him, she told herself again. If that meant he wouldn't force himself on her . . . She could only hope for time—and an opportunity to present itself for her escape.

She couldn't chance failing, because there was no doubt in her mind what would happen then.

Jace watched as the moon rose over the pines and scattered the mountainside with fool's gold. He rested against a large tree trunk as he leaned back into the dark shadow of the boughs and kicked himself mentally for thinking this was going to be easy. He should have known finding someone as complicated as Bo Hamilton wouldn't be easy.

He'd first noticed her at grade school the day she walked into the building. He'd been a second grader, Bo a kindergartener. He'd seen something on her freshly scrubbed face, a stark determination as if she'd made up her mind to take on kindergarten as though it was a battle to be won. He'd loved that about her right away.

His attempts to get to know her had been rebuked, though. She didn't seem to make friends easily, standing like she was in her older sisters' shadows.

Jace rubbed a hand over his face. Since that day he'd been chasing Bo Hamilton, he thought with a curse. And she had been distancing herself from him. Listening to the night sounds, he wondered where she was tonight.

What if she had taken a different way out of the mountains? What if she was already back in town? What if he was on a wild-goose chase?

No. Bo was still up here. Had she been headed back to face the consequences, she would have traveled the most direct route—the same one she'd taken when she left.

She could have camped at any of the spots on the way back into the mountains, and yet she'd kept going. Where had she been headed?

He suspected she hadn't had a plan, or she would have taken a credit card and headed for the airport. Instead, she'd gone camping? He reminded himself that she was a cowgirl. This was her country as much as his. This was where he found peace. Maybe this was also where she found it.

Had she, though? She couldn't have brought enough supplies to last more than a night or so back in here. He also couldn't picture her roughing it for long. So where was she?

Jace told himself that eventually she would have to ride out of the mountains. She hadn't dropped down into the other drainage on the Shields River side—at least not yet. That appeared to be the way the man whose tracks he'd seen had come up.

Oh, yeah, what if she is in a Wilsall bar right now having dinner and a drink with that man?

He shook his head as he studied the moonlit

mountains he would ride into come sunup. The pieces didn't fit. Jace felt a shiver even though the night wasn't that cold. He couldn't shake the feeling that he wasn't the only one now sharing these mountains with Bo.

Praying for sunup, he told himself he should try to get some sleep. He would keep following her trail tomorrow. He would find her if he had to follow her to Mexico.

He breathed in the cooling night air. Even though it was summer, it would get cold tonight. He was glad he'd brought an extra sleeping bag. The dark night sky had filled with white stars that twinkled above the treetops.

Was Bo Hamilton looking up at all those stars right now?

Trying to put her out of his mind, he closed his eyes. The image of his sister filled his thoughts. Em would be worried that she hadn't heard from him by now, but she knew him. She knew how, when he set his mind to something, he stuck with it.

"I wish I was like you," she'd said more times than he wanted to remember. "I let life knock me off course."

"Not anymore. You're strong. You have Jodie to think about now. She will help keep you on the straight and narrow." Even as he'd said the words, he'd known it was more complicated than that. And so had Em.

They both worried something could happen to divert her from her best intentions.

He opened his eyes as an owl flapped by overhead, its wings catching flashes of moonlight. He listened for closer sounds. The crunch of dried pine needles under a boot heel. The sharp crack of a limb as a shoulder brushed against it. The stumbling sound of a horse as it came down the trail.

He heard nothing but the faint breeze high in the pines.

Jace closed his eyes, his rifle cradled in his arms, as he thought about what a surprise it would be for Bo Hamilton when he found her. He couldn't wait to see the expression on her face.

"This is nice," Russell said after he and Sarah had eaten a late dinner out on the porch overlooking the valley. She knew he didn't like leaving her up here alone, and she appreciated his company. He tried to come up every day. He always brought food and water and anything else he thought she needed. He was so thoughtful, so caring that she couldn't help being fond of him.

But it worried her that he might be getting too attached to her. He'd actually mentioned marriage. She'd ignored the comment as if she hadn't heard him, but knew she had to be careful or Russell would get the wrong idea.

"Yes, nice," she said.

92

He cleared his throat. She could tell there was something he wanted to talk to her about, but he wasn't sure how to broach the subject. She waited, half-afraid of what he might suggest.

It had grown dark, but she could still see his face in the starlight. "I've been doing more research on memory loss."

Sarah was relieved he didn't want to talk about the two of them, let alone marriage. But she didn't want to discuss her memory loss, either.

"It's cooling down," she said as she rose and picked up their coffee cups to take them back into the cabin. He had to have known bringing up the subject would upset her, but clearly it was something he needed to say.

"I know you hate talking about your condition," he said as he followed her inside, where he turned on lights to chase away the darkness. "I'm sure it haunts you every day. But the more I read, the more I think I know why you can't remember."

They'd had this discussion before. "You believe Buck did something I couldn't live with."

"I do." He was convinced whatever had happened took place between the time she gave birth to the twins and drove into the river. "You wouldn't have left your children and driven your vehicle into an iced-over river in an attempt apparently to kill yourself unless you felt there was no other way out."

"Maybe you just want to believe that," she said, hating the irritation she heard in her voice. "Maybe I'm a selfish, crazy woman. Or maybe it was postpartum depression from suddenly having so many children that I felt overwhelmed."

"I don't believe that, and neither do you." Russell took a breath and let it out slowly. He appeared half afraid to voice his suspicions because he knew they would upset her. Not to mention that they were outlandish. "How can you be so sure that Buckmaster Hamilton wasn't the man who picked you up that night and took you somewhere, saying he was going to get you help?"

She couldn't be sure, since she had no memory of that night. But Russell had told her the news reports said her vehicle had broken through the ice. With her car half submerged, either she'd been ejected or she'd climbed out, fallen through the ice and floated downriver.

According to what Russell had heard around the valley, she'd been found by an old hermit named Lester Halverson, who'd hauled her out of the river, given her warm clothing and promised to keep her secret.

Just before he'd died, he'd apparently confessed the truth. So much for keeping her secret. He'd told the sheriff that she'd made a call and some-one had picked her up in the middle of the night. He hadn't known whom.

"It makes sense that failing your attempt at suicide, you would call your husband after almost drowning—especially if you were depressed and feeling overwhelmed," Russell was saying. "Was there anyone else you would have turned to?"

Living out on the ranch, she hadn't made many friends. She'd gotten pregnant with Ainsley. Two years later, Kat had come along, and then Bo and then Olivia and then the twins. It was the life she wanted. She'd been happy, she was sure of that. So it made sense that if, at some low point, she stupidly tried to kill herself, she would have called the man she loved, Buck Hamilton, because there hadn't been anyone else to call.

"So you think Buck, convinced that I needed help, took me to a mental hospital and had me locked up? Wouldn't there be a record of it? And if there was, you know the media would have found it by now."

"We're talking about *Buckmaster Hamilton*."

"He wasn't that powerful twenty-two years ago." He might not even have been that powerful today. Sarah paced the small kitchen. "So your theory is that Buck had me locked up in some . . . institution all these years?"

Russell said nothing as he pulled out a chair at the kitchen table.

"And what? I *escaped*? That still doesn't explain why I can't remember those years, why my last memory of Beartooth is the birth of my twins."

Russell sat up straighter, leaning toward her as he spoke. "That was your last *good* memory. Whatever happened occurred after that. It's why you can't remember it."

She shook her head. None of this made any sense.

"What if I'm right and he had your memories . . . wiped away? It's called brain wiping," he said, rushing on before she could stop him. "It's not science fiction. It's being used in treating patients with horrible memories that have kept them from living full lives."

"You can't believe that Buck would have my brain *wiped*." She felt horrified at the thought.

"Even back before he became a senator, he had friends in high places."

"Buck is not a monster, and only a monster would . . ." She couldn't even bring herself to say it.

Russell rose but stayed where he was, as if he realized the last thing she wanted him to do was touch her right now. She was scared. Scared that he might be right.

"Just think about it," he said cajolingly. "Even you can't imagine what would have made you leave your six daughters. But I'm betting your husband knows."

She shook her head in disbelief or denial. She couldn't tell which.

"With modern science, memories can be created —and erased. It's possible now to wipe out only certain memories. Doesn't that feel like what has happened to you?"

She crossed her arms, chilled. "You don't know Buck."

"No, but do you? These memories you have of him—how can you be sure that they're even real?"

Tears welled in her eyes. "If you're right, I don't want ever to remember."

"But you *are* remembering, and whatever it is you're seeing, I know it's scaring you."

She swallowed and made a swipe at a tear that had rolled down her cheek. "Think about what you're saying about the man I married. Even with me showing up like I did, Buck's popularity in the polls is still strong. Maybe even stronger since people see him as a saint for supporting two wives. Unless he pulls out of the race, Buckmaster Hamilton is going to be our next president."

"Exactly, and if I'm right about him, then I hate to think what kind of president he's going to be. It terrifies me. Doesn't it you?"

Sarah shook her head. "I had six children with the man. I *know* him. He isn't the monster you want to make him out to be."

"I hear your words of denial, but I know you're scared. Because if I'm right, you and I both know he can't let you remember. If he thought you were starting to . . ."

Sarah shuddered, tears again filling her eyes, as she looked at him. "Buck would never hurt me."

"He already has."

She fought what Russell was saying. She still loved Buckmaster Hamilton. But if she was wrong, then trusting him would be her down-fall—and Russell's, too, if he didn't quit digging into the past.

Buckmaster couldn't sleep. He stood in the dark-ness on the deck outside his bedroom, looking at the Crazies. He could just make out the silhouette of the towering snowcapped mountain range against the dark sky. The formidable range dominated its surroundings, covering six hundred square miles.

He had always lived in its shadow. At fifteen miles wide and forty miles long, its highest point, Crazy Peak, rose to over eleven thousand feet. It was the kind of place a person could disappear into without a trace—and had.

Buckmaster had heard several explanations as to how the mountain range had gotten its name. The mountains were rumored to have scared the first Native Americans who ventured into them. One story was that they named the range Crazy Mountains for the maniacal storms that raged in the unforgiving terrain. Another story was that the Crow Indians called them the Crazy Woman Mountains because of a woman who went insane and lived in them after her family was killed during the westward settlement movement.

All he knew was that he had great respect for the wilderness beyond his ranch. And right now, his daughter was back in there somewhere. Had Jace Calder found her? Buckmaster feared he'd made a mistake by not calling the sheriff and sending up a posse to bring her back. The only reason he hadn't was that it was premature. He needed to give his daughter a chance to come back on her own given the current situation. He had faith that she would.

He'd never worried about his girls taking horseback camping trips into the mountains. When they were young, he'd go with them. The Crazies were his daughters' backyard. They probably knew those mountains better than he did.

That's why he told himself not to worry. But he couldn't help his growing panic. Bo was in trouble. If not up on the mountain, definitely back at the foundation. He'd thought about calling the auditor, but he didn't want it to appear that he didn't trust his daughter. As much as he would have liked to try to fix things for her, he knew Bo would never forgive him. None of the board members had been contacted yet. As long as Bo returned by tomorrow . . . But what if she didn't?

"Do you know what time it is?" Angelina asked.

"Do I care what time it is?" he returned as she joined him on the deck. She'd pulled on a robe and stood hugging herself from the cold. Even Montana summers were chilly at night. They were even colder up in the mountains. "I didn't mean to wake you. Go back to bed."

"You didn't wake me," she said, looking toward the Crazies. "I can't sleep, either."

"You can't be worried about Bo."

"Why not?" she asked, looking over him. "Do you really think I am so cold and uncaring that I'm not worried about her, too?"

She'd never bonded with his daughters, who called her the Ice Queen behind her back. He'd thought the nickname apt, actually. "If she isn't back by tomorrow noon, I'm calling the sheriff."

He'd expected Angelina to put up a fight. She often complained that his daughters did everything possible to interfere with his political career.

But she said nothing as she looked toward the mountains and visibly shivered. Was she thinking of Bo up there, possibly hurt, alone and scared? He'd certainly imagined that—and worse.

"Come to bed."

He glanced at her, surprised by the tenderness in her tone. Even more surprised by the touch of her hand. Three months of sleeping on his own

100

side of the bed made him ache for a woman's soft, supple body. Desire stirred in him.

But it was Sarah he wanted naked against him. It had always been Sarah. He closed his eyes against the pain of loving a woman he could no longer have.

Angelina took his hand. He let her lead him back into the dark bedroom.

Ray cooked a can of beans over the fire, adding some dried meat and a wild onion. "Used to come up here with my old man," he said as he stirred. The large metal spoon clinked against the side of the equally battered pan. She wondered where he'd gotten the supplies. The pan was black with soot as if it had been used over many campfires—and not just in the past three weeks.

"My old man'd talked about livin' up here," he was saying. "He was gonna build a cabin way back in where nobody'd ever find us."

So he knew these mountains, she realized as her heart dropped into her empty, growling stomach. He'd grown up on the other side of the drainage, he'd told her.

"I was huntin' by the time I could hold a rifle. I weren't never as good as my old man, though. He just don't miss. That's why they made him a sniper when he joined up in the service."

She heard pride in his voice, and both awe and something else. Fear?

"I growed up eatin' venison year-round. Never ate no beef 'til I left home. Hell, elk was as fancy as it got at our house."

Bo let him talk as she watched him. He seemed agitated. She took that as a bad sign. Things could go seriously wrong yet tonight.

"Here," he said, shoving the handle of the pot into her hand. "Ya eat what ya want first. Just leave me a little."

She took the spoon he offered her. It didn't matter that it was canned beans. She would have eaten anything at this point. She was ravenous. Her stomach growled loudly, making him smile.

"I'm a pretty good cook. Not this, but once we get settled way back where no one'll come lookin' for us, I'll kill what we need. There's grouse up here, deer, elk, even bears." He sounded excited about the prospect. "Ya can grow a garden. I can get ya seeds. I can get ya whatever ya need."

Bo blew on the spoonful of beans and took a bite. They tasted slightly burned but, starving as she was, she gobbled spoonful after spoonful as he talked about his plans for the two of them.

"I can't never go back down there, not to live, but that ain't really livin' anyway, you know what I mean? I'm happiest up here in the mountains. Ya must be, too, or ya wouldn't a come up here."

She could feel his eyes searching her face. She took another bite of the beans. She could hardly keep her eyes open. The warm beans hit her stomach and made her even more sleepy. He seemed more relaxed, too. She could only hope he would leave her alone tonight.

After a few more bites, she handed him the pot and spoon.

"Ya rest. We gotta git up early and travel a lot farther tomorrow," he said after he'd finished off the meal. "But 'til we understand each other . . ." He picked up the rope from the ground.

"Please—"

"I ain't gonna tie ya tight if ya promise not to try to git away."

She nodded, wincing as he bound her wrists and ankles. He spread out a dirty sleeping bag for her to lie on. She curled up and closed her eyes, opening them only a crack to watch him, still terrified he would change his mind and assault her before the night was over.

He took the pot down to the creek and came back with it sloshing water that splashed at his feet as he walked. He set it on the fire and dropped the dirty spoon into it. "I ain't been takin' care of myself." He glanced in her direction. She didn't move. Didn't even breathe. "I got reason to now. I kin take care a both a us."

Bo fought sleep, afraid if she gave up to it, something worse might happen. But in the end, exhaustion won out, dragging her down into the darkest of dreams.

Chapter
EIGHT

Before any of the hired help arrived early the next morning, Buckmaster picked up the phone in the kitchen and dialed the sheriff's office. He'd sworn he would wait until noon, but Bo hadn't come home last night. He'd checked first thing this morning, but neither she nor her horse had returned. When he'd tried her cell, it went straight to voice mail, not that he was surprised. This morning, he'd found her cell phone in her vehicle parked in front of the bunkhouse.

That she hadn't taken her cell phone shouldn't have upset him. Service was sketchy at best in the area, let alone up in the mountains. Bo would know that.

But if you got in trouble, often times you could find a mountain peak and get enough bars to call for help. Also, you could sometimes track a phone in an emergency through the GPS.

He told himself it was her stubborn pride. From the time she was little, she was determined to do everything on her own. He'd never seen such a pigheaded child who would just plain refuse to ask for help. It was why she hadn't come to him when she'd realized there was trouble at the foundation. So no wonder she wouldn't take her cell phone. She wasn't about to call even if she got in trouble.

Either that or she hadn't wanted to be found.

Either way, it scared him. His daughter hadn't returned from the mountains, knowing that by now she'd not only be missed, but also that an auditor was waiting for her.

The line to the sheriff's department dispatcher began to ring. From the other side of the room, Angelina sipped a fresh cup of coffee and watched him, her face a mask.

Last night they'd made love. It hadn't started that way. He'd been thinking about Sarah, but that had changed at some point. He'd held his wife, and for a while, he'd felt again the affection he'd had for her when he'd first married her.

It had taken him a while to fall in love with Angelina. She wasn't an easy woman to love. Also, he'd still been mourning Sarah's death even after seven years. But Angelina had wound her way into his heart and his bed. He couldn't discount what she'd brought to his life, if not the lives of his girls.

"Sheriff's department."

"I need to speak with Sheriff Curry. This is Senator Hamilton calling. It's important I speak with him."

"Just one moment, please."

Frank, probably still at home, came on the line right away. "Senator?"

"My daughter Bo went up into the mountains on a camping trip Saturday afternoon. She hasn't returned, and I'm worried," he said without preamble.

"Have you sent anyone up to look for her?" the sheriff asked.

"Jace Calder volunteered. He left yesterday afternoon. I promised to give him twenty-four hours, but I'm worried something has happened up there."

"When was she expected back?" Frank asked.

"Yesterday morning." Buckmaster hesitated. "She had an appointment at her office she didn't show up for."

Silence. He could almost hear the sheriff thinking. "You know that we usually wait forty-eight hours on a missing adult unless there are extenuating circumstances." Bo had been missing not even twenty-four from the time she was supposed to return. "Are there extenuating circumstances?"

Buckmaster thought about the missing money and his daughter. But if he told the sheriff, there was no way he would want to send search and rescue to look for her even after forty-eight hours.

"No," he said. "But if she isn't back by this afternoon or I haven't heard from Jace . . ."

"Then you let me know," the sheriff said. "As it

is, why don't I see if we can't do a flyover? If she's in trouble, she'd know to try to signal the pilot."

Buckmaster felt a little better. "Thank you, Frank. I'd appreciate that."

As he hung up, he looked at Angelina. She'd pulled on a thin negligee and now stood against the light of the window. She really did have a wonderful body.

"You didn't tell him about the problem at the foundation."

"No." He refused to admit that Bo would run away, and if she had, then he had to believe she would come to her senses and return of her own accord. He might not have done a good job raising her, but she still had his blood running through her veins. She wouldn't take the easy way out. She'd come back and face up to whatever was going on at the foundation. Bo was strong like him.

Stepping to his wife, he took the coffee cup from her hand and placed it on the counter. Then he pressed her against the wall.

"In the kitchen?" she asked, sounding breathless but also excited as he slipped his hand under the silken fabric to feel the heat of her bare skin.

As he brushed his lips over the warm skin at her throat, he had trouble even admitting it to himself, but he was running scared. The ground under him no longer felt solid. The life he'd built felt as if it could topple over in the first good gust of wind. He could sense a fierce storm coming, one much worse than what had already hit him and his home.

For a while, he lost himself in the primitive, age-old act of passion. Later, spent and under the spray of the shower, he got down on his knees and did something he hadn't done in a long time. He prayed for Bo and the rest of his family. He prayed for Sarah and for Angelina. Then he prayed for his own soul.

Mostly, he prayed for guidance. While he'd taken a short hiatus, now he needed to get back to Washington, back on the campaign trail. But he couldn't leave until he knew Bo was safe.

Since he'd begun running for president, he'd felt cursed. Was this how his father had felt? Was this why he'd backed out of the presidential race?

He knew it was foolish to pray for a sign from God as to what he should do, but he prayed for it anyway, terrified the curse that had destroyed his father was now on him—and his family.

Bo woke to the sounds and smells of a crackling fire. She opened her eyes and blinked. For a moment, she thought she was still camped in the woods alone. But then she felt the rope biting into her ankles and wrists, and remembered. Her stomach twisted, and she thought she might throw up as her gaze went to the man hunched over the fire. Her skin broke out in a cold sweat. She gulped down breaths to keep from sobbing hysterically again. *He wants to keep me for a mate.*

As he started to turn in her direction, she hurriedly closed her eyes tight and bit back a cry of desolation. Maybe if he thought she was still asleep . . .

The kick to her thigh was anything but gentle. "Daylight's burnin'," he said. "Hafta get movin'. I cooked ya somethin'."

She opened her eyes, pretending that his kick had awakened her. She tried to sit up. Her muscles ached. It was all she could do not to groan in pain. But he'd seemed to like it when he thought she was tougher than she looked, so she held silent.

She had to play along. *He wants to win me over. If I agree too quickly . . .* Well, she knew how that could go. But if she fought him . . .

He bent down to untie the rope at her ankles, his gaze stealing to hers every few seconds. She could tell he was trying to gauge how she was feeling about him this morning. He'd opened up to her last night, telling her a lot about himself and about his life with his father. Did he now regret being that vulnerable with her?

She tried hard to keep her expression pleasant. "What did you cook?"

"Beans. That's all we got, so no complainin'. I'll kill somethin' in a day or two, once we get settled farther in where no one'll hear the gunshot."

Bo nodded, realizing that he planned to make her hike miles and miles back into the mountains as far from civilization as the Crazies went.

He untied her wrists. "I s'pose ya gotta go."

At first she didn't understand.

"Can't let ya go by yerself," he said, pulling her up by one arm. She was still barefoot. As she looked around for her socks and boots, he shook his head. "No shoes. Not 'til I kin trust ya." He made it sound as if he planned to keep her barefoot for a very long time.

Again she nodded, and she let him lead her away from camp to a stand of thick pines. She limped across the dried pine needles and twigs that hurt the soles of her bare feet, but again she did everything possible not to react to the pain.

"In there," he said and handed her a small roll of toilet paper. "I'll be right here. If I hear ya try to run—"

"I won't," she said, taking the paper and limping into the center of the cluster of trees.

She'd had so little to eat that all she had to do was pee, but she left enough of the toilet paper that she thought someone might see it and at least know she'd been here. She'd thought about trying to leave a message, but she knew Ray was listening, half expecting her to do something to lose his trust.

"Ya done?" he asked when she came out and handed him the rest of the roll. He seemed a little surprised and maybe pleased that she hadn't given him any trouble as he led her back to the campfire. The fire he'd built was small, making her wonder if he was worried that her family would be searching for her. What would her father do if someone from the foundation called?

She knew what everyone would think. That she'd run away. How long, though, before her father would send someone up to find her? Or would he wait, assuring himself that eventually she would have to come out of the mountains and face things?

Days, she thought as Ray handed her the pot and spoon. She ate a few bites, knowing she needed to keep up her strength. Ray had made it clear he would be dragging her farther back into the mountains today.

She couldn't bear the thought. Her legs and feet still ached from yesterday's hike—not to mention her wrists, which were raw and painful. Last night, he'd tied the rope on her wrists looser, but still the rough sisal had rubbed against her raw skin every time she moved.

Tears blurred her eyes at the thought of another day of torture, and all the while he would be watching her, waiting. Anything could set him off. She took a few more bites of the beans and handed back the pot and spoon. "I'm not sure I can walk as far as I did yesterday," she said in a small voice, trying hard not to cry. She feared tears would trigger his anger. Or his lust. As she raised her gaze to his, for a moment she thought he might hit her—or worse.

But he just dumped the beans into the fire and stepped to the creek to rinse the pot and the spoon. His back was to her as he squatted by the stream. She glanced over and saw her socks and boots.

Desperately she wanted to run, to go screaming through the forest. Her gaze fell on the crude circle of rocks around the fire pit. Her hands itched to pick up one of the rocks and charge him, slamming the rock down on his head as he crouched over the water.

He wants you to try to get away. He's waiting for you to do it so he can hurt you.

Bo chocked back a sob as she crawled closer to the fire pit. She glanced toward him. Saw him freeze. He was listening. Expecting it. She busied herself by putting out the fire. Slowly she began to scoop up dirt and dump it on the last of the coals as her chest ached with unshed tears and smoke curled up from the dying fire.

Ray rose slowly next to the creek and walked back to her. He glanced at her as she put more dirt on the embers. Smothered, the fire sputtered out, the smoke thinning into a narrow ribbon as it wound up into Montana's clear blue big sky.

He handed her the pot full of icy-cold creek water. "Here, wash yer hands." She did, drying them on her jeans as he reached over and picked up her socks and her boots. "Put these on." He took the pot from her, trading her for her socks and boots.

She watched him pack up everything, knowing he was watching her, as well. Somehow she'd stilled the need to do something risky that would only make her situation worse. She felt stronger, more capable this morning after having lived through the night. But how could she continue with this unbearable situation much longer?

Bo knew that Ray would eventually rape her. She'd seen the hunger in his eyes after weeks alone in these mountains. The man hadn't become an escaped criminal because he could control his impulses. It was only a matter of time.

Her mind whirled as she plotted. She would get him to trust her. Then she would find her chance to escape, and she would take it.

She realized she could never outrun him. If she was lucky enough to get on her horse . . . But she couldn't depend on that. He would expect her to go for the horse. He would make sure she didn't get the chance.

No, she thought. She would have to disable him.

That thought turned her stomach. She'd never hurt anyone—at least not physically, she thought, reminded of Jace Calder. Disabling such a large man would take a great deal of force. A great deal of violence. And even that might not be enough.

Could she kill Ray?

She finished pulling on her socks and boots and looked up at him.

The naked lust was back in his eyes even stronger than yesterday. He scratched his stubbled jaw for a moment, his look burning her flesh. She dropped her gaze to the dusty ground, tried not to move, tried not to cringe, as out of the corner of her eye, she saw him pull the duct tape from his jacket pocket and step toward her.

Chapter
NINE

Alex hadn't known what was bothering Emily Calder the day before. But when she came into the coffee shop for her break the following morning, she looked even more upset.

He hoped it had nothing to do with her accepting a date with him the day before.

Normally he didn't spend much time in any one coffee shop. He liked to divide his time between them. But lately, he'd been making himself useful at the Big Timber one because of Emily. Since he'd started out working in a coffee shop, he still remembered how to make a mean cup of coffee.

When he saw Emily come in, he waved her to an empty table and quickly made her coffee, personally taking it over to her. His cousin and the other barista shared a look that he ignored.

"Here you go," he said to Emily. "Is everything all right?" he asked more quietly.

She looked up to meet his eyes. "Great."

"Really?"

"Maybe not great."

He felt his heart drop, afraid of what she was going to say next. "If it's about our date . . ."

She shook her head. "Things aren't going well at work."

He couldn't help his relief. "I'm sorry to hear that. Is it anything you can talk about?"

She shook her head. "But this helps." She gave him a smile and reached for the coffee.

He watched her take a sip. "Did I get it right?"

"Perfect." Her gaze locked with his. "Thank you. You really need to let me pay you," she said, pulling her gaze away to dig in her purse.

"It's my treat."

"I don't want to get you into trouble with your boss," she whispered.

He started to tell her that he was the boss, but something stopped him. She'd said she would go out with him, thinking he worked at the shop part-time. Would it change things if he told her who he really was?

He feared it would, so he let her count out the cost of the coffee—and a tip. "Thanks," he said and let it go at that. "If you ever need to talk, though . . . well, you have my number."

She smiled. "I might do that."

Bo swallowed hard as Ray came toward her with the roll of duct tape. She avoided his eyes, trying to make herself as small and vulnerable as possible. As if she wasn't as vulnerable as she'd ever been.

"Yer goin' to have to ride the horse," he said as

he knelt down beside her and pulled out a length of the tape. "We ain't never gettin' there if yer the one walkin'."

She was so surprised that she looked up at him.

He must have seen hope spark in her gaze, because his face twisted into a cruel expression. "If ya think—"

"No," she said quickly. "I'm just relieved. I wasn't sure I could walk very far."

He studied her, clearly trying to gauge the truth in her words. "I kin see ya'd be worthless walkin'." He nodded. "Ya'll ride, but I'll be leadin' yer horse and if ya—"

"I won't," she said, not needing to hear any more of this threats.

He grabbed her wrist, his fingers biting into her flesh. "Right. Ya won't." He began to wrap her wrists together so tightly that she let out a cry. She'd made him angry. He'd seen how badly she wanted to escape. She couldn't make that mistake again.

Bo bit her lip against the pain of the tape on her already raw wrists. She wouldn't cry out again. She couldn't if she hoped to keep him from hurting her. She could feel him watching her, taking her measure. She'd never met anyone more mistrustful. What had made him like this? She remembered the myriad of scars on his body and shuddered to think. Not that it mattered how he'd come to be the violent criminal the police had tagged him. She had to learn how to avoid upsetting him. She wouldn't let herself think about how long she would have to appease this man or what would happen when he'd had enough of her.

She told herself she could do this. She would survive this no matter what she had to do.

"I heard Bo Hamilton is missing," Lynette "Nettie" Johnson Benton Curry said as she joined her husband for an early lunch at the picnic table beside the Beartooth General Store. The day had turned beautiful, bright and sunny with a hint of the warmth of the summer to come.

"What?" The sheriff stopped digging out the sandwiches from the bag she'd brought to look at his wife. Her hair, a bottle red, suited her. She'd had her naturally curly hair cut short. That too suited her since she was a small woman, although he'd never thought of her that way. True, he towered over her, but Lynette was such a strong, determined, stubborn and infuriating woman that she'd always felt more like his equal.

"Hadn't you heard?" she asked, blue eyes sparkling with both surprise and pleasure. While she had tried to give up gossip, it still found her doorstep. And whether she would admit it or not, she still enjoyed knowing something that other people didn't—and sharing it. "She went up into the Crazies camping Saturday, planning to be back yesterday, but no one has seen her."

"That much I know," he said as he pulled out a sandwich and freed it from the plastic bag. "Her father called me. What I'd like to know is how *you* know." He took a big bite of his sandwich.

"Anita, who works at the café next to the Sarah Hamilton Foundation office, overheard one of the employees talking. She told her sister, who told Claudia Turner, who told Mabel Murphy—"

"Who told you," he said with a nod of his head. He took another bite of his sandwich. It always amazed him how fast gossip traveled in this county—and the circular routes it took before it reached his wife.

Lynette leaned closer. "The reason everyone is in a panic is that an auditor was to meet with Bo at 11:00 a.m. yesterday morning. Guess why an auditor was called in."

Frank shook his head. He wasn't sure he wanted to hear this, but something told him he needed to.

"There's money missing along with Bo Hamilton. Apparently, a lot of money. Someone has been stealing from the foundation for months."

He put down the half-eaten sandwich as his stomach did a slow roll.

"What's wrong? I thought you liked tuna fish," Lynette said.

"So the assumption on the gossip line is that she's run off with the money?" he asked, feeling a little sick. Buckmaster hadn't mentioned any of this, no doubt purposely.

Lynette nibbled at her sandwich. "Oh, you know the grapevine. Speculation is that there is a man involved."

He bristled. "Why would people instantly think a man was involved?" he demanded more forcefully than he meant to, and more defensively. "Women steal all the time and all by themselves without any help from a man."

She eyed him over her sandwich, looking amused. "What else would make a woman like Bo Hamilton steal from her own mother's charity foundation and take off if there wasn't a man involved?"

He stared at her, fascinated with how her mind worked. "I will never understand women." He stood.

"You aren't going to finish your sandwich?"

"I've lost my appetite." He didn't know why he was so upset. Another Hamilton in trouble, that's all he could think, and now the foundation was involved. Not to mention that all the women in the valley were convinced a man was at the root of the problem.

Lynette put his usual, an orange soda and a

candy bar, back into his lunch bag. "Here, you'll want this for when you get hungry later, especially since you didn't finish your sandwich."

She knew him so well. He snatched up his sandwich and took a giant bite, chewing it as he looked at her, almost daring her to say anything.

She smiled. "I love you, too."

He finished the sandwich before he took the bag she'd offered him. She was right. Later he would want the orange soda and the candy bar.

Right now, he was angry with himself. He wished he had asked more questions about the missing Bo Hamilton when her father had called him. He wondered if he was losing his edge.

"I suppose you don't want to hear the latest on Sarah Hamilton, then?" she asked as he started to walk away.

He sat back down at the picnic table, feeling his anger leave as he looked at his wife. Lynette was the love of his life. She frustrated the hell out of him sometimes, a lot of times, but he never wanted to live without her.

"Nothing you can say will surprise me," he said, realizing it had sounded like a dare. He didn't want to dare Lynette.

She chuckled and leaned toward him conspiratorially, signaling this was going to surprise him whether he liked it or not. With a sigh, he waited. There were no other people around since it was almost two in the afternoon. But still Lynette felt the need to whisper, which meant whatever she planned to tell him was going to be good.

"As you know, when Sarah Hamilton suddenly showed up in the middle of nowhere outside Beartooth and stepped out of the trees in front of Russell Murdock's pickup, Russell took her to the closest doctor, which just happened to be old Dr. Farnsworth."

Yes, he knew all this and said as much. Dr. Farnsworth was retired, lived just down the road from where Russell had found the woman and had moved to the area a few years ago with his wife, so he hadn't recognized the senator's first wife whom everyone else had thought dead for twenty-two years.

Lynette nodded. "The doctor was checking Sarah for injuries and getting her cleaned up, since apparently she was scraped up along with being confused, so he had his wife help him with her."

Frank was losing his patience. "Lynette—"

"The doctor's wife saw something."

"Saw something?"

Lynette leaned closer. "A tattoo."

"A lot of people have tattoos." He told himself this wasn't news, and yet when he thought of fiftysomething Sarah Hamilton, she was the last person he'd expect to get a tattoo.

But he reminded himself that the woman

couldn't account for twenty-two years of her life. Who knew what could have happened to her during that time? Did any of them know *this* Sarah Hamilton?

"Not everyone has a tattoo like this one." Lynette was still looking like the cat who'd eaten the canary.

"Like what?" he demanded.

"Very unusual. The doctor's wife had never seen another one like it."

"How many tattoos has the woman seen?" he grumbled. "Is she an expert in tattoos? The woman is in her seventies. I really don't think—"

Lynette reached into her pocket and pulled out a small white piece of paper. "I had her draw the design to the best of her memory." She held the paper out triumphantly. "I thought you might also like to know where this tattoo is located." As he started to tell her he was getting tired of having to guess, she held up her hand and said, "On her right buttock. Kind of like the way you brand your cattle."

He took the scrap of paper and looked down at the crudely drawn design. Then he looked at his wife. "What the hell is it?"

"If I had to guess, I'd say it was a pendulum."

"A pendulum? Why would someone get this tattooed on their butt?"

His wife shrugged.

"But what does it mean?"

"You're the detective. I can't do it all for you," she said as she finished her sandwich. "You have to admit it's interesting, isn't it?"

He wanted to grab her and kiss her. "I really should hire you for the department," he said as he looked again at the design. It did remind him of a brand. "A pendulum, huh?"

"I have to get back to work." She'd married the Beartooth General Store when she married her first husband, Bob Benton. He had hated the store. He gave it to her in the divorce because she loved working there. After it burned down, she'd sold the property, thinking she'd put that part of herlife behind her.

But now she was back working for the new owner part-time because the store was still her baby, the only baby she'd ever had. Also, the store was the epicenter of the county's gossip and, like it or not, Lynette was a gossip magnet.

"Hey," he said as she put her trash in her paper lunch bag and stood to leave. He rose, as well. Taking her arm, he drew her to him. "You really are something."

"I know. That's why you married me."

"That was one reason," he admitted with a chuckle. Then he kissed her, picked up his bag with his soda and candy from the picnic table and headed for his office, hoping someone somewhere could tell him what this tattoo meant, because it damned sure meant *something*.

• • •

"Tell me again about how you met Sarah."

"Angelina, must we do this now?" Buckmaster asked with a groan. He suspected she was merely trying to keep his mind off Bo. All through lunch, he'd been looking out the window, praying that he would see her come riding out of the pines in the distance.

"Please just indulge me."

"I've told you. I took a load of horses up into the park for the summer. I was unloading them when I noticed her standing next to the corral."

"So it was love at first sight?"

He heard the edge to her voice. Why did she put herself through this? She'd never shown any jealousy before Sarah's return. Or had he just missed it?

"It wasn't love at first sight." As he said it, he realized how true that was. Sarah had been cute, but he came across a lot of cute girls. At twenty-five, he hadn't even given a thought to settling down . . . But somehow that had changed the day he met Sarah, he realized.

"Who made the first move?" Angelina asked.

He let himself remember. He could almost smell the dust, the horses and the pines. The warm, early summer breeze stirred her long blond hair. Even now he could feel the summer sun on his back.

"Have you ridden all of these horses?" she had asked.

It had seemed like an odd thing for her to say. Most girls said things like "I love horses" or "Would you show me how to ride one?" Things he'd heard many times before.

He'd looked at the horses he'd released into the corral and laughed. "Yep, I think I *have* ridden them all." They took only the gentlest of horses to Yellowstone for the tourists to ride, so these had been around the ranch for some time.

"Which is your favorite? Wait. Let me guess." She seemed to study the horses as they milled around the corral, her gaze so intent he'd wanted to laugh again.

"That one!" she'd finally said excitedly. "What's her name?"

"What makes you think that horse is a mare?"

She'd smiled at him. "I'm right. She's your favorite, isn't she?"

Sarah had chosen a palomino mare named Sunny, a mare who just happened to be one of his favorites. He'd given Sarah another look. It wasn't just because she was flirting with him. He had time to kill. He didn't have to be back to the ranch until morning.

"You must be psychic," he'd said as he joined her at the corral fence.

They'd got to talking, and the next thing he

knew, he'd asked her to the movie in Gardiner. Had it been her idea? He couldn't remember. She could have asked what was showing and said she was dying to see it. He couldn't be sure.

He frowned. She'd definitely come on to him.

"Well?" Angelina asked.

"Well what?"

"Was she the instigator?"

"What if she was?" he demanded. "What does that prove?"

"That she knew who you were, knew you were bringing horses up that day, knew you were the son of Senator B. D. Hamilton."

He shook his head. He was often confused lately by what Angelina was talking about. "Even if all of that were true, what possible difference could it make now?"

"Admit it. She came after you. She must have had a reason."

"Think about what you're saying, Angelina. What? Did she trick me into marrying her, hoodwink me into impregnating her with six daughters so she could try to kill herself and disappear later for twenty-two years?"

"There has to be a reason for all of this," Angelina said stubbornly.

He couldn't see that there was a reason for anything and said as much. "You're going to drive yourself crazy looking for sense in something that makes no sense."

"That's what she wants you to think," Angelina said cryptically. "You wait and see. Sarah knows exactly what she's doing."

Jace had awakened before the crack of dawn. The night had been long. He'd dozed, but his sleep hadn't been restful. All night, his senses had been on alert to any sound other than the usual forest hum.

He'd had a dream, one of those crazy ones that hadn't made any sense and yet had been disturbing. It had been about the night his parents had died. Even with the light of day, he could still feel a cloying darkness, imagine the smell of the smoke rising up from the wrecked plane and hear the heart-rending cries of his little sister.

Unsettled by the nightmare, he'd eaten some jerky and saddled up, anxious to find Bo Hamilton and put his waking nightmare to rest.

Riding to a high ridge, he tried his cell phone. He wanted to see if Bo had returned. He got a few bars and punched in Senator Buckmaster Hamilton's number.

The man answered on the second ring. "Have you found her?"

"Not yet." He'd hoped that somehow Bo had surprised him and found her way back to the ranch. He knew it was wishful thinking that she might have returned on her own. He'd picked up her horse's tracks again this morning. They were headed up the ridgeline and deeper into the Crazies.

"I'd hoped . . ." Jace could hear the distress in the older man's voice.

"I'm on her trail, headed deeper into the mountains." Jace heard nothing but silence and looked down to see that he'd lost the senator. He tried again but couldn't get enough service for the call to go through this time.

He had wanted to ask whether Bo had been seeing someone. It could explain why the only other tracks he'd found were a man-size boot print that had crossed her path several times. He knew that was a long shot. The two probably weren't connected.

The tracks bothered him. He should have seen other horseshoe prints. If Bo were meeting someone, wouldn't the man be on horseback? Had something happened to his horse? Or was it a backpacker? Most backpackers didn't wear cowboy boots with worn soles, though.

It was almost as if the man had been tracking Bo on foot.

As he looked ahead into the shadowy, dense pines, he worried even more about who was up on this mountain with him and Bo.

Chapter
TEN

Sarah felt at loose ends. She hadn't seen Buck for days now. She wanted to know how her daughters were doing. If she didn't get out of this cabin, she would go stir-crazy.

Russell had left last night, saying he had some business to take care of at his ranch but he'd check in later with her today. She knew calling Buck, the man she still considered her husband, was probably a mistake. Russell didn't think she could trust Buck.

"Did I catch you at a bad time?" she asked when he answered.

"No. In fact, I was just thinking about you," Buck said. "I have something for you."

"Buck, I don't need—"

"Please, let me do this. Is there any way I can see you?"

Sarah hesitated. Russell would be furious with her, but he didn't understand that in her mind, Buck was her loving husband with whom she'd had six children. Those missing years were just that: missing.

"I could give you the directions to where I'm

staying," she said. "Just be careful so no one from the press—"

"I will."

Thirty minutes later, he drove up in front of the cabin. Every time she saw him, she felt those old emotions roiling inside her. This was her husband. This was the man she loved.

But then she would hear Russell's voice in her head. *If you loved him so much, why would you have driven your car into the Yellowstone River in the middle of winter in an attempt to kill yourself? Then, when that failed, why would you leave for twenty-two years?*

That was the question, wasn't it? Maybe that was what she hoped to find out by seeing Buck. But as she watched him climb out of his SUV, she reminded herself that this man was married to someone else now and on his way to the White House. A whole lot had changed since that night she plunged into the Yellowstone.

"So this is where Murdock's been keeping you," Buck said and shook his head. "Did he mention that I want you to move onto the ranch?"

She nodded.

"And?"

Not wanting to argue with Buck for the short time they would have together, she said, "I'm thinking about it."

That seemed to appease him. He relaxed a little,

reminding her of the old Buck Hamilton she'd fallen in love with.

"I want you to have this," he said, reaching into his pocket and pulling out the handgun.

Sarah stared at the .22 pistol as Buck laid it on the table. From his other pocket he pulled out a cell phone.

"I want you to be protected. I also want you to be able to call me anytime—and not with Russell's phone."

She didn't want him going off about Russell, so she asked, "Protected from *what?*" She still hadn't touched the gun, could barely look at it.

"I don't know. *Whatever.*" He waved an arm through the air impatiently. "Until I'm around to make sure you're all right . . ."

"*Until?* Are you planning to make some changes in your life that I don't know about?"

He dropped his arm and looked at her. "You know I spend most of my time in Washington as it is, and now with this damned campaign . . ." He rubbed a hand over his face. "I hate not knowing where you are, what's happening with you or if you need . . . anything." He took a breath and let it out slowly. "This is just so damned confusing."

"It seems pretty simple to me. You're married to another woman. Angelina is your concern now. Not me."

Buck swore. "You know it's not that damned

simple." His eyes filled with sadness. "I worry about you."

"You just don't like me being around Russell."

He seemed to chew at the inside of his cheek for a moment. She almost smiled because she *did* know this man. He was fighting to keep from saying anything derogatory about Russell Murdock. When he had before, she'd defended Russell, which only angered Buck more.

"Hell, I've always liked the man," he said now. "Until he became involved with my wife."

"Russell and I are not *involved*. And I'm not your wife."

"You know what I mean," Buck said, studying her openly as if trying to decide for himself how involved she was with Russell. Wouldn't he have a fit if he knew that Russell had mentioned marriage? Well, what was good for the goose was good for the gander, she thought, surprised that she was angry at Buck for remarrying.

She knew that wasn't fair. She'd left Buck—not the other way around.

"I'll feel better if I know you at least have a cell phone of your own and a weapon, should you need one," he said.

She looked down at the .22, knowing what it would mean to him if she took it. He'd feel he'd done something, and Buck couldn't stand feeling otherwise.

The small gun was nothing more than a peashooter. She wanted to laugh. But she also wanted to cry as she picked up the small, useless thing. It felt light and ridiculous in her hand. She felt an aching longing for something heavy and powerful as she quickly put it back down and hugged herself against the memory of a much more powerful weapon in her hands.

"Sarah—"

"So you think I need a gun? That's why you had to see me." She couldn't help feeling disappointed. What had she hoped he would say when he got here? "You're assuming I know what to do with a weapon?"

"I know you never showed an interest in guns."

She shook her head, wondering why he didn't remember that she'd wanted nothing to do with any kind of weapon. She hadn't even wanted them in the house, not with six small children.

"I thought you might have learned to shoot sometime since . . ." He let that thought fall away, but his gaze searched hers. He was wondering again about those years she'd been missing. Everyone wanted to know where she'd been and what she'd being doing. Herself included.

Buck suggested they go outside and do a little target practice. He found some rusted cans and set them up on the fence. Then he patiently walked her through how to use the weapon. As he droned on, she let her mind wander. When he finally handed her the .22 pistol, she turned out to be an excellent shot. The only person surprised was Buck.

Deputy Bentley Jamison, a former New York City homicide detective, studied the scrap of paper before looking up at his boss. "Sometimes a tattoo is just a tattoo."

"Not this time," Frank said as he sat back in his chair. He'd called Jamison in because the man had seen more tattoos than any of his other deputies. He'd hoped that Jamison might have recognized it. "It isn't like any tattoo I've ever seen. Is it possible it's a jailhouse tattoo?"

"If it's as crudely done as this drawing, it's possible. I'd have to see it to tell you."

"Seeing it could be a problem. Who gets their butt cheek tattooed?"

The deputy laughed. "More than you might think."

"I should have added, a woman fifty-some years old?" Frank said.

"She could have had that tattoo since she was a teenager. Have you asked her about it? Or Buckmaster. He'd know if she had it before she disappeared."

He hadn't. "I might ask the senator. He's in town right now. He's going to wonder why I want to know, though."

"You haven't told him about the way his first wife returned from the grave?"

135

"That she parachuted down from a low-flying plane wearing a paratrooper's chute as if the whole thing had been some kind of special ops undercover operation? No. He never asked. He's probably like everyone else who thought she'd been dropped beside the road after maybe hitchhiking back here. But maybe it's time I did tell the senator," the sheriff said with a sigh as he rose from his chair. "He needs to know that Sarah might not be the woman he married anymore. Also, I want to see his face when I tell him in case he knows more about this than I do. I'll question him about the tattoo, as well."

"Are you going to share your suspicions?" Jamison asked.

"I would think he'd have his own suspicions when he hears what I have to tell him, wouldn't you? Meanwhile, I've talked to search and rescue. They're going to do a flyover tomorrow and see if they can find Bo Hamilton. Given what I know about why she left when she did, I'm not as concerned that something has happened to her. I think she might not *want* to be found."

The bright sun was blinding. It speared down through the trees to pierce Bo with an intensity that made her head ache. A thin trail of smoke rose from the fire pit, the smell irritating her throat and eyes.

She blinked as she fought to get her wits about

her. Now that breakfast was over, they would be traveling farther north into the mountains. All her instincts told her that she had to find a way to escape.

It was dangerous to even try. Just the thought made her pulse pound in her ears and her body go weak with fear. He wanted her to like him. Every time she met his gaze, she saw a hopefulness that would have broken her heart under any other circumstances.

He wanted so desperately to trust her—and yet he didn't. She had seen him wavering, had felt that knife edge of control over his rage and violence, and knew that if she failed, he would kill her. Eventually. Her instincts told her that he would make her pay in the worst possible ways until then.

She pushed that thought out of her mind, because if she didn't get away from him, it was inevitable that he would attack her. She could hold him off for only so long. Eventually he would realize that this idea of his of the two of them living up here together was just a stupid dream on his part. That alone would burn him and make him furious. That alone could get her killed.

After he'd taped her wrists together, he pulled her to her feet by one arm. She saw that he'd saddled her horse this morning before she'd woken up. Her heart began to pound so hard she thought it would bruise her ribs as he led her over to her horse.

Her mind raced as she ordered her limbs not to shake. She held her head high and desperately tried to keep her expression neutral. She could feel him watching her. The man was no fool. He had to know that once she was on the horse, she would try to get away. It was her only chance.

A plan had been stirring in her brain. It wasn't a great one because it depended on Ray giving her the opportunity she needed. Since her wrists were bound, she would have to kick him. Ideally, he would step far enough away that she could put a boot to his head. Her only other choice was to kick him hard enough in the chest or stomach to at least knock the air out of him and give her those precious seconds she needed to get away.

Would the kick be enough of a surprise that he would drop the reins? It had to be. She must make the kick count. Then if she could spur her horse and get away quickly enough, he wouldn't be able to catch her. But riding hard through these trees wouldn't be easy. She reminded herself again at how big he was. How determined. How strong he was. He would come after her.

For a moment, she questioned whether she could do this. Whether she should. Maybe if she waited for a better opportunity . . .

She couldn't chance that *he* could wait. Nor that he would give her another opportunity. She'd caught him staring at her more and more, the hunger in his eyes growing. He'd said he'd been up here for weeks, alone, and now he had her.

Ray dragged her over to her horse, and she realized he wouldn't have to help her into the saddle. Even with her wrists bound together, she could pull herself up. Maybe she should kick back at him when she was already in motion. But wouldn't he expect that?

As he untied the reins from the tree limb, he let go of her. She started to reach for the saddle horn when she saw him pick up the rope. He dropped a loop of the sisal over her head and, tightening it around her neck like a noose, he jerked her back against him, his arm coming across her chest, crushing her breasts.

He leaned down next to her ear. She felt his hot breath on her neck just above the spot where the rope was cutting off her air. "Yer mine. Ya accept that and I'll treat ya right. But if ya don't, I'll do things to ya to make ya wish ya were dead."

Buckmaster was trying to keep his mind off Bo as he watched the clock. The sheriff had said he would see about sending a search and rescue plane out. Shouldn't he have heard something by now?

He reflected on his visit with Sarah. He'd been surprised when she'd told him where she was staying and allowed him to come up to the cabin. He knew it was only because Russell Murdock wasn't around. Which meant that he was right about Russell trying to control her. Control all of them, he thought, remembering his call a few days ago.

When he'd called, Russell had answered Sarah's cell phone.

"It's ridiculous that I don't even know where my own wife is," Buckmaster had snapped. "And now you're answering her phone?"

"Sarah isn't your *wife*."

"Just let me talk to her."

"She isn't here right now. Do you want to leave a message?"

"If this is your attempt to keep her from me—"

"If you knew where she was staying, you'd just harass and bully her like you do everyone," Russell had said with a calm that had made Buckmaster grit his teeth.

"Fine." But it had been far from fine. "Sarah doesn't need protecting from me."

Russell had answered with an insulting silence.

"Damn it, Murdock."

"You should thank me for making sure she is safe," Russell had said.

But is she safe from you? Buckmaster had wanted to ask, but he had held his tongue. "I have something for her."

"I can pick it up later."

"I want to give it to her myself." He hadn't wanted Russell knowing about the cell phone—let alone the gun.

"I'll have to get back to you."

Buckmaster had hung up. Then unexpectedly today, Sarah had called and given him the directions to where she was staying. He wondered where Russell had been, what he was up to. There was no doubt in his mind that the man was after his wife . . . after Sarah, he corrected himself and swore.

This was so damned confusing, having two wives. In his mind and heart, Sarah was still his. Now that he was back at the ranch, he felt guilty as if he was cheating on Angelina. He hadn't told her about the money he'd given Sarah, the account he'd set up for her or the gun and cell phone he'd bought her. He knew she would make too much out of it. Especially since he had gone to see Sarah today, sneaking off to avoid an argument.

Angelina would have known he brought Sarah the gun only as an excuse so he could see her. He told himself that he shouldn't have to make excuses to see his wife. His first wife, he corrected himself.

That was the problem. He didn't know what his and Sarah's relationship was supposed to be. She'd been dead to him for the past twenty-two years. Now that he knew she was alive . . . was she as confused by all this as he was? Angelina wanted him to forget all about Sarah. Russell Murdock seemed to want the same thing.

He pulled out his cell phone, thinking he would call Sarah and make sure she was all right. Maybe the gun had been a bad idea. But she'd been a natural shot. He'd been amazed since she'd said she hadn't used a gun before.

At a sound behind him, he turned. Angelina stood in the doorway. He instantly felt guilty and swore under his breath.

"Trying to reach Sarah?" she asked, her tone flat.

"I need to call Ainsley and see if she's heard from her sister." Not a lie. But too close for his comfort.

"Not Sarah?" She was looking at him as if his guilt was written all over his face.

He'd prided himself on being honest. Or that had been the case before all this. "I saw her earlier. I took her a gun."

Angelina raised one plucked eyebrow in surprise. "*A gun?* Whatever for? Are you hoping she'll kill herself?"

"Why in the hell would you say something like that?" he demanded.

"She tried to kill herself once before—at least, that's what she made it look like. But it is probably just my own wishful thinking. Sorry."

"You're talking about the mother of my

children," he said through clenched teeth. He didn't want to be angry with her. He knew this was hard on her. But she stretched his patience to its limit.

"Some mother," Angelina said under her breath.

He ignored it, not wanting to fight with her. "Russell Murdock has hidden her away from the press in a cabin up in the woods. I don't like the idea of her being alone up there." He thought about mentioning that he wanted to bring Sarah down to stay in the bunkhouse. But now didn't seem the best time.

Also, Sarah had said only that she was considering it.

"So Russell is looking after her. That's good, isn't it?"

She knew damned well how much he hated Russell spending time with Sarah, but he didn't need to admit it.

"I don't want to fight with you," he said. Angelina was a beautiful, desirable woman. He thought of the two of them in the kitchen earlier this morning. Without thinking, he stepped to her and brushed a kiss across her lips.

"What has gotten into you lately?" she asked, a laugh at the edge of her voice. She liked the attention. Had he been ignoring her with everything else that was going on? Angelina had never seemed to need his attention before, though.

He met her gaze. "Do you feel loved?"

She looked surprised by the question. *"Loved?* You and I have more than love."

Was that how she saw their marriage? More than love? Or no need for love? "Like what?"

"What do you mean *like what?*" She frowned, looking flustered. "We have the same dreams, the same goals. We're compatible, comfortable with who we are as a couple."

Or were they just complacent? "The same goals? You mean the presidency."

"Yes, that and whatever else you want."

"What about *you?* Isn't there something more you want out of life, out of this marriage?"

She stepped away from him, looking angry. "Why are you—"

"I'm not sure I've been a good husband to you."

Her gaze narrowed. "I don't understand all this introspection." But her tone said she understood it only too well. *"Sarah."* She shook her head, tears filling her eyes. "Is everything you do and say now going to be about Sarah?"

He shook his head angrily. "Earlier in the kitchen, that was just you and me, and you know it. But, Angelina, how can I not question what kind of husband I've been, given that my first wife tried to kill herself and then disappeared for twenty-two years?"

"Did you ever consider that all of this might

be Sarah's problem and not yours? Public opinion certainly sees it that way."

He let out a sigh. "She isn't like people are painting her."

Angelina let out a bark of a laugh. "You have no idea what Sarah is really like or you would know why she drove into the river twenty-two years ago. She's not that sweet, innocent girl you think you married. I wonder if she ever was. If you knew Sarah, then you would also know where she's been and why she's back now. And you would be able to see through this ridiculous claim of hers that she has . . . amnesia."

He started to argue that you could know someone well, but that didn't mean you were a mind reader. She didn't give him a chance, though.

"When I asked you about Sarah's past, it quickly became clear that you really didn't know anything about her. You took everything she'd told you at face value. I think it's time you find out who she really is."

"As I've told you, Sarah doesn't have anything to hide or the press would have found it by now."

She smiled smugly. "Oh, you can bet they're looking, but they're having the same problem I did when I tried to find out if anything she told you about herself was true. Her early years look as if they were perfect. Too perfect. Something is wrong, Buckmaster, and always has been. The Sarah Johnson you think you know? I'm telling you she doesn't exist and never has."

When Bo heard the buzzing, she thought it was bees at first. But as the sound grew louder, she realized with a start that it was a plane's engine. She'd been staring at Ray's back for several hours as he led her horse farther and farther into the mountains. The man seemed to have the stamina of a mountain bear.

He'd tied the noose around her neck so that if she tried to get away, the rope would tighten, pulling her off the horse. Then the horse would drag her by her neck. Had he stayed up all night figuring out how to do that? Or had someone once done it to him?

She thought of his scars. She'd read somewhere that psychopaths were often abused when they were younger. She'd also read that they were very intelligent and clever and could often create intricate, complex plans. They weren't just smart, they were . . . sneaky smart, and sometimes capable of great feats of strength when "on." She figured Ray was on now. He had a plan and he wasn't going to let anything—or anyone—change it. Especially her.

By the time she'd realized the buzzing she was hearing was an approaching plane, so had Ray. He stopped walking and turned to look back at her. His frown was accusing as if he thought she was responsible for it. The plane was getting closer, flying low. Looking for her? Or just sight-seeing?

"They're lookin' for someone," he said, still frowning at her.

Did he really think he could abduct her and no one would ever look for her? She swallowed at the hateful look in his face. "They're probably looking for you."

He shook his head, blue eyes boring into her like lasers. "They gave up looking for me over a week ago. That plane's lookin' for *you*."

She couldn't believe he was blaming her because someone was searching for her. Then she reminded herself who had taken her captive. She couldn't expect rational thought from a man like him. More than likely he'd blamed his situation on bad luck or someone else all of his life. He wasn't a man who could be reasoned with. She'd be smart to remember that.

Hope filled her at the thought that the plane really was a sign someone was looking for her.

"Well, they ain't gonna find ya," he said with a sneer as he glanced around. She hoped he was searching for a place to keep them out of sight of whoever was in the plane and not one to kill her. Fear coiled in her stomach. Just because rescuers might be looking for her didn't mean they would find her in time.

As he tugged hard on the rope around her neck, she nearly fell from the horse. She clung to the saddle horn with her hands still duct-taped together and said nothing as he led her over to a wall of rock. The trees were thick, the branches woven together over their heads. The chance of anyone in the plane seeing them was slim to none. But still Ray seemed worried.

The rock wall cantilevered out, leaving a space just large enough for the two of them sans her horse. He dragged her off the horse and shoved her back into the hole. She saw that the rope was still tied to the horse. If for any reason her horse spooked, she could be dragged to death.

"Don't move," he ordered her.

She was desperate to remove the tightening rope from her neck as he tied the reins to a branch in the dense pocket of pines. If she walked toward him and the horse, the rope would loosen. She could pry it off her neck and then . . . She looked around for an opening in the trees where she could run to before the plane reached them. If she could get the pilot to see her . . .

The roar of the engine filled her ears. It was flying so low, it had to be someone looking for her, just as Ray suspected.

She took a step toward Ray and her horse, her fingers already reaching for the noose, when she realized the pilot couldn't save her. Even if he saw her and realized by the way she was bound that she was in trouble, no one could reach her before Ray threw her to the ground. When he was finished with her, she doubted even the search and rescue people would ever find her body.

Bo stepped back, her arms dropping. Ray shoved back into the tight space, driving her against the rock cliff with his body, as the plane flew over. It was so close that Bo felt she could reach out and touch it. The sound echoed against the rocks, the loud drone echoing in her chest. A sob of frustration rose in her throat. She choked it back as the rumble of the plane's engine grew fainter and fainter until it was gone.

Chapter
ELEVEN

Frank drove up to the ranch's main house, and
Senator Hamilton came out before he could exit
his patrol SUV.

"Bo?" Buckmaster asked, his voice filled with
hope.

Frank shook his head. "Someone from the
search and rescue team is flying up to see if
they can spot her right now. I'll let you know as
soon as I hear."

Buckmaster looked relieved but said, "If she
isn't back soon, I'm going to take some men
and go look for both her and Calder." He seemed
to realize that the sheriff wouldn't have driven
all this way just to tell him again about the
search and rescue flyover. "If this isn't about my
daughter . . ."

"I need to talk to you about your . . . about
Sarah. Is there somewhere we could talk in
private?"

The senator glanced back at the house. Frank
saw the man's wife standing at the window,
watching. "Why don't we walk down by the
creek?" Buckmaster suggested.

They hadn't gone far when he asked, "What's this about Sarah?"

Frank turned to face the man. He'd known Buckmaster for years, but they didn't travel in the same social circle and never had. "I need you to know that Sarah has been under investigation since she returned."

"Under investigation? *For what?* If you know something more about where she's been—"

"Did she tell you how she happened to be on that road in the middle of nowhere?" the sheriff asked.

His question seemed to catch the senator flat-footed. "No. She told me that she can't remember anything except waking up lying on the road after Russell Murdock apparently ran her down with his pickup."

Frank thought about correcting him, but realized it probably wouldn't do any good. When Sarah had come stumbling out of the trees, Russell had managed to get his pickup stopped in time.

"Russell took me to the spot where she came out of the woods," he told the senator as they walked a little farther along the path. He could hear the creek, smell the sweet scent of the water and the cottonwoods that grew up around it. "I followed Sarah's trail back into the trees for a good quarter mile." Buckmaster was frowning. He knew the area. Nothing was back in there. "I found the spot where she'd landed."

Buckmaster stopped walking. Behind him, the clear stream burbled as it snaked its way through the trees and rocks. *"Landed?"*

"She was dropped from a plane. I found her parachute caught in a tree."

The senator staggered back. "What? That's not possible."

"Her DNA and blood were found on the parachute's harness."

Buckmaster walked down to sit on one of the large boulders at water's edge. "I don't understand."

"Neither do we."

"We?" he asked as Frank joined him, taking a seat on an adjacent boulder.

"I called in the FBI." The senator couldn't have looked more surprised. "With you running for the presidency . . ."

Buckmaster let out a curse and rubbed his hand over his face. "You think Sarah . . ."

"We don't know what to think. The chute she wore was the kind used for undercover operations."

"You think she's some kind of special ops . . . what?"

"That's just it, Senator. We don't know. We don't know where she's been or why she's back, but the timing makes us suspicious."

Buckmaster let out a bark of a laugh. "Sarah? You know her. Do you really think—"

"Does she have a tattoo?"

The question stopped the senator cold. *"A tattoo?"*

"Did she have one before she disappeared?"

"Don't you mean before she drove her vehicle into the Yellowstone River trying to kill herself? Or maybe that was just a ruse and she just wanted us all to believe she was dead?" Buckmaster shook his head, visibly upset now. "No, she didn't have a tattoo. Are you telling me she does now?"

"I need to show you something in confidence. I'd like as few people knowing about this as possible."

Immediately the senator looked worried. Frank reached into his pocket and pulled out the drawing Lynette had given him. "Do you recognize this?"

Buckmaster stared at the drawing. "This is a *tattoo?* A tattoo that you say Sarah has now?"

Frank nodded. "Do you have any idea what it is or what it might mean?"

"No," Buckmaster said, handing the paper back as if he didn't want to touch it any longer than he had to. "Sarah has this tattoo?"

"I haven't seen it, but a witness did."

"And you think it means something. Like what?" Buckmaster demanded. "That she's joined some militia or some cult or some mercenary group that dropped her from a plane to take over the government?"

Frank said nothing as he watched the senator absorb what he'd told him.

After a moment, Buckmaster let out a curse.

"We still don't know who picked her up that night after Lester Halverson fished her out of the Yellowstone River," the sheriff said. "But it explains why we couldn't find her body. You have any idea who she would have called?"

The senator shook his head angrily. "I only know it wasn't me." He raked a hand through his graying hair. "You said you've been investigating her. What have you learned, or is it beyond my pay grade?"

Frank knew he had to be honest. The senator had friends in high places. It wouldn't take much for him to find out that the FBI didn't see Sarah as a threat to Buckmaster or to national security. He told him as much.

"So why are you asking me about some tattoo?" Buckmaster demanded.

"Because I don't agree with the FBI." The senator raised a brow at that. "It's too much of a coincidence that she shows up now."

"You sound like Angelina." He cursed under his breath. "But if the FBI doesn't think she's dangerous—"

"What if you get the Republican presidential nomination? What if you get elected?"

Buckmaster stared at him. "What is it you think she'll do?"

"That's just it. I don't know. But she had help coming back here. Someone was flying that plane. Someone wanted her back in Beartooth, Montana."

"She said she came back to see her daughters."

"Then why didn't she take a bus? Why did she leave them in the first place?"

The senator rubbed a hand over his face again. "She swears she doesn't remember. That she doesn't know how she got here, that her first memory is waking up on the ground in front of Russell Murdock's pickup. Is it possible he's involved in all this? Maybe he picked her up that night after she went into the river."

"I don't think so, but of course we're looking into that, too."

Appearing dazed, Buckmaster said, "She really was dropped from a plane by parachute?"

Frank nodded. "Other than the lawmen who were at the site, no one else knows about this. I haven't even told Sarah."

"I know Sarah," Buckmaster said, even though the sheriff wondered if it were still true after twenty-two years. "Let me ask her about all of this. If I think she's lying, I'll let you know."

He knew he couldn't keep the senator from telling Sarah. "All right. But I'd appreciate it if Sarah is the only person you tell."

Buckmaster scratched the back of his neck.

155

"This tattoo. Where exactly is it on her? I didn't see one when I talked to her."

"You probably wouldn't have. According to the witness, it was on her right buttock like a brand."

Jace heard the plane long before he saw it. He knew even before he recognized the county search and rescue emblem on the side that the pilot was looking for Bo Hamilton. Buckmaster had promised to wait twenty-four hours. He hadn't. Not that Jace could blame him. It was definitely time to call in reinforcements.

The pilot spotted him riding along the ridgeline and tipped a wing at him. Jace waved back and kept riding to the north. He heard the plane continue along the same path he was headed. He was looking for Bo.

Jace stayed on her trail as the sound of the plane died away. Had the pilot seen her somewhere ahead? He had no way of knowing since he didn't see the plane again. How long would it be before the senator sent some of his men into the mountains to search for her? Or would he talk the sheriff into sending search and rescue ground teams before the required forty-eight hours?

At least one question was answered. Bo Hamilton was deep in the Crazies. That alone concerned him more with each passing hour. He wasn't sure how much food she'd brought. She could drink from one of the snow-fed streams safely enough, but she would need food to survive. She did hope to survive, didn't she? She wasn't fool enough to think that missing money at the foundation warranted taking her life?

His concern deepened even before he'd ridden a little farther and saw her horse's tracks drop down into a ravine. Reining in, he considered why she would have ridden there. He swore under his breath. Maybe her horse had spooked and taken off down the hill.

He swung out of the saddle. Ground-tying his horse, he took his rifle and started down the mountainside. He could see that her horse hadn't been running when it left the trail.

Jace hadn't gone far when he again saw the man's boot tracks in the dust. Like before, they crossed the horse's prints. A little farther, he saw the dirt disturbed as if there had been a scuffle. He looked closer, half expecting to find grizzly bear prints near the area. Because the Crazies were like a large island in the middle of civilization, they were crawling with grizzlies.

But what he found instead was a fire ring where someone had camped. Next to it were the man's boot prints and the distinct print of a hand in the dust. A woman's.

After work, Emily picked up her daughter from day care and drove the few blocks home to the small house she'd rented on the east side of Big Timber. She'd been thinking about Alex all day but hadn't contacted him. She was afraid she'd blurt out everything that was worrying her. He made her feel comfortable. Maybe too comfortable.

The house she rented was small. Jace called it her dollhouse. Just the thought of her brother made her feel anxious. Why hadn't she heard something from him? Surely he wasn't still up in the mountains. But then again, as far as she knew, Bo hadn't returned, either. Could they both still be up there?

She tried not to worry. Jace was as capable as any man she'd ever known. He knew these mountains, and he was practically born on a horse.

Jodie chattered away about her day as they walked from her car to the front door of the dollhouse. The door was painted bright red while the rest of the house was turquoise.

"Did they let you decide on the colors?" Jace had joked.

"I know you don't mean that as a compliment," Emily had said, "but I would have chosen these same colors if I'd been asked. It's as if I was always supposed to rent this house."

He had laughed and shook his head. "I hate even to ask who your landlord is."

When she'd told him, he'd said, "Well, that

explains it. She's long been keeping the sixties alive. You two should get along fine."

Opening the door with her key, she and Jodie stepped inside. The first time she'd entered the tiny house, she'd been transfixed by the bright-colored walls, the built-in cubbyholes, the painted white wood floors. The house had smelled of patchouli oil, but that scent had faded.

Now the house smelled more like the pepperoni pizza she and Jodie had eaten the night before. That and . . . She frowned. Cigarette smoke.

Her landlady, a throwback to another era as Jace had said, didn't smoke cigarettes. But Emily would have sworn someone who smoked had been in the house.

"I want pizza," Jodie said as Emily dropped her purse on a chair by the door and carried the groceries into the kitchen.

"Not tonight. Tonight we're having breakfast, remember? Waffles and bacon."

Jodie began to jump up and down as Emily put the bag of groceries on the counter. She sniffed the paper bag the clerk had filled for her. It smelled like produce. "You set the table, and I'll change clothes and make us something to eat." She stepped into the small bedroom, following the scent of cigarettes.

She'd given them up when she was pregnant with Jodie and hadn't had one since. But she knew the smell too well.

The house had two small bedrooms, a galley kitchen with a breakfast nook, a miniature living room and one rather large bathroom.

It had been perfect for the two of them, and Emily really had believed that the house, like the job, had been a gift from her higher power. That's what they called it in the recovery program she'd attended.

Now she pulled out her cell phone and called her landlady. "I was wondering if you came by the house today for repairs and maybe brought some- one with you," she said without preamble. "No? I only ask because the house smells like cigarette smoke. Okay. Probably just my imagination."

After she'd hung up, though, she realized maybe it was her imagination, because she really would have loved a cigarette right now. "It's the stress of everything at work," she said to herself as she changed clothes and headed for the kitchen, where Jodie hadn't gotten any farther along than folding the napkins.

"Better get busy setting the table, slowpoke," she said as she put the bacon on to fry and her daughter got out the syrup and butter.

"A bird made a mess in my room," Jodie said.

Emily had been distracted with worrying about Bo and Jace and the desire to have a cigarette. She'd seen too many addicts give up booze or drugs only to pick up some other addictive bad habit.

"A bird?" she repeated, thinking she'd heard wrong. "A bird made a mess in your room?"

"I guess it was a bird."

She pulled the bacon off the stove and headed for her daughter's room with Jodie leading the way.

"See. The bird came through the window and left dirt on my bed," Jodie said.

Emily stared at the open window and the torn screen flapping in the breeze, then at the dirty footprints on her daughter's bed.

She grabbed Jodie and pulled her into a tight hug as her mind raced. Was the person still in the house?

There was only one room she hadn't looked in. "Stay here. Mommy needs to do something."

As she headed toward the bathroom, she saw that the door was closed. She made a detour to pick up the baseball bat she kept by the front door.

At the bathroom, she eased the door open with the business end of the bat.

Empty. She stepped in to make sure no one was behind the shower curtain before she breathed a sigh of relief.

The relief, though, only lasted an instant. *Someone had been in her house.*

The question was who and, on its heels, why?

As Jace came back up the mountainside to where he'd left his horse, he found more odd tracks. He stopped, crouched down and studied them. His pulse took off like a shot as he realized what he was seeing. Bo's horse's prints in the dust followed by the tracks of a woman's boots.

Why would Bo be following her horse? That made no sense. Except for the familiar man's boot prints in the dust. He looked up the trail. *The man was now riding the horse and Bo was walking?*

What the hell?

Climbing back on his horse, he began to follow the new tracks. They still headed farther back into the mountains, but he noticed that Bo's boot prints were becoming more and more indistinguishable as he rode—as if she was dragging her feet. It was almost as if she was being— The thought was lost as he saw a spot in the trail where something had been dragged.

He let out a curse and looked up the mountainside. Heart pounding, he spurred his horse. He'd thought she'd met the man up here. Now he didn't know what to think. Had the man double-crossed her? Had he only been after the money? That was if Bo really had taken the money from the foundation and run with it.

None of this made any sense. But he moved faster now, even more confused by what he was seeing. The trail wound through the pines. He dropped down a mountainside, crossed a shallow creek and climbed again, switchbacking up the next mountain. It was getting late by the time he found where they had camped the night before.

Swinging down from his saddle, he inspected the site. The ground had been disturbed around the small fire pit. He found the man's tracks but not Bo's. Glancing at the nearby creek, he started toward it, when he found the barefoot tracks in the dust. Like the handprint, they were woman-size. Bo.

He looked at the angle of the sun and calculated how many hours he was behind them before climbing back on his horse. As he started down the trail, he realized that the man was now walking. Did that mean Bo was riding the horse? It would appear that way since he'd seen her tracks at the campsite.

Worry burrowed into him as he rode. He had to catch them, and yet daylight was waning. He'd been gone more than twenty-four hours. All his instincts told him he had to find Bo Hamilton—and soon.

Chapter
TWELVE

Buckmaster had planned to send men into the mountains to look for Bo, but the sheriff had talked him into waiting until he heard from the pilot who'd gone up to look for her.

When Buckmaster got the call, he snatched up the phone, praying the pilot had seen her.

"All he saw was a cowboy headed in," Frank said. "We're assuming it was Jace Calder since you told us he was tracking Bo. Senator, he was way back and still riding farther into the mountains. I've talked to search and rescue, but given the area that we're going to have to cover . . . I think Jace Calder might be your best bet. Apparently he's on her trail. Also, there's a storm coming in. It could mean snow in the mountains, and that would hamper a search."

"I just can't believe she went that far," Buckmaster said.

Frank cleared his throat. "Is there any chance she's on the run? Because if that is the case, then we need to know now."

The senator swore. He hated the way gossip moved through this county faster than the winds that blew down out of the Crazies.

"Is there a chance she only wanted us to believe she'd gone into the mountains?" Frank asked.

"No. Her vehicle is out front. She left her purse and all of her credit cards in it. She didn't even take her cell phone no doubt since she knew it doesn't work up there worth a darn." Buckmaster felt his face crumple as he fought back tears. When he spoke, his voice broke. "I know my daughter. She wouldn't . . ."

"We'll try to find her, Senator," Frank said. "Keep me informed if you hear anything. Search and rescue will have to get prepared, so I doubt we can do anything until morning given how far she's apparently gone."

"I'm going to send some men up to look for her."

"I wouldn't do that. Let search and rescue handle it. Too many people up in those mountains will only make it harder. If she's as far back in as Jace Calder seems to think she is, it would take more than a day for your men to catch up anyway. There is some flat land farther back where search and rescue might be able to set down a helicopter and get a party out looking."

Buckmaster could hear the sense in what the sheriff was saying. He wanted to get on a horse himself and ride out, but he realized the foolishness of that. "All right," he finally agreed. "Tomorrow morning." Jace had said to give him twenty-four hours before sending in the cavalry.

He was sending in the cavalry tomorrow. He just hoped it wasn't too late for his daughter.

He disconnected only to have the phone ring again. Hoping it was Bo or at least word about her, he quickly picked up.

"What's wrong?" Sarah asked the moment he answered.

"Sarah." When he'd seen her, he hadn't told her about Bo because he didn't want to worry her. That wasn't the only reason. She hadn't been a part of her daughters' lives for so long, he'd almost felt as if she didn't have a right.

But damn it to hell, she *was* Bo's mother. Now he felt guilty for keeping it from her.

"Buck, I know something's wrong. What is it?"

"Bo's gone up in the mountains and hasn't come back out yet." He filled her in on what little he knew.

"You sound scared."

He realized that if he didn't tell her, she'd hear about it eventually anyway. "There's a problem down at the foundation, missing money apparently. Bo was supposed to meet with the auditor yesterday morning. She took off up into the mountains Saturday afternoon on what we thought was a weekend camping trip."

"You think she took the money?"

"No. She has no reason to take the money," he snapped, angry that she would even ask that.

"Something must have happened up in the mountains. One man has already gone up tracking her to see if he can find her, and tomorrow the sheriff is involving search and rescue."

"I hate those mountains," Sarah said. "They've always terrified me."

He blinked, astounded by her words. Had he known that? He thought about what the sheriff had told him. He would have argued that he knew Sarah better than anyone. But after everything that had transpired? He didn't know her as well as he'd thought.

"But you didn't call about Bo," he said. "Is something wrong?"

"No, you're going to think I'm silly. I just wanted to see if the cell phone you gave me worked."

"I don't think that's silly at all," he said, recalling how he had planned to do the same thing and would have if Angelina hadn't interrupted him. "I need to see you. I'm coming up to the cabin."

"No," she said quickly. "I'd rather meet at the swimming hole." It was a spot not far out of Beartooth where they'd spent time together so many years ago. "Russell just drove up. I'm sure he'll take me. I can be there in thirty minutes."

Gritting his teeth, he told himself not to make an issue of Russell right now. Once he was with Sarah . . . "See you then."

• • •

Feeling the day slipping away, Jace stopped on a high rise to search the mountains ahead with his binoculars. He kept thinking he would catch a glimpse of them at some point on one of the mountainsides ahead.

Bo and her companion were traveling faster today, making better time than yesterday. But then, so was Jace. He could feel that he was getting closer. It was only a matter of time before he caught up.

But then what? Bo wasn't alone. Near the drag marks, he'd seen where a rope had cut into the earth.

What were they dragging up into the mountains? The money? A body?

What he'd seen made no sense. It was another reason he was anxious to catch up to Bo. But he was also wary. Something about this felt . . . wrong.

He put away his binoculars and gathered up the reins. The sun had set beyond the peaks to the west. Cool air moved restlessly through the shadowy pines. It wouldn't be long before he couldn't follow their trail any longer.

He wanted to push on. He knew he was getting close. Maybe too close. What if they had already spotted him following them? He didn't want to stumble into anything he wouldn't be walking away from. He needed to be more careful than ever since he had no idea who Bo was with or how desperate she was to get away.

He spurred his horse and headed on down the trail. They would be stopping soon to make camp if the tracks he'd been following were any indication. The man was limping, his boots worn thin. That was another thing that bothered Jace. Who was this man she was traveling with that he didn't have proper boots if Bo had stolen a potful of money? Why didn't the man have his own horse? Or had something happened to it?

So many questions, all of them making him more anxious to get to Bo.

Buckmaster kicked small rocks into the stream as he waited for Sarah to arrive. When he heard Russell drive up, he didn't turn around. The less he saw of the man, the better. He hadn't been able to sleep last night except in fits and starts. He'd finally gotten up, cranky and out of sorts.

Bo still hadn't returned. He was beyond worried. Something was wrong. He could feel it, and that only made him more frustrated and irritable.

Even Angelina had known to give him a wide berth this afternoon. When he'd told her he was meeting Sarah, he'd expected her to put up a fight. But she'd said nothing as he'd left.

At the sound of a pickup door opening and closing, he waited, keeping his back to the road until he heard Sarah's tread on the bank behind him and stepped out of the shade as she came toward him.

She looked beautiful, her blond hair like spun gold in the dramatic light of afternoon. She must have bought herself some clothes, because she was wearing what appeared to be new clothing. When had she gone shopping since she was hiding out from the media?

He hadn't meant to voice the thought, but apparently had when she answered his question.

"Russell picked up a few things for me in town," she said.

Russell. Of course. "The man has good taste."

"I hope you didn't get me here to argue about Russell," she said with a sigh.

He shook his head. He wanted to pull her to him. To comfort her as much as himself. It had been so long that he couldn't remember what it was like hugging let alone kissing her, and that made him sad. They'd shared years together as well as six children. He could no more forget that than he could take his next breath.

While he could deny his feelings for this woman until the cows came home, it was a totally different story when she was standing in front of him. She was his true love. He'd married Angelina because Sarah had been gone for seven years. Angelina had been a marriage of convenience. But Sarah . . .

"I've missed you," he said, again voicing the

thought without thinking. "The past twenty-two years," he added.

She smiled sadly, but she kept her distance from him as if wary of him. What was that about? "I've missed you and my girls, as well."

Missed me and the girls? She didn't sound as though she had. A woman who missed her husband and children didn't stay away twenty-two years.

"Have you heard from Bo?" she asked.

He played down his concern half hoping that by doing so there really wasn't anything to worry about. "There are people looking for her. If we don't hear something today, I'll be going up in the mountains to look for her myself."

"Oh, she has to be all right. I need more time to get to know my daughters. I haven't hardly seen them, not with their busy lives and the press hounding me." She looked embarrassed. "I don't mean to complain but between me turning up and you running for president, we seem to have set reporters off. I keep thinking they will tire of this and let me live a normal life."

Buckmaster wondered what she thought a normal life was. Certainly not being married to the next president of the United States.

He was used to public scrutiny, but apparently she wasn't. If she'd been in the public eye the past twenty-two years, then the sheriff and FBI would have discovered where she'd been. So

171

for Sarah this must be agony. She'd never liked being in the limelight. Or at least, the Sarah he had known hadn't. She didn't even like her photograph taken. He had lots of photos of the girls but not many of their mother before she'd left them. What few there'd been, Angelina had apparently discarded.

A thought struck him. Had Sarah gotten rid of all the photos of herself before she'd headed for the iced-over Yellowstone River that winter night?

He was beginning to realize that he didn't know this Sarah. But then again, maybe Angelina was right and he'd never known the other one, either.

The problem was that he remembered the feel of her body, the scent of her skin, the taste of her . . . He would have sworn twenty-two years ago that he knew this woman better than he knew himself. But, he reminded himself, he would have been wrong, because he never saw the suicide attempt coming.

"I need to ask you something. It's . . . personal." He glanced toward the pickup parked on the road above the stream. He didn't see Russell, but he knew the man was there waiting. Maybe even trying to listen. But the sound of the rushing water and the breeze in the trees should make it difficult if not impossible if they kept their voices down.

"If this is about Russell—"

"Sarah, do you have a tattoo?"

She stared at him for a long moment before she laughed. "That's your question?"

"Do you?"

"No." She looked shocked that he would even ask. Maybe he still knew her better than he thought. "Why would I get a tattoo?"

"That's a good question. The doctor and his wife who took you in after you stumbled out of the woods and into Russell Murdock's pickup . . . the wife saw a tattoo."

Her eyes widened. "Who told you that I—"

"The sheriff."

She turned away as if embarrassed. "I knew everyone was talking about me, but—"

"It's on your right buttock. If it exists and isn't just some old woman's imagination running wild . . ."

Sarah turned back to him. "Wouldn't I know if I had a tattoo?"

He shrugged. Wouldn't she know where she'd been for years? Or how she'd suddenly reappeared? "There's something else. The sheriff said you returned to Beartooth in a rather unique way. You parachuted in and not with just any chute. It was one that allows the pilot to fly low, the kind used in special ops."

"That's . . . ridiculous." Her voice broke. "Why would he say something like that?"

"Frank Curry wouldn't unless it was true."

She shook her head then glanced toward a spot on the creek where the trees were thicker.

He watched as she stepped over to trees, out of sight of Russell sitting in the truck up on the road. She hesitated for a moment and then peeled down the top of her pants and panties.

Buckmaster moved closer, saw nothing and felt a rush of relief until she pulled the fabric down a little farther. He cursed under his breath.

There it was. The design the sheriff had shown him. Not as crude as the drawing, but it didn't look professionally done. He thought of the jailhouse tattoos he'd seen on television.

"Buck?" She sounded scared. "Tell me there's nothing there."

He wished he could. "It's there, a tattoo. But it's more like a brand. You really didn't know it was there?"

She pulled up her pants and turned to look at him. Tears welled in her eyes as she shook her head.

He could see how scared she was. But when her gaze met his, he saw something that shocked him. "What?" he demanded at the accusation in her eyes.

"Did you have anything to do with this?"

Buckmaster stared at her. "The tattoo?" he asked incredulously. "You think I was the one who . . . branded you? Or you think I was flying the plane that dropped you back here?"

She shook her head as if realizing how stupid a question that had been.

"Sarah." He reached for her, but she side-stepped away from him.

"You should stay clear of me," she said in a small, frightened voice. "I don't know who I am."

"*I* know who you are," he said, even though he was realizing more and more that it might not be true.

"I need to go," she said as she started up the bank.

"Sarah," he called after her, but she kept moving without turning around. He thought about going after her, but he had a feeling she might be right. Staying clear of her was the smartest thing he could do for a variety of reasons. But it was one of the hardest things he had ever done.

Right now, though, it was the only thing he could do.

Sheriff Frank Curry glanced up in surprise to see a local outfitter standing in his doorway. His mind had been miles away. Ever since Sarah Hamilton had returned from the grave, his thoughts were often on her. He'd turned the investigation over to the FBI, but they hadn't been concerned. That didn't keep him from worrying.

"John," Frank said and got to his feet to extend a hand. John Cole had taken him down the Yellowstone River in his drift boat last summer for some of the best trout fishing Frank had ever experienced. John spent his summers guiding on the river and his winters guiding in the mountains.

"Frank, I was at one of my fall camps, the one on the Wilsall side of the Crazies, and someone had broken into my supplies and tack I keep up there. I was thinking it might be that escaped fugitive I'd seen on TV since one of my neighbor's horses was stolen, as well. The horse came out of the mountains a few days ago in bad shape. It had one of my stolen saddles on it."

Raymond Spencer. Frank had heard that deputies on the other side of the mountains had been searching the area but had stopped when there'd been a sighting of Spencer in Butte. A few days later, there was another sighting in Reno. The general consensus was that he'd left the area.

"Thanks for letting me know," the sheriff said. "I'll contact the Livingston sheriff's office. Any idea when this break-in might have taken place?"

John shook his head. "That rain a few nights ago wiped out any tracks. The camp and shack aren't far into the mountains. I heard he was from the area, so he might have known about it and is now several states away."

Frank nodded. "Or he could still be in the Crazies." He remembered a case years ago in which a man and his son had hidden in the mountains for months without anyone being the wiser. Their mistake had been coming down far enough to look for a woman for his son.

"I'll be going back into the mountains to check on my high camp in the next few days," John was saying. "I'll keep an eye out."

He didn't need to tell John to be careful, but he did anyway.

"Bo Hamilton is in there. Jace Calder went looking for her. We haven't heard from either of them." Even if Bo was on the run, Jace should have caught up with her by now.

"I'll keep an eye out for them, as well," John said.

After John left, Frank put in a call to search and rescue, making sure everyone was ready to move out first thing in the morning.

As he hung up, he told himself there was a lot of country back in there. What were the chances the three of them would cross paths? Had already crossed paths?

Chapter
THIRTEEN

Emily's landlady came over and fixed the window and screen. "Is anything missing?" Ruby asked.

"Not that I know of. I didn't think to look."

Ruby glanced up at that.

"I . . ." Why hadn't she thought to look? "I just thought it was kids. It's not like I have anything anyone would want to steal."

"Kids?" Ruby studied her for a long moment. "It looks to me like the footprints were man-size, not kids."

Emily said nothing because she could tell that her landlady thought it was some man she knew sneaking in.

"I'll have someone install steel grates on the windows tomorrow."

She nodded. "Thank you."

That night she let Jodie sleep in her bed, not that she slept much. Someone had been in the house. Her first thought and worse thought was that it might be Harrison.

She quickly checked the browser on her phone. On the prison site, she saw that according to their latest records, he was still behind bars.

Emily reminded herself that her lawyer had assured her she would get a call before he got out.

She tried to relax, but it was hard with Jace up in the mountains, Bo still on the lam and someone having broken into her house. What next?

"There have been a few break-ins in the past few weeks in the neighborhood," Ruby had said before she'd left. "Must have been that."

Emily hoped that was all it had been. A break-in by someone looking for money or items to sell sounded better than someone breaking in looking for her. Or worse, her daughter.

It wasn't until she climbed into bed beside her daughter that she realized she'd been wrong. Something was missing.

She stared at the spot on her nightstand where she kept the photograph of her and Jodie. It was gone. She got up quickly, telling herself it must have gotten knocked down.

But when she knelt on the floor, it wasn't there. It wasn't anywhere.

Why would someone break into her house for a photograph of her and Jodie? Her heart leaped to her throat. Harrison was still locked up. He couldn't even know about Jodie, could he? Was it possible he thought Jodie was his?

As she climbed up on the bed, she felt a fissure of fear move through her. If he'd heard she'd had a baby . . .

She moved closer to her daughter, snuggling against her. What would Harrison do if he thought Jodie was his? Surely he wouldn't try to get one of his no-count friends to take her, would he?

"What did he do now?" Russell demanded angrily when Sarah got into his pickup.

She shook her head. "Please, can we just go? I can't talk about it right now."

He started the truck and pulled away from the stream. She saw him glance back. Buck was standing where she'd left him, looking as shell-shocked as she felt.

"Would you mind taking me to the sheriff's office?" she asked.

Russell shot her a look of both surprise and concern. "I'm not sure what happened, but I have to ask. Are you sure that's a good idea?"

"In this case, it is. He has some answers that I need."

"Buckmaster told you that?" Russell asked in surprise. "You didn't mention what I talked to you about?"

"Brain wiping?" She let out a laugh. "All I need to do is mention that to Buck or the sheriff. Everyone already thinks I'm unhinged. If I started talking conspiracy theories and brain wiping . . ." She shook her head.

"Then what—"

180

"I can't talk about it right now." She reached over and touched his hand. "I'm sorry." All she could think about was what Buck had told her. *She'd been dropped by parachute from a plane?* That was impossible. She was terrified of heights. Wasn't she? She wasn't even sure where the thought had come from. Buck would know. Or would he?

Her head ached, and she felt sick to her stomach. Her last memory had been of giving birth to her twins who were now college graduates. All she knew of the days after that were what she'd been told. She'd asked herself dozens of times why she would have left her children to drive into the Yellowstone River in the middle of winter. How could she leave her babies? It was what the media had been demanding to know for months. They'd labeled her a bad mother, a head case and a liar.

Russell was convinced something had happened between her and Buck to make her so . . . desperate? Scared? Out of her mind that she would do something like that. She couldn't imagine it and thought of that woman as another Sarah Hamilton, certainly not her.

The drive into Big Timber didn't take long. Russell had remained silent, although she could tell he was worried. He didn't think she should talk to the sheriff. She knew he was only trying to protect her because, like her, he feared what was in her past, and he didn't even know about the latest.

What would he say when she told him? She hated to think. He was the one who'd suggested she not give the sheriff her DNA or her fingerprints when Frank Curry had asked. She knew it made her look guilty of something, but then again, wasn't there a good chance she *was* guilty of something?

What fifty-eight-year-old woman parachuted back into her husband's and children's lives after twenty-two years with only dark, frightening flashes of memory? A woman with dangerous secrets.

Frank put in a call to the Livingston sheriff's department, hoping he would hear that Raymond Spencer Jr. had been caught and was now behind bars. "Any word on Raymond Spencer?"

"Last seen in Reno, Nevada," he told him.

"You have a positive identification on that sighting?"

"Why do you ask?"

Frank explained about the camp, the stolen horse and supplies, and the outfitter's concern Spencer was in the Crazies.

"Spencer *is* from that area, but a used-car dealer in Reno sold a car to a guy matching Spencer's description a week ago. I can't see any reason he would return to Montana with everybody and his brother looking for him, can you?"

Frank couldn't. But no one had picked up the car that the salesman had sold the man. Nor was there a positive ID on the buyer. He wished he was as sure that Spencer was miles from the Crazy Mountains as the sheriff in Livingston was. He remembered that Spencer's father, Raymond Jay Spencer Sr., had done time recently at Montana State Prison. He put in a call to the warden up there.

"What do you know about Raymond Spencer?" he asked.

The warden laughed. "A model prisoner. Served in the military as a sniper. Got in a bar fight and ended up killing a man with his bare hands. Last I heard he'd become one of those antigovernment survivalists. Why are you asking about him? Isn't it his son who's in trouble?"

"I thought his father might know where he was. A local outfitter said a neighbor's horse was stolen, he lost supplies and a saddle, and he thought he might have stumbled across Spencer's camp up in the Crazies."

"Possible, I suppose. His father was one of those militia guys who lived off the grid. Apparently he took Spencer with him from the time the kid was a boy. Not sure where the mother was or if she was even in the picture."

"They were from Wilsall, right?" Just on the other side of the Crazies.

"Which means he knows the area."

It made sense that if Spencer needed to disappear, he would go to land that he knew in a place that he was least likely to be discovered. But what about the car he'd allegedly bought in Reno?

"You thinking of sending some men up in the mountains to look for him?" the Livingston sheriff asked.

"I'm worried because he is listed as a violent criminal and we have a young woman possibly lost up there in the mountains."

"Do you want me to talk to the sheriff with you?" Russell asked Sarah as he pulled into the sheriff's department parking lot and killed the engine. He wished she'd tell him what had happened at the stream with the senator, but Sarah clearly wasn't talking. At least not yet.

"If you don't mind, I need to do this alone."

He nodded, tempted to tell her he thought this was a mistake. But he had no right to tell her anything.

"Are you sure you don't mind waiting?" she asked as she opened her door and climbed out. "I'm sure one of the deputies can give me a ride—"

"I'll be here if you need me." He watched her

close the pickup door and hurry into the sheriff's department, all his instincts telling him he should stop her. But only one person could stop her, the only person she listened to. Buck, as she called the senator.

Russell swore under his breath, something he seldom did. The sheriff had wanted her DNA and fingerprints. That alone told him that Sarah was being investigated.

Why investigate her? Shouldn't they be looking into Senator Buckmaster Hamilton? The man had said something to her that had her scared. Was that the senator's plan, to make her look even more crazy than she'd already been portrayed? What if he was behind all of this?

Bo didn't know how long she'd ridden. At some point, she thought she might have fallen asleep in the saddle, because she jolted upright as the horse stopped. Her hands went to the noose around her neck, terrified that she was about to be pulled from the saddle and dragged behind the horse.

She sensed the change in Ray even before she saw his expression. He stopped walking, cursing under his breath, as he pulled off a boot to look at the soles. Even from the back of the horse, she could see that he had a large hole. The boots also seemed too big for him as if he'd borrowed them from a man with larger feet. Or took them.

Realizing that was probably exactly what he'd done, she felt another shudder. Who knew what this man had done before he'd crossed paths with her? When he looked up, she saw the anger and frustration and that ever-present lust. The other times he hadn't acted on it. This time she could see things were different.

He kept his hard gaze on her as he pulled on his boots. She tried not to move, not to breathe, as he got to his feet and limped toward her.

When he touched her leg, she willed herself not to, but she flinched. He grabbed the rope around her neck and jerked it hard toward him, almost dragging her from the saddle. "Ya got a problem?" he demanded, studying her.

"Just tired."

"Yeah? Ya rode all day while I walked." He sounded bitter, anger lacing the edge of his words, meanness in his eyes.

Was he really trying to make her feel guilty because she rode today instead of him? It was her horse! She didn't want to be here. He was the one holding her prisoner. A spark of anger wove through her exhaustion, but she quickly smothered it before it could burst into words. The irony of the situation would be lost on Ray Spencer.

He dragged her off the horse. Her legs felt weak. She leaned against her horse as Ray removed the rope from her neck. Like her wrists where the rope had worn through the tape, the skin on her neck was chafed and sore from the rough sisal. All she'd had to eat all day was a few spoonfuls of canned beans earlier that morning and the piece of dried jerky he'd given her in the afternoon. She hated to think how far they'd traveled. All day she kept thinking he would stop. He had to be getting tired. At one point after the sun had set, she saw that he was limping badly.

But nothing had stopped him until the growing darkness had forced him to call it a day, apparently. She looked around. The sky over the trees was a dusky gray. Here in the branches of the pines, pockets of inky black spread toward them on a cold breeze as the air quickly cooled without the sun.

Where were they? All she knew was that she'd never been this far back into these mountains. She felt as if they'd left all civilization behind. No one would ever be able to find her back in here.

The thought brought tears to her eyes.

"Ya start blubberin' and so help me . . ." Ray raised a hand, and she quickly wiped at her tears as she stepped back from him. He was tired and cross, and she sensed that it would take very little for him to take it out on her.

Tired of walking, tired of waiting, just plain tired of everything, Ray glared at the woman. That plane had definitely been searching for *her*. If her father really *did* have a lot of money, then this could be a problem unless the woman was found —or completely disappeared and soon.

On top of that, his father, RayJay, was on his way. Ray couldn't help but worry. His old man would be angry about this. The last thing his father had said was to make sure he didn't cross paths with anyone.

RayJay was no fool. He might have even heard about the search for the woman. Ray realized it had been a mistake taking her. If he had let her go on without her seeing him, then there wouldn't be anyone looking for her. He'd covered his own trail, getting a former inmate friend who resembled him to take a trip to Reno. Everyone would think he was still in Reno. No one would know he was up here.

He cursed his impulsiveness in taking her. Maybe he should just have some fun with her, kill her, bury her body and send her horse off. Once her searchers found her horse, they would think she was thrown. They might look for her, but they would never find her. But they might find *him*.

He swore again. No matter what he did now, he couldn't keep searchers from the mountains. He hated to think how furious that was going to make his father. Worse, now that he had her, he didn't want to give Bo up. He sure as hell couldn't release her. She'd go straight to the cops.

No, he would keep her, no matter what it took. And if anyone came looking for her? Well, they, too, would disappear.

Ray glared at her, wanting to blame her. If she hadn't been so tempting . . .

"Can I help you with dinner?" she asked.

He blinked. *"Can I help you with dinner?"* he mocked her. "Ya plan on settin' the table or what?"

"I can cook."

Tilting his head to the side, he eyed her. "A classy bitch like you knows how to cook?"

"I *like* to cook."

He appraised her. "That's good. I ain't no cook so ya kin do *all* the cookin'. I'll kill the meat for us." He softened toward her. Maybe this would work out. He was risking his life for this damned woman. It had to work out.

Bo felt some of the tension loosen inside her. Earlier, Ray had looked as if he wanted to kill her. Now he seemed . . . pleased. She didn't know how long that would last, but for the moment, she could breathe again.

"Tonight, all we got is more beans."

She told herself to be careful. One wrong step . . . "I like beans fine."

The darkness of the mountains seemed to flow into the pines like ink. Had they not been standing so close, she wouldn't have been able to see his features.

"This'll work out," he said, so close she could smell his sour breath. There was something pathetically hopeful in his voice, in his face. "Ya will learn to like me."

Her sisters had always told her she'd make a lousy poker player because her every thought surfaced on her face. She prayed that wasn't true now as she did everything possible not to show her true feelings. She also held her tongue, afraid that no matter what she said, it would be wrong.

After a moment, she held out her taped wrists and waited. She could feel the heat of his gaze on her face. He was looking for any small tell. His gaze fixed on her, Ray slowly pulled his knife from the sheath at his hip and reached for her hands. His hand brushed against her skin. She flinched again and felt his fingers tighten roughly over hers.

"Your hands are cold," she said, her voice cracking.

His gaze bored into her as he slipped the knife between her wrists. "Not as cold as this knife."

Ray froze as he must have heard the same sound she did in the distance. To Bo, it had sounded like a foghorn.

He let out a curse as he quickly cut the tape at her wrists. Just moments ago she'd thought she might live through the night. Now, she could feel the tension coming off Ray in waves.

"What was that?" she asked in a hoarse whisper. She hadn't realized how close she was to tears. Ray had recognized it, she was sure of it. Whatever it was, she feared it didn't bode well.

"Daddy's on his way. He'll be here by mornin'."

She thought she might throw up and would have if there'd been anything in her stomach to come up. The thin thread of hope that had kept her going shredded before her eyes. "*Your father?*"

"Who else's?" he snapped as he moved over to his pack and pulled out what looked like a buffalo horn.

She waited for him to blow it, but instead he stood in the growing darkness, more still than she thought she'd ever seen him. She looked past him to the blackness beyond the trees. *Run! It's dark enough that maybe he won't be able to find you.*

His gaze shifted to her as if he sensed her thoughts. "Wait 'til he gets a load of you. Wonder what he'll do."

Not as much as she did.

He slowly dropped the horn back into his pack. When he spoke, he ground out his words. "The old bastard'll want ya for himself."

Just when she thought she couldn't be more frightened . . . She wished she'd run when she'd first had the thought. She probably wouldn't have gotten away, but maybe this would be over. Because all her instincts told her that once his father found them, things were going to get much worse.

From the growing dark, Ray stepped to her so quickly she started. "Come over here where I kin see ya while I make the fire."

She did as she was told, watching him as he expertly got a fire going. He opened a can of beans and set them into the coals.

"You didn't expect your father so soon?" Bo asked, trying to understand the relationship between father and son and whether there was a chance she could use it to her benefit.

"He weren't sure when he'd get away." Ray looked up at her. His blue eyes gleamed in the firelight. "Don't worry. Yer mine. I ain't sharing ya. Not even with my old man. He wants ya?" His voice dropped to the low growl she'd become accustomed to. "He'll have to kill me first."

She shivered and looked down at the beans. They were bubbling hot, but he hadn't offered her any. He seemed more worried about his father's arrival than he did the search party that would eventually be coming to look for her. She hadn't expected him even to build a fire tonight, worried about the smoke letting any searchers know where they were. She realized that the fire might have been Ray's first mistake.

"I kin handle my old man," he said without much conviction. "But there's somethin' yer goin' to have to do." He pulled out the knife. The rising moon caught the blade as Ray held it up in front of her face. "Do I have to tell ya what'll happen if ya don't do what I say?"

Even though the coming night was cold, Bo began to sweat, her pulse a panic against her skin. She had looked past him to the dense shadows of the pines, terrified that what was coming could be far worse than the man standing before her. Now, though, she feared she shouldn't have worried about Ray's father. She doubted she would last the night.

Chapter
FOURTEEN

Jace reined in and listened. He'd heard something. It had almost sounded like an elk bugle, but it was the wrong time of the year. He sat on his horse listening, waiting to see if he heard it again.

The breeze sighed in the tops of the pines. He could hear water running somewhere close by. An owl hooted from a nearby tree, and he caught the flash of wings before it disappeared overhead. But he heard nothing else.

He should have caught up with Bo by now. Even as he spurred his horse forward, watching the mountain slopes ahead, Jace had to question what he was doing. He'd made mistakes with his kid sister. Hell, he'd been a kid himself when he was trying to raise her alone after their parents died.

While he'd done everything he could to protect her, she'd only rebelled all the more. Maybe if he'd been more understanding . . . Now he knew that Emily had been hurting. Losing her parents at such a young age. Then having a bossy big brother telling her what to do . . . No wonder she'd rebelled. He would have, too.

So was he doing the same thing now, going after

Bo Hamilton? He felt as if he should have learned that there were some things he couldn't control. Bo was definitely one of them. He should have let the senator's men round her up. It probably wouldn't have made any difference in the long run. Bo had bolted, so there was a good chance she was scared or in trouble.

While he hated to think what it would do to Emily, there was nothing he could do now to make this right even if he found Bo and took her back to face the consequences.

Jace kept riding, though, telling himself he was tired and discouraged, but he wasn't the kind of man to give up. He'd find her. It might not matter in the grand scheme of things, but he'd do what he said he was going to do.

After this, he should be able to put Bo behind him for good.

Buckmaster jumped at the sound of the phone. He snatched it up, hoping, praying it was news of Bo. Instead it was his oldest daughter.

"How is Mother?" Ainsley asked after they'd spoken for a moment.

"She's fine. I saw her earlier today. Have you heard from Bo by any chance?"

"No, why?"

He didn't want to worry her. "You know Bo. I just haven't heard from her for a few days. How is your job going?" She'd taken a position scouting locations for a movie production company.

"The job is great. Since I know Montana, it's easy to find locations for the various films."

"But?" he asked, hearing something in her voice.

Ainsley sighed. "A reporter has been hanging around. At least, I think that's what he is. He keeps turning up wherever I am."

Buckmaster couldn't imagine why a reporter would be dogging Ainsley. But as the oldest of his daughters, she would remember her mother better than any of the others. The media couldn't seem to let go of the story about Sarah's return and how it impacted his upcoming presidential race. Still . . . "Maybe this man's interest in you is . . . personal."

She chuckled at that.

"Is he handsome?"

"Dad."

"So he is." Buckmaster smiled to himself. He would love to see Ainsley find a good man. "I hope you're at least considering going back to law school. That was always your dream."

"Dreams change."

How well he knew that.

"I think I just need a little time off, is all."

He didn't believe that was the problem, but he didn't push it.

"I have to go. You're sure everything is all right there?" she asked.

"I'll let you know if we need you." Ainsley had practically raised her sisters. It was time he had a life of her own. "You're missed, though."

"Thanks." She hung up, and he stood holding the phone for a moment. Should he have told her that Bo was missing and so was a lot of the Sarah Hamilton Foundation's money?

No. He would wait until he knew something definite. No reason to worry Ainsley when it wasn't yet necessary. Same with Kat, who was off shooting photographs for her upcoming exhibit, and Olivia, who was due to have her baby any day. Harper and Cassidy were a world away. None of them could do anything anyway. It was bad enough that he had to wait, feeling this helpless.

He felt time slipping away. Bo had been missing too long. Jace Calder, who'd been so sure he could find her and bring her back, had been gone more than his estimated twenty-four hours.

Buckmaster tried to console himself in the knowledge that tomorrow the search and rescue team would be going back into the mountains looking for Bo.

He planned to saddle up and go with them, no matter what the sheriff said. He had to know his daughter was all right.

"You're investigating me?" Sarah demanded as she stormed into the sheriff's office. The woman at the front had followed her back, saying the whole way that she couldn't just barge in like this.

"It's all right, Ann," Frank said to the woman before turning his attention to Sarah. She could see that he'd been about to leave his office for the day. She didn't care. "Why don't you close the door and have a chair?"

Her anger surprised her. She'd always been passive, letting trouble roll off her like water off a tin roof. Or at least, that's what she'd been told she was like. Meek, sweet Sarah.

Well this Sarah was boiling mad. Her anger was almost scary. She felt as if she was capable of anything. Maybe what Buck had told her was true. Maybe she *had* dropped back into town via a parachute. A woman who was terrified of heights? How was that possible? What if she hadn't jumped? What if someone had pushed her?

Even more frightening was the idea that it hadn't been her first leap from a moving plane. Maybe she'd done it dozens of times—this other Sarah, the woman she only sensed inside her.

"Would you like some water or maybe a cup of coffee?" the sheriff asked.

She shook her head. "I'm fine." But she wasn't fine, she thought as she sat down in a chair across from his desk. "Buck told me you were investigating me." She'd known Frank Curry when he used to ride around on a motorcycle and had long blond hair and an attitude. No one had been more surprised when he'd joined the sheriff's department as a deputy. And now here he was, the sheriff.

"There were extenuating circumstances that made an investigation prudent."

Sarah scoffed. "How dare you investigate me. This is why you wanted my DNA and my finger-prints."

"I also wanted to help you find out who you've been the past twenty-two years."

"For my sake? Or is Buck behind this?"

"For everyone's sake, including your daughters."

Just the mention of her daughters was like a bucket of ice water on her blazing anger. When she spoke again, her voice was little more than a whisper. "You're afraid for my daughters?"

"Wouldn't you be given what information we have?" Frank asked.

She met his gaze. "Is it true about the parachute?"

He nodded. "We found your DNA and blood on the chute's harness."

"How could you know it was my DNA?" Unless her DNA had come up in some criminal database. She held her breath.

"Your daughter Kat was kind enough to offer hers so we could match it."

Kat, dear Kat. Of course she would be the one.

But they could have also gotten it off the broken mug that they'd taken the day she'd refused to give them her DNA. So why involve Kat? Because they had taken the mug illegally and now they were covering their asses. Or were they simply building a case against her?

"You think I'm dangerous not only to my daughters but also to society? No, not to society," she corrected herself as she realized why she was under scrutiny. "To the future president. What is it you think I've come back to do?"

The sheriff shook his head. "I don't know. Do you?" When she didn't answer, he said, "I'm hoping you can fill in some of the gaps. This is what I know so far."

Sarah listened, feeling more afraid by the moment as he told her about the night at the river, about the hermit who found her, about her calling someone to pick her up before she disappeared for twenty-two years.

Russell had been right. She shouldn't have come here. She shot to her feet. "I have to go."

The sheriff rose, as well. "Sarah, I want to help you. If you remember anything—"

"I appreciate that, Frank. I do. Right now, though, no one can help me." The truth of her words felt like a knife to her heart. Worse, she felt as if she didn't know whom to trust. Her instincts told her that the sheriff was the last person she should confide in—just as Russell

200

had worried—because she had something to hide and didn't even know it.

Buck said that she knew she could trust him, but could she really? Russell didn't think so. And while she trusted Russell, she feared that could change, though, when they found out where she'd been the past twenty-two years.

With that disturbing thought simmering in her brain, she turned to leave.

"Did Buck mention the tattoo to you?" Frank asked before she reached the door.

"That silly thing?" She laughed as she stopped and half turned. Even to her, the laugh sounded hollow. "Too much tequila."

The sheriff looked surprised, and she realized her mistake even before he spoke. "Then you remember getting the tattoo? So you must also remember what the symbol means."

She shook her head. "I don't remember getting the tattoo. I can only imagine it must have involved alcohol. If it means something, I have no idea what. Probably the tattoo artist didn't, either."

Frank nodded as he sat back down. His look of disappointment made it clear that he didn't believe her. She couldn't blame him. She'd always been a terrible liar. Was that true? Was anything she thought or saw in her dreams even true? Russell believed her brain had been wiped of the memories. But he'd also said that false memories could have been planted there.

"Sarah, are you sure you don't have some idea why you would get a tattoo in that particular spot, let alone that particular design?"

"I have no idea about a lot of things," she said from the doorway and left.

Alex checked his phone periodically for the rest of the day, hoping Emily would have gotten back to him about their date. She'd said she might call to talk. She hadn't.

She has a daughter, he reminded himself. She would have to get a sitter for whatever night they went out. He had to be patient. He didn't want to push her. He got the feeling that if he did, he could frighten her off. And that was the last thing he wanted to do.

He saw something in her. It wasn't even something he could explain to his cousin Jeff. He liked making Emily smile. It was that simple and that complicated. He looked forward to seeing her every chance he got. It made his day.

"You all right?" Jeff asked.

Alex blinked. He hadn't realized he'd been staring out the front window until he focused on what he'd been staring at. The battered older-model brown Ford across the street. Usually, the man in the cowboy hat would be sitting in it. Right now it was empty.

Grabbing a pen and a scratch pad, he hurried out the front door and across the street. He'd expected to see the man appear before he could reach the car. Alex did his best to act as if he wasn't up to anything. He almost laughed at the thought as he walked along the sidewalk until he was at the back of the car.

He scribbled down the plate information surreptitiously as he kept walking. At the end of the block, he quickly crossed the street. He was almost to the Big Timber Java entrance when he finally stole a glance across the street.

The man in the old black cowboy hat was bigger than he'd looked sitting down in his car. He was dressed in a faded black T-shirt, baggy, worn jeans and what looked like combat boots. Both forearms were covered in tattoos as well as his neck. He came out of the hardware store carrying a large sack. As he reached his car and started to open the rear door, he looked in Alex's direction.

Alex quickly stepped into the coffee shop and leaned against the nearest wall, out of sight. He saw Jeff give him a what-the-hell look. He didn't think the man had seen him take down his license number. But he couldn't be sure. When he dared peek again, the man was still standing next to his car, his gaze on the coffee shop.

"What was that about?" Jeff asked when Alex joined him behind the counter. He was still shaken by the intense look on the man's face and the fact that this man had been watching Emily for several days now.

"I got the man's license plate number."

"What man?" Jeff asked and glanced toward the window.

"Is he still looking this way?" Alex asked without looking up.

"I don't see anyone." Jeff glanced at what he'd written on the notepad. "What are you going to do with that?"

"I'm not sure, but the man has been watching Emily from across the street in a large older dark vehicle."

"So you're going to find out who he is and what, kick his ass for looking at your girl?" Jeff asked with a raised eyebrow. "How do you know the guy isn't her boyfriend and he's planning to kick *your* ass?"

"She said she doesn't have a boyfriend."

"Uh-huh." Jeff began refilling the napkin bin on the counter.

"She wouldn't lie to me."

His cousin shook his head. "Just be careful. You have no idea what you're getting yourself into."

Alex pocketed the paper with the license number on it. Now that he had it, he wasn't sure what to do with it. He could take it to the sheriff and have him run the plate . . . Probably not.

Wouldn't the sheriff need a good reason to do that?

Jeff was probably right. He didn't know what he was getting into. But when he checked his phone, he saw that he had a text from Emily, and his pulse took off.

Friday night would work fine, if it's okay with you.
Great. Pick you up at six for dinner first, then the movie?

See you then.

He smiled to himself as he pocketed his phone and the slip of paper with the license plate number on it. When he glanced across the street, the car and the man were gone.

Chapter
FIFTEEN

"You were right," Sarah said as she climbed into Russell's pickup parked outside the sheriff's department. It was late now, twilight deepening. The Crazy Mountains had turned a midnight blue against the lighter sky. They looked cold and dark. At the thought of her daughter being up there . . .

But they were Buck's daughters and always had been, even before she'd left. He'd put them on horses before they could even walk. He'd taken them to the mountains camping when they were toddlers. He'd wanted them to be like him, fearless. He hadn't wanted them to be like their mother, meek, mild Sarah, afraid of everything.

"I probably shouldn't have gone in there."

"What happened?" Russell asked as he started the engine and backed out.

"I'm being investigated."

Russell glanced over at her. "What about that surprises you? The sheriff asked you for your fingerprints and DNA. Did you really think he was just trying to help you find your past?"

She was surprised at the anger she heard in his voice.

"You were married to a man who will probably

be the next president of the United States if he doesn't screw it up."

"Or if I don't. Isn't that what you mean?" When he said nothing as he drove out of the parking lot, she demanded, "Why do you think you know what is best for me? You and Buck? What makes either of you . . ." Her voice trailed off. "I'm sorry. All you've done is try to help me. Buck, too. If anyone is to blame for this, it's me. The sheriff told me how I literally dropped back into Beartooth and everyone's life by parachute. He also asked me about a strange tattoo on my butt that I've never seen and had no idea was there. If it really is."

Russell threw on the brakes. "*What?* You parachuted into the woods where I found you?"

"So you *didn't* know," she said. "He didn't tell you about the tattoo?"

Russell shook his head. "It's just a tattoo, right?"

"More like a brand, I'm told. I can't see it unless I use a hand mirror. I'm going to need you to take a photo of it for me. Would you do that?"

He glanced over at her. She could tell that he was touched she trusted him with this. "You know I'll do whatever you ask me to."

She nodded distractedly. "The rumors you heard were true. The sheriff told me about a man named Lester Halverson finding me. This man, a hermit who lived on the river, told him that I called someone that night. Whoever that some-one was, they picked me up, and that's the last anyone around here saw of me."

"Did he ask you again for your DNA and fingerprints?" Russell asked, worried.

"He didn't have to. Apparently he had them all along, taken from the chute's harness. He then compared it with the DNA from my broken coffee mug—and backed it up with Kat's DNA."

"But nothing came up in any of their criminal databases." He sounded relieved.

Sarah, though, didn't seem to feel better. When he questioned her about why she wasn't relieved, she said, "Whatever I might have been, I just didn't get caught." She shook her head, not believing any of this. "The sheriff knows more about me than I do. And you were worried about what I might tell *him?*"

"Sarah." Russell reached over and took her hand. She started to pull away but changed her mind. Her hand felt so warm in his big callused one. She wanted him to wrap his arms around her and hold her. In Russell's arms, she told herself, she would feel safe. "It's going to be all right. You're going to remember everything."

That's what terrified her given the sheriff thought she might be a national security risk.

Darkness closed in quickly over the mountains. As the moon rose, Jace caught glimpses of the full gold orb through the pines. The air was colder this far back into the mountains, the pine scent crispier. He breathed it in and thought for a moment that he'd caught a whiff of smoke.

He rode up to a high knob to camp for the night. He'd lost his light and didn't dare keep going in the dark. He chose the knob so he would be able to see if anyone was approaching in the bright moonlight. Originally he'd ridden into the mountains thinking he would find Bo and simply take her back. Now he had no idea what he would be facing when he did find her.

Where are you, Bo? Still running?

He breathed in hard, his anger boiling up again. What the hell was he doing? This was none of his business. He'd taken it on himself to bring the woman back to face . . . To face what? Until that moment, he hadn't let himself believe that she'd had anything to do with the stolen money. But what if she had? What if her actions led to the dissolving of the foundation— and Emily's job?

He realized he hadn't thought this through. Finding Bo and taking her back might not solve anything.

He took another breath. This time there was no mistaking it. He caught the acrid smell of campfire smoke. He froze for a moment before sniffing the air. Definitely campfire smoke.

He had thought he must be getting close. Bo

and the man she was traveling with apparently only had the one horse. They were traveling slower than he was—but not that much. Why were they pushing so hard?

Because now the two of them were on the run?

He tried to gauge where the smoke was coming from. It could travel great distances on a wind. But tonight there was only a slight breeze coming out of the north—the same direction as Bo Hamilton and her companion.

Tying his horse to a tree, he took his rifle. His handgun was already strapped to his hip, loaded and ready. The moon topped the pines, splashing the mountainside with light. He could make out a smudge of gray below him to the north. A campfire less than the distance of a football field away.

He started down the mountain, unsure what he was going to find once he reached the campsite. The man she'd met up with, whoever he was, complicated things. Jace expected him to be armed—Bo could be, too, for that matter.

So he wouldn't be storming into the camp until he knew what he was getting into. If she was on the run with the money, she wouldn't take kindly to him showing up. And neither would the man with her.

Bo was terrified Ray was going to cut her. He ran the flat part of the blade down her arm, his gaze locked with hers as he did it.

She fought not to shudder at his touch or, worse, the knife's. When she tried to take a step back, he'd grabbed her with his free hand, cupping the back of her neck and squeezing until she cried out.

The knife still in his hand, he pulled her closer until they were only a breath's width apart. Behind him, the campfire crackled, the beans bubbling. She caught a whiff of them, and her stomach growled even though she could tell they were burned.

The moon had risen above the tops of the pines and now poured a silver sheen down on them. She could see Ray's angry face clearly. She'd prayed that this moment would never come, but time had run out—just as she'd feared.

"I *am* goin' to have ya, one way or another," he said from between gritted teeth. "Ya want it rough?" He gave her a shake. "Ya'll get it."

She didn't want it at all, but her options had run out.

"I been patient. Now I'm tired of waitin'. My old man'll be here tomorrow. I have to know that yer . . . mine. Ya understand?"

She feared she understood only too well. He no longer cared if she liked him. He needed her to be his before his father arrived in the morning. Tonight he was going to take what he wanted, and if she fought him . . . Well, that would be the worst thing she could do. But how could she not?

Still holding the back of her neck in a viselike grip, he shoved her back until she collided with the thick base of a tall pine. In the darkness of the boughs, his free hand went to her breast. He rubbed his palm over it, and when she didn't respond, he squeezed it hard through her clothing, making her wince.

He let out a guttural sound that could have been pleasure. Or pain.

She closed her eyes, filled with the terror of what she knew was about to happen. She would fight him with her last ounce of strength. That thought almost made her laugh. Weak with hunger, exhausted from fear and pain from her injuries, lack of sleep and hours either walking or in the saddle, how in God's name would she be able to fight him off?

No, she thought as she opened her eyes and looked into his. She had a feeling that she wouldn't be the first woman to fight him, and that it would only get her hurt worse.

Gain his trust. It's the only way you're going to get off this mountain alive.

He released his grip on her neck at the same time he let go of her breast.

She kept her gaze locked with his, afraid of what he would do next but willing herself to keep calm. Something softened in his face.

Then he froze. "Did you hear that?" he asked in a hoarse whisper.

She hadn't heard anything except the frantic pounding of her pulse in her ears. Glancing around, all she saw past the campfire was darkness. She caught the sound of the beans bubbling in the can. "The beans—"

He clamped a hand down over her mouth as he shoved her hard against the trunk of a pine tree—and deeper into the darkness of the pine boughs. "That weren't no beans," he whispered, tilting his head as he listened.

What was it he thought he heard? Surely not his father. Ray had said he wouldn't be here until morning.

She listened. The night had gone incredibly still beyond the black shadow of the pine boughs where they stood. Bo felt as if she'd gone deaf. Closer she heard the pounding of her heart in her ears and Ray's ragged breathing. His face twisted in anger. Or was that fear?

He sheathed the knife. He reached into his jacket pocket, pulled out the duct tape and began to wrap her wrists together with an urgency that filled her with both panic and hope that what he'd heard was someone out there coming to save her.

After taking the back road to his ranch, Russell let her inside the door and turned on the lights. He took her cell phone from her and blushed to the roots of his hair.

"Are you sure you don't mind doing this?" Sarah asked. She'd known how uncomfortable this was going to make him. Was it modesty or the feelings he had for her? The fact that he'd fallen half in love with her was no secret to either of them. It was just a mistake on his part.

"You know I would do anything to help you." But he looked as if he was about to face a firing squad, not take a photo of the tattoo on her butt.

She still couldn't believe the tattoo even existed. The doctor's wife, Sarah realized, was the only person who'd seen her naked since her return from the dead.

That was before Buck had told her about the tattoo's existence and confirmed that it was true. Something like a brand was on her right buttock. But Sarah hadn't believed it until she'd seen it with her own eyes with the use of a hand mirror moments ago.

"I need a clear photo so I can try to tell what this is," she said to Russell as he stood holding the phone. She turned her back and pulled the waistband of her pants down enough that he would be able to get a shot.

She heard him behind her, heard the snap of the cell phone camera and heard him take a second photo.

"Done," he said, sounding odd.

She fixed her clothing before turning to look at

him. He was staring into the phone. Russell had been her protector since that first day that he'd found her in the middle of nowhere coming out of the woods.

But right now, he looked uncomfortable.

"Is it that bad?" she asked, seeing that he was upset.

He shook his head. "It's just . . . seeing you half-naked." His gaze met hers. The raw desire she saw there shouldn't have surprised her.

She didn't dare respond to the need in his eyes, although she obviously couldn't remember the last time she was with a man. If it wouldn't have complicated things, she might have taken Russell up on it. She could definitely use a good roll in the hay—a thought that was nothing like the old Sarah whom Buck had married. She'd been shy about sex with Buck—even after they'd brought six children into the world.

She had a feeling that if she let herself go, there would be nothing shy or reserved about her lovemaking. Another reason she wouldn't be having sex with Russell.

"May I see the photo?" she asked, anxious to defuse the situation.

He nodded and handed her the cell phone.

"This is so odd," she said as she stared at what appeared to be a pendulum. She couldn't imagine why she would let anyone puncture her skin to drive ink into the dermis of her rear, let alone pay someone for the privilege. Not for a pendulum.

"No more odd than returning from the dead with no memory of the past twenty-two years to find your husband married to another woman, your children all grown and the press hounding you for all the sordid details," Russell said. "Compared to that, well, it's just a tattoo."

She smiled at him. How easy it would have been to step to him, put her arms around his neck and pull him down for a kiss. She could see him carrying her to the bedroom. He would be a tender, considerate lover. So why didn't she give into it? Did she really think Buck wasn't having sex with his wife?

"You have no idea how it got there or what it might mean?" Russell asked.

"None. You said you can plug the phone into your computer and make a printed copy of it?"

They'd come to his ranch, taking the back way to avoid any press that might still be lurking around. The cabin where she was staying was nice, but Sarah missed staying down here in his guesthouse. But she knew Russell was right about it not being safe—and not just from the media.

Buck's new wife had come to see her before Russell had moved her to the cabin. No surprise that Sarah had taken an instant dislike to the woman. What had scared her wasn't the other woman, but the violent impulse she'd had in Angelina Broadwater Hamilton's presence. She'd realized then that she was the one who might be dangerous.

Russell sat down at his computer, plugged in the phone and loaded the two photos he'd taken. The tattoo came up on the screen. The hand mirror or the cell phone screen hadn't done the design justice.

"Does it look like anything you've ever seen before?" Russell asked.

She shook her head, but with a heated rush her skin remembered the bite of the needle into her tender flesh and a feeling of both pain—and pleasure.

"Can you make me a copy?" Sarah asked, her voice cracking.

He didn't move to print the image on the screen. She looked over at him. His gaze was both sad and disappointed.

"You remember getting it, don't you?" He sounded accusing.

She shook her head, but she could tell he didn't believe her.

"When I was a boy, a friend and I took a knife and cut a slice in our palms becoming blood brothers. Sarah, is there a chance this tattoo connects you to whoever flew you back here?"

Ray froze to listen. He'd developed a sixth sense when it came to trouble. It was as if he could feel it bone deep.

He'd been feeling it since he'd taken the woman. Why hadn't he thought this out? Like his old man always said, sometimes he was dumber than a tree stump. Of course someone would come looking for her. He stared at her for a long moment as he listened, regretting that he hadn't just had his way with her and killed her. Someone would still have come looking for her, but at least he would have had the satisfaction no matter how fleeting. Now . . .

He hurriedly finished wrapping her wrists, taping them tighter than he probably should have in his anger and frustration. This was all her fault. If he was right and someone was coming after her . . .

Too late to change anything now. He had her, and damned if he wasn't going to keep her. If he was right and there was someone out there . . . Well, they'd never have her. He'd kill her before he'd let anyone take her.

But he told himself it wouldn't come to that. Whoever was looking for her wouldn't know about him. Surprise! He'd kill the person. Once his old man got here, if he still had the woman, then he would take her with him deeper into the mountains. He wasn't giving her up. She would learn to love him. Or wish she had.

He stopped again to listen. And if he didn't still have the woman? Then he'd take the horses his father was bringing and get out of these mountains. He'd go to Mexico and start over.

But it hurt to think that he would be going alone since his father hated Mexico—and would be so angry with him that he wouldn't go with him anyway. Ray had it in his head that this woman was his. He wasn't sure he cared what happened to him if he didn't have her at least once before he had to kill her.

Bo hadn't heard *anything*. But Ray seemed to think someone was out there. Or some*thing?* Given the large number of grizzlies that lived in the Crazies . . .

"Is it a bear?" she whispered.

In answer, he tore off a piece of the tape and plastered it over her mouth as he shoved her to her knees on the ground.

"No." Her cry was muffled by the tape. "No!" she cried again, terrified that all this had been a ruse so he could bind her and finally take what he wanted roughly, the way she suspected he liked it.

"Shut up!" he whispered hoarsely against her ear as he threw her facedown in the dirt so hard that she had trouble catching her breath.

She was screaming inside as she saw him grab the rope from where he'd dropped it earlier. Pulling her to her feet, he forced her to turn against the trunk of the pine tree and then began to wrap the rope tightly around her and the tree.

He stopped twice, both times freezing for a moment as if listening again to the night, before he continued tying her.

Her face against the rough bark, she, too, listened for any sound coming from the trees or mountains around them. She heard nothing. Was it possible Ray Spencer was losing his mind? She almost laughed at the thought. The man was a psychopath. He'd been locked up before he escaped. Ideally, he would be locked up again and soon.

But she didn't dare hope there was someone out in the darkness who could make that happen. Hope would make her cry, and if she cried, Ray would give her something more to cry about. It was better to believe he was having a psychotic incident.

What happened, though, when he realized his mistake? She squeezed her eyes shut, feeling hot tears leak from her lashes and run down her cheeks. She would be lucky to live through this night, she thought as she heard Ray douse the campfire. The acrid smell of smoke wafted over her. She tried not to cough.

She turned her head to the side as far as she could. She saw him through the smoke. He was standing a few yards from her out of the moon-light, his face twisted in an expression she hadn't seen before. He looked like a trapped animal. He was scared. He'd looked this same way when he'd heard the horn and realized that his father would be arriving soon.

What if it was a grizzly? She knew that if it came to a choice between saving her and saving himself, Ray would leave her as bear bait.

Her chest hurt from trying to hold in the tears and the frantic pounding of her heart. What was out there? Ray wasn't stupid enough to try to kill a grizzly with a pistol, was he? But he didn't have his pistol, she saw with a start. The barrel of his rifle glistened in the moonlight at the corner of his open pack. His pistol was in there, as well. She had the feeling he much preferred a knife, and that's why he didn't carry the guns.

But if it was bear, did he plan on killing it with his knife? No, whatever he thought he heard, he believed it to be human.

With a start, she realized that was why he was keeping to the darkness of the pines—so he couldn't be seen. Which meant he was afraid to get his guns out of the pack because it was a good distance away and in the moonlight.

A twig snapped, sounding like a gunshot somewhere out in the forest. Ray heard it, too. He glanced toward his pack, clearly debating whether to race across the camp in the moonlight for the guns, but he didn't move. She listened hard, thought she heard the sound of a boot heel on the dried forest floor. Was someone really out there?

Not his father, since Ray had said he was hours away. Could it be someone looking for *her?* Hope filled her like helium. She tried to call out, the sound muffled against the tape. Out of the corner of her eye, she saw Ray, the knife gripped in his fist, motioning for her to shut up. But he didn't move toward her—that would have meant crossing a stretch of moonlit ground, making him a target.

Closer, she heard the sound of something brush against a pine bough. There *was* someone out there! She saw Ray slip deeper into the darkness of the pines.

She pressed her face into the rough bark of the tree as she worked to get the tape free from her mouth. If searchers had come to save her, she had to warn them about Ray.

Chapter
SIXTEEN

"Russell, what is all this?" Sarah asked as she looked at the stack of papers he placed on the kitchen table. He'd made them dinner, and they hadn't talked about the damn tattoo, something she was glad of.

"I've been doing some research. I mentioned it before, but I thought you'd like to check it out yourself."

So that's what he'd been doing when he wasn't visiting her. She picked up the top article. Last time he'd brought up the subject, it had scared her. It scared her even more now that he wasn't letting it drop.

"Brain wiping," she said and sighed. "I appreciate what you're trying to do, but the neurologist—"

"I know, he said there are all kinds of reasons for your amnesia." She hadn't told him that the neurologist had suggested her memory loss was psychological. She hadn't wanted to admit that even to herself.

"He also said it might be permanent. I may never get my memory back." She could tell that Russell didn't want to believe that any more than

Buck did. Russell had asked her about what she was remembering, though, making it clear that he was aware some memories seemed to be coming back.

She'd told him they were just flashes. True enough. But she feared they *were* memories and that one day they would all come flooding back. It terrified her given the strange, distorted images she'd seen.

"I should have told you but I've been searching for articles on brain wiping from back more than twenty-two years ago. I knew someone had to be doing research then. I figured once I found the scientist, all I had to do was locate a facility that would have been easy for him to get you to without calling attention to either you or himself. Remember, everyone believed you were dead. So it had to be one he could drive you to and get back from before he was missed."

She was amazed at the lengths he would go to to prove this theory. Russell really believed Buck had her locked up all those years ago after her botched suicide attempt.

"I found an article published in a medical journal twenty-three years ago—a year before you disappeared."

Sarah stared at him. Even when he'd shared his theory, she hadn't considered it was a real possibility. "What are you saying?"

"A doctor by the name Ralph Venable was doing

brain wiping research long before anyone thought it possible."

She'd read one of the articles Russell had given her on brain wiping. "But I thought the experiments have only been on *rats!*"

"So you *did* look at the other information I brought you." He sounded pleased by that, and encouraged. "Yes, recent experiments have been done on rats. But Venable was sure it would work on humans. I know it all sounds like science fiction. Targeting certain parts of the brain where a memory is stored while leaving the rest entirely intact. If modern science was now able to do this, then why not a doctor ahead of his time twenty-two years ago?"

"Because it's so . . . diabolical."

"Diabolical if I'm right and your husband was the one who picked you up that night. If he had heard about this doctor, he would have known where to take you."

"That's a lot of ifs."

"You've been looking for answers? Well, here's one right under your nose."

She rose from her chair to move around the kitchen. "So Buck somehow found out about this man's research and took me to what? Some hospital?"

"I doubt it was a hospital. Probably more like a private clinic. You'd just tried to kill yourself. Taking you to a doctor made sense, right? If word should get out, well, he would look like a caring husband trying to protect you."

Sarah hugged herself, chilled at the thought as she turned to look at him. "But Buck's true reason was so this mad scientist could wipe out whatever horrible thing I knew about my husband that made me drive into the river."

"Yes."

"Then why didn't Buck bring me back home after my memory was erased?"

Russell shook his head. "Maybe he didn't trust that you wouldn't remember."

"So instead, he kept me a prisoner for the next twenty-two years?"

"I'm not sure where he kept you."

"And the good doctor?"

"I'm still trying to track him down. But I suspect you saw him again—right before I found you coming out of the woods a few months ago."

"Saw him again? You mean Buck had him wipe out the past twenty-two years so I thought I'd just given birth to the twins. You do know how crazy this all sounds, don't you?" He was making her head ache with this off-the-wall theory.

She'd told Buck she would meet him in thirty minutes. She had to get going and yet . . . "You say this doctor was years ahead of his time in this type of research? Why take a chance experimenting on humans when I would assume if he were caught he'd lose his license to practice medicine, maybe even be imprisoned?"

"The story was that Venable's wife was brutally raped by some drunken soldiers on leave. The men were never caught. Apparently, his life's work was to make her horrible memories go away."

She had to ask. "Did he succeed?"

Russell sighed and shook his head. "She killed herself."

"So his brain wiping failed."

"Not necessarily. According to what I've read, emotional memories are very powerful and can have strong physiological effects on a person— so much so that they can't be entirely wiped away. Which could explain the flashes of memory you're having."

The thought sent a chill through her. Was it possible the man she'd married was capable of the things Russell suggested?

"If scientists are now able to wipe out some memories without affecting other memories," Russell continued, "why isn't it possible Venable could do it twenty-two years ago?"

"But you weren't able to find a facility where he'd worked near here?"

Russell shook his head.

"And he wasn't able to save his own wife."

"No. But if I'm right, Venable succeeded

beyond his wildest dreams with at least one patient."

She met his gaze. "Me."

Ray froze at the sound of a twig snapping some distance away. He'd already crossed paths with one grizzly on his way back into the mountains. Fortunately it hadn't been a mama grizzly with a couple of cubs. He'd heard too many stories about hunters getting mauled to death.

But tonight this was no bear out there, he thought as he listened from the dark shadows under the pines. Nor was it his father. So who had stumbled onto their camp?

The full moon was so bright that it looked like daylight out of the darkness of the pines. Ray glanced toward his pack by the still smoking fire. With a curse, he realized two mistakes he'd made. The fire. He should never have built it after seeing the plane earlier. Of course the pilot wasn't the only person looking for Bo-Peep. Worse, he'd been so busy putting out the fire and taking care of the woman that he'd left both his rifle and his handgun inside the open pack in the middle of camp. But to get to the weapons, he would have to cross a dozen yards of moonlit ground.

He listened, heard nothing. Maybe that's all it had been, nothing. Maybe he was just jumpy because his old man would be here by daybreak.

Ray had spent his life being afraid of his father—and at the same time knowing the old man was all he had.

All his instincts told him to stay where he was. Whatever was out there was dangerous, and it was coming for him.

The smell of smoke was so strong, Jace knew the camp was just on the other side of a thick stand of trees. He slowed. He didn't dare go stumbling into camp, and it would have been easy in the dark of the pines.

He'd purposely stayed in the deep shadow of the trees as he'd moved. The moon was bright as day, almost blinding when he stepped out into it. He could be spotted too easily in its light spearing down through the pine branches—and get himself shot. After following Bo's tracks and the man's, he had a bad feeling about what he was going to find now that he'd caught up with them.

Ahead, he saw a break in the stand of pines and moved toward it. He tried to be careful where he stepped. It was hard enough to be quiet in the forest in broad daylight, let alone in the darkness of the pines. He'd already stepped on a twig. The snap as it broke had sounded like a cannon going off to him. Had they heard it in camp? He had to assume so.

He'd reach the edge of the dense stand of pines

when through the narrow opening, he saw the source of the smoke. A small, dying campfire billowed the smell of wet coals into the night sky. The fire had only recently been doused with water. That meant they had heard him coming.

Probably also the reason there was no one near the fire. Had they left? Or were they only lying in wait?

A horse whinnied some distance away. He heard the scuffle of boots in the dried needles of the pines and then nothing.

He had to get closer. This was Bo's camp, he was sure of it. And that horse he'd just heard would be hers if he was right.

So where were they?

Cautiously and as quietly as he could, he worked his way through the pine trees closer to the camp. He hadn't gone far when he saw movement out of the corner of his eye. He swung his rifle but came up short, thinking he must be seeing things.

Bo Hamilton was bound with rope to a tree.

What the hell?

He could hear her muffled pleas from behind her duct-taped mouth but couldn't make out what she was saying. She seemed to be struggling to get the tape off her mouth by rubbing her face against the bark of the tree.

Jace felt his heart drop. What had he stumbled into? He wanted to call out to her, but something told him the last thing he should do was let whoever had done that to her know where he was.

"Help!" Bo cried as she got most of the tape from her mouth. Her voice was still muffled and hoarse, but he got the message. "He's in the trees. He has a knife!"

Rage filled Ray. He'd had such high hopes for his future with his little Bo-Peep. It would have worked, too. If they could have reached a spot deep in the mountains, he would have built them a cabin. They would have been happy. He would have done anything to make her happy.

A bloodred film blurred his vision. He thought he might explode with fury as he clinched the knife harder in his hands until he thought he might crush the handle. He couldn't let it end like this. If he could reach his pack, get his rifle, he'd kill whoever had come for her. He had no idea who was out there in the darkness. Or even how many of them there might be. He'd heard only one. But what if there were more? What if he moved and they gunned him down? He could feel death knocking at his door.

Don't do nothing stupid. It was his father's voice. *Too late, Daddy.* He'd already done something stupid. He'd taken the woman, and now he would rather die than give her up.

Don't do it. Run! You don't want to die tonight in the dirt up on this mountain. His own voice this time. Raging at the thought that all he could do was run away, he cursed under his breath. Bo was *his*.

He heard Bo call out again, pleading for help. She'd managed to get the tape off her mouth. For just a moment, he'd actually thought she was calling to him to help her until he heard her say "He has a knife."

His heart had seemed to detonate in his chest, the pain worse than any beating he'd ever had—even his father's beatings. Just like that, she'd turned against him. Every woman he'd ever known had turned against him. But none of their betrayals hurt as much as this one.

She thought she was saved by whoever had come looking for her? He wanted to laugh out loud. She was dead wrong. Nothing could save her from him. No matter how many of them had come for her.

Ray knew it was suicidal, but he shoved to his feet from behind the tree where he'd been hunkering and sprinted toward his pack. He told himself that if he could reach his gun and get off only one shot, he'd kill the bitch.

How had he thought she would ever be his willingly? He should have taken her the moment he'd pulled her off her horse. She'd played him for a fool, and now she was going to pay for her betrayal.

With a tortured cry, he sprinted toward the

open pack next to the campfire. Even as he ran, he wished there was another way. He still wanted her, still hoped in some destroyed part of his heart that she could be his.

A bullet whizzed past his ear. He changed course, realizing there was only one way to end this now. With the knife gripped in his fist, he raced toward the woman, the blade raised. He saw her eyes widen as she realized what he was about to do. She didn't know how lucky she was that this was the worst he could do.

Jace had heard what sounded like a war cry an instant before a huge man came charging out of the woods. Jace swung his rifle, taking aim, expecting the man to charge him. The moonlight caught the glint of the knife clutched in the man's hand.

But to Jace's surprise, the man had run toward his open pack next to the extinguished campfire.

"He's going for his gun!" Bo yelled.

Jace took aim, pulled the trigger—and missed.

The man abruptly changed directions, this time heading for Bo, the knife raised in the air, a horrible sound coming from the man's mouth.

With the jump of his pulse, Jace saw what the man intended to do and fought to steady the rifle. He couldn't miss this time. If he did . . .

He pulled the trigger and heard the *thwunk* as the bullet hit the man's body.

The man stumbled but didn't go down. Jace fired again, but the man abruptly turned and quickly disappeared into the cover of the trees.

How badly had he wounded him? He had no way of knowing. He watched for movement in the darkness at the edge of the camp. Nothing. "Are you sure he doesn't have another weapon?" he called to Bo.

"No, his gun and rifle are in his pack near the fire." So that's why he had run toward the pack. But then he'd changed course, his intentions all too clear.

He could hear Bo sobbing. He had to get to her. As he advanced, keeping to the shadows in the trees and away from the moonlight, he heard the sound of a horse whinny.

"Where's your horse?" he called to Bo.

He heard her try to stop crying to answer. Her words came out barely intelligible. "Hidden in the trees."

The man had gone for Bo's horse.

Jace reached her. Leaning his rifle against the tree, he pulled his knife and quickly cut the rope, freeing her.

She sank to the ground, sobs racking her body.

He wanted to take her in his arms and hold her, tell her she was going to be all right now, but as long as whoever had done this to her was out there . . .

"Who was that bastard?" he demanded as he picked up his rifle again, still watching the dark trees around them.

"Ray Spencer," she said in a hoarse whisper between sobs. He'd heard the name, but it took him a moment to realize where. Then he remembered the fugitive who'd been on the run for the past three weeks after a convenience story robbery in which someone had been killed. He swore under his breath as Bo sobbed, "He . . . kid-napped . . . me."

"Did you see where he tied up your horse?"

"No." She looked around as if terrified the man would reappear. Jace shared that same concern.

"He's alone?"

She nodded.

"What weapons does he have?"

"Just a knife."

Jace glanced to the man's pack near the fire ring. He could see the stock of an old rifle and the barrel of a handgun shining in the moonlight.

Quickly stepping away from the darkness of the tree, Jace dragged the pack over to Bo. "Can you stand?"

She nodded but couldn't seem to stop the sobs. He helped her to her feet. "Can't . . . believe . . . you found me." As she held out her wrists for him to cut the tape binding them, she said, "I . . . thought . . ." She cried harder as if she'd given up on ever being rescued.

"Listen to me," he said, taking hold of her shoulder and giving it a shake. "I need you to be quiet. I have to be able to hear him if he comes back." *When* he comes back, Jace thought. The man had left everything behind, including the woman he'd abducted.

"He wouldn't let me go." She managed to stop crying, hugging herself but still looking terrified. She leaned against the trunk of a tree as if too weak to walk. He hated to leave her, but he had no choice.

He pulled the man's pistol from the pack, checked to make sure it was loaded and handed it to her. "Tell me you know how to use this," he said.

She nodded, wide-eyed, as she held it tightly, her whole body trembling.

He reached down to flip off the safety for her. "Just don't shoot me. Stay right here."

But as he started to step away, she grabbed his leg and cried, "Where are you going?"

"I just need to see how badly he was shot. I'll be right back."

Letting go of his leg, she clutched the gun in both of her hands. She looked even more terrified as he moved cautiously to the spot where he thought he'd hit the man. In the bright moonlight, he could see the blood on the ground. Not a lot, though.

He saw that the drops had left a trail. He

followed it to a spot where he picked up horse-shoe tracks. The man had taken off on Bo's horse.

As Jace started back toward the camp, he looked to where he'd left Bo. She wasn't there.

His heart did a quick drop before he spotted her. She stood yards away in the moonlight, turning in a circle, the gun in her shaking hands. She looked distraught and beyond petrified. He doubted she could hit the broad side of a barn in the condition she was in, but he wasn't taking any chances.

"It's me," he called, and she instantly slumped to the dirt.

He quickly stepped to her. "I have to go after him. He's wounded but not badly. If I don't—"

She grabbed hold of his leg and began to cry again. "You can't leave me."

"You have the gun—"

"He'll kill you and then he'll come back for me."

"Thanks for the vote of confidence," he said more gently as he pulled her to her feet.

Bo looked up into his face as if until that moment she hadn't recognized him. *"Jace Calder? Of course it would be you."* Her reaction didn't surprise him given the bad blood between them. She began to cry again.

"Bo—" But he could feel time slipping away. "I have to go after him. If I don't go after him now—"

She took a step back, shaking her head, the gun clutched in both hands. Her words came out choked with fear. "You can't leave me. If you leave me . . ." She started to slump to the ground.

He grabbed for her, his fingers closing on her wrist. She let out a cry. He'd hurt her. Jace mentally kicked himself as he took her in his arms. She leaned into him as if terrified of letting him go. He hadn't had time to consider what she'd been through. Now, though, he took in the raw skin at her wrists and her neck. Those would heal. He feared her other injuries went much deeper than her bruised and scraped skin.

Looking toward the darkness of the trees, he cursed under his breath. If he left her and the man circled back around and got to her, he'd never forgive himself.

He knew what it took to kill a man. In her condition, he couldn't trust that she could pull the trigger.

"All right," he said, knowing that this, too, was a mistake they both could live to regret. "I won't leave you alone, but we can't stay here. We have to get moving. He has your horse. We have to get to my horse before he finds it."

She nodded mutely as if all the fight had gone out of her. He had to let her go to pick up the man's pack. No way was he leaving it so the man could get to the weapons. When he turned back, Bo stood like a small sapling rocking in the breeze. He could see how weak she was from her ordeal. He'd seen a can of beans in the doused fire. When was the last time she'd had something to eat? Lack of food was probably the least of it. He couldn't bear to think what the man had done to her.

"Can you walk?"

Bo glanced toward the darkness. She nodded and started to hand back the gun.

"Keep that. You may have to use it."

She looked up at him. He saw a tremor move through her. "If I have to use it . . ."

He nodded. He would already be dead.

Chapter
SEVENTEEN

Bo followed Jace from the moonlit camp into the darkness of the pines, half expecting that any moment she would wake up and this would have been nothing more than a dream.

What were the chances that Jace Calder would be the one to save her, given how she'd hurt him? She must have been hallucinating. Maybe Ray had stabbed her, and this was some subconscious fantasy. If she was dying, it made sense that she would think of Jace—and her biggest regret. Or this could be a nightmare in which things got even worse.

She stumbled as she trudged through the pines and almost fell. When she looked up, she didn't see Jace. Even when he appeared out of the trees for a moment, she thought it was Ray and all of this really was just delirium.

Jace had stopped ahead of her to wait. She'd tried to keep up with the long-legged cowboy, but she felt as if she was moving through quicksand. When she reached him, he didn't move for a long moment. She could tell he was listening.

Fear coiled again inside her. She was far from rescued. Ray Spencer was still out there. An eerie quiet had fallen over the night. She listened, terrified that Ray was tracking them like a mad dog. But all she could hear was the thunder of her pulse in her ears and the sound of the ground cover under them as they began walking again.

An owl hooted from a nearby limb, startling her. She stumbled on a root and fell face-first into the dirt. Jace quickly hoisted her to her feet.

"Try to stay up," he whispered, impatience and worry in every line of his body.

She nodded. But exhaustion, lack of food and fear had left her limbs as weak as water. She wasn't sure how much farther she could go.

Just when she thought she couldn't take another step, she heard a horse nicker nearby. Fear spiked through her. What if it was her horse and Ray was waiting for them?

But ahead, Jace moved to a large bay horse tied to a tree. Swinging up in the saddle, he rode over to a downed log and reached for her. "Now," he snapped. She stepped up on the log and he helped pull her up behind him. Wrapping her arms around his waist, she held on as he reined the horse around.

"We're not going after him, right?" she had to ask.

"No. We're going to try to get out of these mountains before he finds us."

"Maybe he's dead. Or running away. He knows you have a gun. He wouldn't be stupid enough to come after us." She knew she was voicing her hopes, but still she wanted Jace to agree with her.

Instead, he said nothing. She leaned into him and closed her eyes. Numb, she let the rocking of the horse lull her into an exhausted sleep.

The next morning, Emily was glad to drop Jodie off at day care where she knew she would be safe. By the time Emily had gone to Big Timber Java for her first coffee break of the day she had almost put the break-in out of her mind.

She hadn't realized how glad she was to see Alex Ross until he came out of the back and flashed her a smile. She saw him look past her to the street outside and frown.

Turning in her chair, she followed his gaze in time to see a battered large old dark-colored car go by. When she turned back, Alex was no longer frowning. He was looking at her, his eyes shiny and bright as he walked toward her.

"You should know I went to jail for a while," she said when he joined her with two cups of coffee.

"Do you always blurt out details about your past?" he asked with a laugh.

"I've found it's best to be honest. It's taken me a while to learn that."

"I'd heard." She should know that news in a small town moved faster than mouth.

"And you still asked me out?"

Alex grinned shyly. "I like you."

"You don't *know* me. Aren't you curious why I went to jail?"

"Tell me if you want. But you don't have to if it makes you uncomfortable."

Uncomfortable? It embarrassed her, made her feel stupid, and made her worry that no nice man would ever be interested in her.

"I had this boyfriend."

He chuckled. "I already don't like it."

"Yeah. I was on my way to work that morning. I was waitressing at this dive of a diner. Anyway, Harrison, that was his name, asked me to give him a ride."

She went on to explain that he'd wanted her to stop in front of a jewelry store. She'd actually thought the jerk was going in to get her a ring to ask her to marry him.

That was until he came running out and she heard the wail of an alarm go off and he told her to drive!

She'd been young and foolish. Part of Harrison's appeal had been that he was dangerous. She never knew what he was going to do next, so it wasn't a big surprise that he'd also been moody and abusive one minute and sweet the next. She never knew which Harrison would come through the door.

"Where is he now?"

"Prison. He's not supposed to get out for a few more years."

"Is he Jodie's father?" Alex asked.

She hadn't remembered telling him her daughter's name. "No. That's another story."

A weighty silence fell between them. "You're having second thoughts, aren't you?" she asked.

He looked up in surprise. "No, I was just thinking how strong you are. To have lived through all of that, and look at you now."

His words knocked her off balance. "I don't feel like I've accomplished anything yet."

"You're wrong. I've seen you with your daughter. You're a great mom, and you have a good job."

She eyed him warily. "I'm sorry, but when anyone is nice to me, I start looking for their motives."

He laughed. "I only have one agenda. I want to get to know you. That's it."

Still she eyed him skeptically. She considered telling him about the break-in at her house but hesitated. She didn't want him to think she was the kind of girl who knew the kind of men who would break into her house—even though she was.

Alex had to take a call, so Emily finished her coffee and went back to work. The foundation office was like a morgue with everyone waiting to see if they even had a job when Bo returned.

Her mind miles away, Emily didn't notice the old brown car parked down the block or the man sitting behind the wheel.

Russell hated that he woke up thinking about Buckmaster Hamilton. The man was adored by thousands, soon maybe millions. So wasn't it possible that Russell was wrong about the senator? His dislike for the man was based on nothing but speculation, admittedly. He'd never even given the man a thought—until the senator's first wife suddenly appeared in front of his pickup.

It all came down to why Sarah had tried to kill herself. It had to have been because Buckmaster had done something. True, public opinion had sympathized with the senator. The consensus was that Sarah probably had postpartum depression, but her disappearing from her children's lives had most people suspecting an underlying mental problem.

One reporter in particular, Chuck Barrow, from the *Herald*, had tagged her a bad mother for leaving behind her six daughters all these years. He questioned how long postpartum depression—if that was what it was—could be blamed.

The rest of the media had followed suit, making her sound deranged, especially given that she said she couldn't recall the past twenty-two years.

But they didn't know her, Russell argued with himself.

He had always considered himself a fair man. What did he really know about Sarah and Buckmaster's marriage? Nothing. When it came to marriage, only the two people in the marriage knew what really went on behind closed doors, he reminded himself.

He remembered when he was in high school and his fiftysomething teacher, Margaret Winslow, disappeared. Everyone talked about how her husband, Ed, had doted on her and wondered how he would be able to make it without her if, God forbid, something terrible had happened to her.

No one suspected foul play—especially from Ed. Nor could anyone believe she might have run away or committed suicide.

They found Margaret's car two hundred miles away, abandoned on a lonely stretch of gravel road in the middle of nowhere. They found her body twenty yards from it, the gun she'd used to blow her brains out lying next to her body. The suicide note was tucked in her underwear.

It read, "Don't blame Ed. I'm the one at fault. He deserved a better wife."

It wasn't until the autopsy that the truth came out. Margaret was covered with bruises, some new, some old. She'd suffered numerous broken bones, many that had healed on their own. Ed had been beating her for years, leaving more scars than the ones hidden under her clothing. The woman must have been in horrible pain most of her married life before she couldn't take anymore and killed herself.

Russell thought of his own marriage. He would have said that after more than forty years, he knew Judy. But how well had he really known her? Did she have secrets she never told him? Desires she never expressed? Regrets and disappointments she'd kept bottled up?

He wondered what secrets were locked in Sarah Hamilton's brain. Whatever they were, they had something to do with Buckmaster Hamilton. Russell would stake his life on that. What had the man done to drive his wife to attempted suicide and into exile for the past twenty-two years?

If that's what had happened to her. Russell still believed that the person who had secreted her away after her failed suicide attempt was her not-so-loving husband, never dreaming she would ever escape.

But she hadn't just escaped. Someone had helped her return, he reminded himself. He had trouble believing she'd parachuted back into Beartooth. But apparently she had. So whoever had assisted her . . .

Who had those kind of resources? Senator Buckmaster Hamilton.

Russell shook his head. Or maybe someone just as powerful who didn't want the senator to win the presidential race?

His head ached from trying to figure out what had happened all those years ago. If he was right, though, Buckmaster had a lot to fear when Sarah finally remembered. He wondered what the senator was thinking now. Did he believe Sarah didn't remember? Or did he live in fear that she would remember and destroy his political career?

What had driven a mother of six daughters to suicide? Unfortunately, the only way they would ever know was if Sarah remembered.

"Can you talk about what you're remembering?" he'd asked Sarah recently.

She'd looked up. He'd seen the denial in her expression before she even opened her mouth. "I'm not . . ." She'd swallowed, and her gaze had locked with his. "They don't make any sense. They're just dark . . . images." She'd shuddered. "Nightmares without any basis in reality."

"I know they scare you, but don't push the memories away, if you can help it. You *need* to remember."

Her smile had been full of sadness. "Do I?"

"Yes. Sarah, you have to remember before your . . ." He had been going to say husband, but Senator Buckmaster Hamilton was sharing another woman's bed, had another wife, the one he'd replaced her with. "Before Buckmaster wins the Republican presidential nomination. If I'm right about him, you can't let him become president."

He was more convinced than ever that Buckmaster Hamilton had been behind Sarah's disappearance and memory loss. But he still didn't have proof.

Buckmaster was pushing for Sarah to move onto the Hamilton Ranch. All the polls had the man leading in the race for the Republican nomination and taking the presidency by a landslide.

What if there was only one person who could keep that from happening? He reminded himself that Sarah was still in love with the man. But once she remembered . . .

Russell could feel the clock ticking.

"What's wrong?" Nettie asked when her husband came through the door. She could tell by the slump of his shoulders that it wasn't just the hour that had him dragging.

The sheriff shook his head as he lowered himself into a chair. "I'm just tired."

"Frank," she said as she sat down across from him and took both of his big hands in hers. "It's more than being tired. What are you so worried about? Tiffany?" When he was down, the cause was often thoughts of his deranged daughter who had tried to kill him. Fortunately she was safely locked up where she couldn't hurt anyone else.

"No," he said with a sigh. "She's someone else's problem now. I'm riding up in the Crazies in the morning with search and rescue to look for Bo Hamilton and Jace Calder. Apparently he went looking for her and neither has been heard from since." He met her gaze. "There's a chance an escaped killer is up in those same mountains."

"You think they crossed paths?"

"I certainly hope not. It's big country. But it's odd that neither Bo or Jace has returned when Jace went up there with every intention of bringing her back."

Nettie shook her head as she studied the man she'd loved since she was a teen. "But that isn't what's really worrying you."

He opened his mouth as if to deny it, then seemed to stop himself. "It's one of my other cases. Hell, it's not really a case just my own investigation, and I can't get it out of my mind. Now I'm starting to question myself."

"What do your instincts tell you?"

"That no matter what the state crime boys or the FBI says, I should keep investigating."

She let go of his hands to sit back and study him. Her first thought was, *Frank, what have you gotten involved in?* But while she might worry about having a sheriff for a husband, she'd known when she married him that he was a lawman through and through. "If your instincts tell you to keep investigating, then you should. It must be something big for you to be this worried."

His smile was sad. "You know I can't tell you."

"Even if it isn't an official investigation?" Before he could answer, she laughed and said, "You don't have to tell me. I already know. It's Sarah Hamilton, isn't it?"

"Lynette—"

"I'm no fool, Frank. Don't you think I question why she came back right after the senator announced his candidacy for president?"

"It could be just a coincidence."

"Posh! A woman who claims she doesn't remember the past twenty-two years?" Nettie shook her head. "You need to watch her like a hawk. She's hiding something, mark my words, and it's more than some weird tattoo on her skinny ass."

He laughed. "Do you have any idea how much I love you?"

"If you're just trying to change the subject—"

"I'm not," he said and leaned back, looking more relaxed than he had in months. "I trust your instincts if not my own lately. You've been right about so many things."

But not everything. She'd married the wrong man all those years ago. She ached to turn back the clock to relive all those wasted years that she could have been with Frank. She was with him now, though, she reminded herself, and she was worried about him.

"Why do I feel as if it is more than worrying about what Sarah Hamilton is hiding?" she asked.

He shook his head, then seemed to change his mind as if there was something he needed to get off his chest. "I've always gone by the book. But a few months ago, I took evidence without a warrant to get a suspect's DNA. That's not like me. I keep thinking it's time for me to retire and let Dillon and Jamison take over."

She shook her head. "If you stepped down tomorrow, would you quit worrying about Sarah Hamilton? That is who we're talking about, right?"

He laughed, a sound that warmed her heart. "If only that's all it would take."

"Then stop talking nonsense. I've never understood our legal system anyway. Everyone but the crooks and killers has to follow the rules. Don't you see something wrong with that?"

He smiled. "The problem is that I swore to uphold the law. If I can't do that anymore . . ."

Nettie hated to hear him talking like this. She knew her husband. This kind of talk scared her. "What is it you're so afraid is going to happen?"

Again he met her gaze. She felt a chill as he

said, "I don't believe that Buckmaster Hamilton will ever see the Oval Office."

"Sarah coming back doesn't seem to have affected his popularity. If anything, people admire the way he's handled it, and others feel sorry for him. But you aren't talking about him losing the election."

Frank shook his head. "Unless something drastic happens, he'll win the election. It's Sarah. I know it sounds crazy, but if I'm right, she's not working alone. I think her . . . mission is to stop him, one way or the other."

For a moment, Nettie was speechless. "Her *mission?* You make her sound like she's a paid assassin."

He said nothing.

"Frank, why would she want to kill him?"

"I have no idea."

Chapter
EIGHTEEN

The sun was rising in the east, a bright line of
pale color, when Jace finally found a place he
could stop. Exhausted, Bo had fallen asleep
immedi-ately. He'd had to loop a rope around
the two of them to keep her from falling off the
horse. But he knew she also needed food and
medical attention. He had no idea what Ray
Spencer had done to her.

Unfortunately, they'd had to keep moving. He
didn't know how badly Spencer was hurt. He
couldn't take the chance that the criminal might
catch up to them.

As Jace reined in, Bo stirred and then
straightened with a start. She instantly began to
fight the rope around them, perhaps still thinking
she was Spencer's prisoner.

"You're okay," Jace said as he quickly untied
them and swung out of the saddle. As he helped
her down, she looked around as if half expecting
to see Spencer. "You're safe."

He tried his cell phone again, noticing that his
battery was low. As before, he couldn't pick up
any coverage and pocketed it again.

When he looked at Bo, he saw that she was still

scared. "You didn't happen to bring your phone, did you?"

She shook her head and glanced toward the dark pines. "You think he's dead?" she asked, hugging herself. The morning this high in the mountains was cold. He could see her breath as she spoke.

"No. I don't think he was wounded that badly."

"But he's probably taken off. He'll know we'll tell the sheriff where he is as soon as we get back to the ranch."

Jace hesitated. "No, he'll come after us."

She cut her eyes to him as if she thought he must not have realized she was looking for reassurance.

He would have loved to reassure her, but he would have been lying. All his instincts told him that Raymond Spencer, who should have been trying to avoid getting caught, would be hot on their trail.

"Why would he do that?" she demanded.

Jace debated how much to share with her. Their chances of getting out of these mountains alive weren't good. He didn't want to scare her any more than she'd already been, but he also needed to be honest with her. The only chance they had was if they both knew the score.

"You have a gun," she was saying. "He has to understand there might be others out looking for me. Why would he—"

"Before I shot him, he was going after you.

I believe he'll come after us to finish the job."

She stared at him as if she hadn't heard him correctly. "Because of *me?*"

"I need to know how badly you're hurt." He paused. "Did he—"

"No! He didn't rape me."

"But he did hurt you."

"If you hadn't come along when you did, he would have forced himself on me. He talked about making me *his*. He wanted me to . . . like him. I swore I would survive no matter what happened, but fortunately it never came to that. If faced with him again . . . I'd use this gun on myself before I would let that happen now," she said, touching the weight pulling down one side of her jacket.

"Let's hope if it comes to that, you'll kill him instead," Jace said. "There's a creek just over the rise. Clean your scrapes as best you can. I'll bandage them when I get back."

She looked down at her wrists then. The skin was raw and red, and she was clearly in pain. Her gaze went to her clothes. She was beyond filthy, her shirt torn in places. From her expression, he saw that it was the first time she'd noticed. She'd probably been too busy trying to stay alive.

"Wait," she said as if just realizing what he'd said. "Where are you going?" He could hear that edge of panic in her voice. He felt the full weight of what she'd been through.

"I have some jerky in my pack," he said. "The sun is almost up. I'm going to double back a ways to see if I can spot him so I know how far behind he is. Then we have to get moving again. There's a storm coming."

"What makes you so sure he's behind us? If you're right and he's chasing us, he has my horse, and there is only one of him," she said as she glanced toward the creek. Darkness still hunkered in the pines. The growing light on the horizon made the trees cast long shadows that seemed to move like dark ghosts in the breeze. "What if he got ahead of us?" she asked in a small voice.

He shook his head. "I wounded him. He would have to take care of that before he could come after us. I'm betting he's behind us, but probably not far. As you said, he has a horse, and he's the only one on it."

Jace saw that she wasn't convinced. "If I'm wrong and he's waiting for you at the creek, then use the gun," he said as he swung up on his horse again.

"If you're trying to scare me . . ."

"I won't be long. Be ready. We leave as soon as I get you bandaged when I get back. If you need me . . ." He met her gaze.

She stiffened her spine and placed her hand into her pocket, where she'd stuffed the pistol. "Just hurry."

He nodded. "I will."

• • •

Bo watched as Jace disappeared through the trees, willing him to come back quickly. All her nerves on end, she looked through the dim light toward the creek. The moon still hung on the horizon, round and white. Behind her, the sun was starting to rise.

She could see well enough that if Ray approached, she would have a little time before he was on her. The thought of him sent a shudder through her as she moved toward the creek. Her movements were jerky, her body so tense the she almost jumped out of her skin when a hawk let out a cry high above the lofty pines. Closer a squirrel chattered down at her.

Everything seemed as it should have high in the mountains. Jace had mentioned a storm was coming in, but there was no sign of it this morning other than the cold. At the creek, she laid the gun on a rock within reach and pulled off her boots and socks, all the while watching the trees. Every shadow looked like Ray Spencer to her. Every sigh of the breeze in the pine boughs sounded like his worn boots coming toward her. Rolling up the legs of her jeans, she stuck the gun into her waistband and stepped into the water.

The snow-fed creek took her breath away. Her feet ached from the cold water. As she rolled up the sleeves of her ragged shirt, she looked around, half expecting to see Ray's grinning face on the opposite shore. The sun fingered its way through the pines to throw a golden sheen on the creek's surface. While it did little to warm the day yet, she turned her face up to it and tried to breathe. Where was Jace? He'd said he'd hurry.

Scooping up a handful of water, she splashed her face, gasping at the cold. The water made her ache even though her feet felt as if they'd gone numb. At the sound of a horse, she started and drew the handgun from her waistband to point it toward the pines.

"It's me," Jace called out a moment before he rode into view. He reined in and leaned on his saddle horn as he gazed at her. "Take off the rest of your clothing and wade in."

She quirked an eyebrow at him as she stuck the gun back into her waistband.

"Not to worry. You're safe with me."

He'd saved her, and she felt grateful. Not that she'd forgotten what their relationship had been before, despite the current circumstances.

"I have a change of clothing for you," Jace added as he swung down from the saddle. They'll be a bit too big, but they're clean. I thought you'd feel better with a change of clothes."

She was touched by that simple, kind thought. She watched him dig through the pack he'd brought and bring out a long-sleeved shirt and a pair of jeans.

He carried them over to where she stood. "I

have some rope we can use to keep the jeans on you." His gaze met hers. "What are you waiting for?" With a curse, he set the clothes down and turned his back. "It isn't like I haven't seen you naked. But try to hurry. We aren't out of the woods yet."

"Did you see him?" she asked as she quickly stripped and stepped back into the icy water to wash.

"No, but he's following us. All we can hope is that he's hurt badly enough that he won't catch us."

She dunked her head under the water and instantly got a brain freeze. Closing her eyes tight, she waited for it to pass before she dunked her hair again and then squeezed out the excess water before climbing out of the creek. She dried off as best she could before she reached for Jace's clothes.

He was standing over by his horse with his back still to her.

"I can't believe you came along when you did," Bo said, wondering again at why it was Jace Calder who'd rescued her.

"I didn't just *happen* along. I came looking for you."

She turned to stare at his broad back in surprise. "Why would you—"

"My sister told me what was going on and asked me to come find you."

Her surprise turned to astonishment. "And you agreed?"

"I've been tracking you for two days."

She couldn't believe this. She'd just assumed his finding her had been an accident. "And what were you going to do when you found me?"

"Take you back." His voice had an edge to it. "Emily's been disappointed enough in this life. I didn't want you adding to the list."

She pulled on his shirt. It was huge on her. So the only reason he was here was because his sister had asked him to come find her. And the only reason he'd agreed was because he thought she'd run off. Bo Hamilton, the woman who ran when things got too tough.

"You thought I stole the money?" She couldn't keep the astonishment out of her voice. Didn't he know her better than that? As she rolled up the sleeves to her wrists, she repeated, "You thought I stole the money?"

"Not for yourself."

She shot a look at his back. He thought she stole it for someone else? "A man." Bo almost laughed. Even if there had been a man in her life . . . Angrily she pulled on the jeans, rolled up the bottoms and tied the rope he'd given her. She didn't have to ask why he thought that. But it still made her mad. She wished there was a man in her life. That, too, added to the anger, since for the past five years, every man she met she'd compared to Jace. They'd all come up lacking.

As she pulled on her socks and boots, she said, "I'm the one who called in an independent auditor when I realized how much was missing."

"How much is missing?" he asked, his back still to her.

She swallowed. "Close to a hundred thousand."

He let out a low whistle.

"I haven't been on top of things lately," she admitted. "My mother came back from the dead. Surprise. And my sister Olivia . . ." She waved a hand through the air. "I blew it, all right. But if I hadn't been captured by some escaped criminal who wanted to make me his . . ." Her voice broke.

"I'm sorry," Jace said, turning around. He took a step toward her, but she held up her hand to stop him.

She hated how close she was to tears as she met his gaze. If he gave her any sympathy right now, she would fall apart again. She couldn't bear the disappointment in her that she'd heard in his voice.

"I just came up here to clear my mind like I always have," she said. "Like I did when you and I . . ." The words *broke up* hung between them. She'd been the one who broke up with him after he'd asked her to marry him. "I would have made the meeting with the auditor. I will make it right, whatever—"

"Hey," Jace said as he closed the distance between them. Taking both her shoulders in his hands, he waited for her to raise her gaze to him. "I'm sorry I brought it up. Sorry I thought . . . Right now, that's the least of our worries."

Jace eased Bo down onto a flat rock and went to get the first aid kit out of his saddlebag. He mentally kicked himself. Bo had been through so much. Worse, he couldn't bear to hurt her, and he had.

But right now he had to get them off these mountains. The day had grown too quiet. No breeze. The sun still hadn't topped the pines, leaving shadows at their base. He thought they had a good lead on Ray Spencer, but he couldn't be sure of that. All his instincts told him they had to get moving.

As he walked back to where he'd left Bo, he saw that she had pulled herself together. He couldn't imagine the horror she'd been through. Something like this could break any woman, even Bo Hamilton.

The cold creek water had put some color back into her face. That and the clean clothes and she looked a little stronger.

Pushing up the sleeves of his shirt he'd given her, he inspected the scraped, raw skin of her wrists and winced. Fury ran like a blaze through his veins at the man who'd done this to her, followed on its heels by gut-wrenching sympathy for Bo. He cut his gaze to her as he opened the tube of ointment. He'd always known that she was a remarkable woman, but this . . . He gently applied the salve to her scrapes. She flinched once but seemed to steel herself, even though he knew it had to hurt like hell.

"Can you lift up your hair?" He put ointment on her scraped neck and elbows and then closed the first aid kit.

"Thank you," she said and met his eyes.

He looked into her luminous, wide green eyes and felt that old heartache. This was the woman he'd asked to marry him, the woman he'd planned to spend the rest of his life with. It was all he could do not to take her in his arms, hold her and tell her everything was going to be all right.

Except that if they didn't get moving, it wasn't going to be all right. This ordeal she'd been through wasn't over by a long shot. Ray Spencer was still alive, and he was tracking them as surely as Jace's next breath. It was one reason he'd wanted her out of those bloody, torn clothes. She'd appeared and acted beaten down. She was going to have to be strong to get out of these mountains.

And yet he couldn't look at her without feeling sick for what she'd gone through—and wanting to kill the man who'd put her through it.

"You can ride. I'll walk. I'm worried the horse will go lame if we both continue to ride," he said as he retrieved her soiled clothing from beside the creek and stuffed it into his pack. Although he never wanted to see them again—and he doubted she did, either—he didn't want to leave them for Raymond Spencer.

Ray knew he was in trouble. He didn't think the wound was bad, but what did he know? He'd stopped the bleeding after managing to get to the horse, untie it and pull himself up into the saddle. He'd been bleeding bad. All his instincts had told him to find a place to hole up, to see how badly he was wounded, to figure out what to do.

He'd expected the man to come after him. His only hope had been to get away as quickly as possible and find a place where he could set up an ambush when the man came looking for him.

What worried him was that he couldn't be sure how many would be coming for him. He'd seen the one man, had heard the one shooter. But only a fool would have come up into the mountains looking for the woman alone. Then again, the man wouldn't have known that little Bo-Peep had gotten herself captured, would he?

Ray knew he was in no shape to fight off even one man, though. He'd spent the night hidden in some pines on a rise, waiting for an end to his pain. He'd fought to stay awake, but he'd passed out. When the sun had come up, he hadn't been able to understand why he was still alive. If he hadn't bled to death, then he'd thought for sure that the man would have found him and killed him.

With the new day, he felt stronger. He'd considered his options. Get out of the mountains as quickly as possible and seek medical help and go straight to jail. Or go after his woman.

He'd almost laughed. There was no contest. He was going after her. He had nothing to lose. This gunshot would probably get infected and kill him anyway. After he'd managed to pull himself up into the saddle, he headed south, figuring that was the direction the man would have taken the woman since he hadn't come after him. He figured the man would have tried to put some distance between them by riding through the night.

But with only one horse, they couldn't have gotten far. Ray would catch them before they got out of the mountains.

The sound of his father's horn pierced the morning air. He flinched. It was much closer than he'd expected. His father blew his horn again, waiting for an answering one from him.

Ray knew his old man would want to kill him and put him out of his misery. But they were blood. His father wouldn't let the bastard who'd shot him get away with this. He reached into his saddlebag, pulled out the horn and blew it. The throaty low sound echoed in the trees around him.

The old man would find him.

Chapter
NINETEEN

"What the hell is this?" Buckmaster demanded, holding up a sheet of paper. He'd gotten to the personal mail before Angelina, and from the expression on her face she'd hoped that wouldn't happen.

He watched her brace herself, straightening to her full height of five-nine, her shoulders locking back and her beautiful face setting like granite. She was up for a fight, and he was ready to give her one.

"A retainer fee? You hired a private detective?" All he could think was that she had some bastard spying on him.

"You weren't going to get the goods on Sarah, so I had to do it," she said, blue eyes sparking with defiance.

"Sarah?" It took him a moment, because this wasn't what he'd expected. "You're having someone trail Sarah?" So basically, that would mean he'd been right in the first place. Every time he met Sarah, she would know about it.

She waved a hand through the air as she shook her head. "He's finding out if any of what she told you about her life was true."

He found himself staring at Angelina more and more since Sarah had returned from the dead. She thought he didn't know Sarah? He wanted to laugh. What the sheriff had told him about his first wife had proven that. Hell, he'd thought he knew the woman standing in front of him, but boy had he been wrong about that.

So maybe he didn't know who Sarah was— just as Angelina said. What difference did it make at this point? The sheriff was worried that Sarah would do something, though he had no idea what. Angelina was convinced Sarah had ulterior motives, as well. But so far Sarah had done . . . nothing.

The woman couldn't even remember most of her life. She didn't seem like much of a threat to him. Unfortunately, Angelina was clearly not letting it go.

"I understand you're suspicious, but hiring a private detective? You're the one who's so paranoid about scandal. Did you give any thought to what the press would make of this if it got out?"

She glared at him, all her defenses up. "Someone needs to protect you from yourself."

He laughed at that, one of his big, hearty laughs. It felt good. He hadn't realized how long it had been. "Angelina, you are the most amazing woman."

Her eyes narrowed, as she tried to decide if he was being sarcastic.

"I mean it. You never cease to amaze me. You get your teeth into something, and you're like a rat terrier. No way you're letting go. I love that about you."

All the defiance and belligerence that had made both her expression and her stone face soften in that instant seemed to drain from her face. She looked so vulnerable that he reached out and pulled her to him.

Unlike Sarah, she'd never felt small and fragile in his arms—until that moment.

He pressed his lips against her hair and breathed in her scent. "I'm sure glad you're on my side." He thought about telling her that the PI had been a waste of money. That Sarah Johnson Hamilton wasn't a threat. That it wouldn't be long before they would be living in the White House.

Instead, he simply held her and tried not to worry about what this very expensive private investigator might find.

The sheriff along with Senator Buckmaster Hamilton, a half dozen of his men and a small group of search and rescue personnel rode up into the Crazy Mountains not long after sunrise.

Buckmaster said he'd told Jace Calder that if he didn't hear from him in twenty-four hours, he would be sending in the cavalry. But this was ridiculous.

"Senator, let the trained personnel—"

Buckmaster cut him off. "I'm going, and so are my men. We need as many as we can to find her."

Frank made another attempt, knowing he was talking to the wind. "This many people can destroy leads up there if—"

The senator gave a shake of his head as he swung up into his saddle. "No more standing around talking. I'm finding my daughter, and that's all there is to it."

Frank gave up, mounted his horse and rode after the senator. He had chosen to accompany the senator and his men rather than ride in one of two helicopters that would be searching for Bo and Jace later. If they didn't find her, several National Guard helicopters would be called in the next day.

The early morning was bathed in mist. Dew glistened on the grass and pine boughs as the sun began its arc skyward. A chill still hung in the air that even the summer sun couldn't chase away as they headed up the well-worn trail from Hamilton Ranch.

The leader of the search and rescue team would be going up in the helicopter with several of their dogs. Buckmaster had provided some of Bo's clothing to help in the search. Frank had more faith that they would find the missing woman— if the forecasted storm didn't hit first. They would be going past a spot where the county search and rescue plane had spotted Jace Calder.

The storm right now was a concern even more than the unforgiving Crazies that rose above them. The mountains were dense with towering pines, jagged sheer cliffs and fast-moving streams. Even in early summer, snow still clung to the north side of some of the peaks. The terrain looked as forbidding as it was. There were too many miles of canyons and gullies up here. So much wild country. It wouldn't be the first time someone had gotten lost in it. Or the last.

He didn't want to think about what the chances were that they would find Bo Hamilton. He just hoped Jace Calder wasn't lost, as well. As for Ray Spencer . . . well, his hope was that the man really was in Reno right now playing penny slots somewhere off the Strip.

Frank waited for his radio to squawk with news as he heard two helicopters fly over on their way along the ridge to the last spot Jace Calder had been seen while following Bo.

He kept telling himself that Jace was smart and experienced. But he was tracking Bo. If she got off the trail . . . Even seasoned outfitters like John Cole got turned around occasionally. After a while, all the pine-covered mountainsides looked alike. Throw in a storm . . .

Frank remembered getting lost up there when he was seventeen. He'd been elk hunting and had left camp. When it had started to snow so quickly, he hadn't been prepared. Before long he couldn't see his hand in front of his face. He realized he was walking in circles when he crossed his own tracks. If John Cole hadn't found him . . .

As he looked toward the mountains, the sheriff couldn't shake the feeling that something bad had happened. The options up in these mountains were limitless—even without a man like Raymond Spencer possibly in the mix.

Ray felt a wave of relief at the sight of his father, even knowing that the shit was about to hit the fan.

"What have ya done?" RayJay Spencer asked in a slow drawl as he took in his son's condition.

"The bastard shot me," Ray said. He'd ridden in the direction of the sound of his father's horn— southwest. The ride had done nothing for his wound. It was bleeding again, leaving him feeling weak. Like the blood, his anger had run out, as well. Now he was shaking and scared.

"How bad is it?" the old man asked impatiently as he swung down out of his saddle.

"Bad." He practically fell off his horse as he got down holding his side. "Hurts like blazes."

"Let me see it." His father shoved his hand away from the wound. "Who done this to ya?"

Ray shook his head. The old man was mad enough that he'd gone and gotten himself shot. He hated to think what RayJay would do once he heard about the woman.

"Over here," his father ordered, motioning to a downed log. "Sit." Pulling up his shirt, RayJay probed the wound, making him howl in pain. "Stop bein' a crybaby. Let me see yer back. The bullet went straight through. Don't look like it hit nothin'."

He watched the older man go to his saddlebag and come back with a quart of whiskey. Picking up a stick, RayJay shoved it at him. "Here, bite on this." He stuck the stick between his teeth an instant before he felt the booze hit the wound.

He must have passed out. The next thing he knew, he was lying on the ground, blinking up at the sun bright above the trees.

" 'Bout time," his old man said. He looked down to see that his side was bandaged. "Take these." He handed him two pills, which he swallowed without water. "That should keep ya alive. Least for now."

He nodded. "Thanks."

"So where's this bastard that shot ya?"

Ray struggled to get up, but his old man pushed him back down.

"What ain't you tellin' me?" RayJay asked.

He spilled the story in between his old man cussing and threatening to kill him.

"Ya have any idea what ya've done?" his father demanded with a shake of his head.

"I want her."

RayJay kicked him hard in the thigh and

mimicked, " *'I want her.'* It's cuz a her ya got shot. Cuz a her they'll be crawlin' these mountains lookin' for all a us."

"What we goin' to do, Daddy?"

His father turned and started for his horse. He thought for a moment that his old man would leave him right where he lay to die alone.

"I don't know what yer goin' to do," RayJay said as he turned back to him, a gun in his hand. "But I know what I'm doin'. The only thing I can under the circumstances."

"Jace," Bo called. He'd been walking ahead of her and the horse, watching the country in front of them, calculating how long it would take them to get out of these mountains. Worse, whether they could stay ahead of the man he was convinced would be coming after them.

"Jace." He heard the squeak of leather as she reined in and swung down out of the saddle before he turned.

"What is it?" he asked as she stooped to look at his horse's right leg. He swore under his breath. He could see at a distance that his horse was favoring that leg. He'd feared an injury after they had both ridden the horse last night.

Bo said nothing as she moved out of the way to let him inspect the horse. "We're going to have to walk him," he said, rising again. Just when he thought things couldn't get worse.

She nodded, clearly trying to look stronger than she actually was.

At the sound of a rifle shot in the distance, they both started.

"I thought you said he didn't have a firearm other than the ones in his pack that he had to leave behind?" he demanded in a hushed voice.

"He didn't," she said, her voice not above a whisper. "That couldn't have been him." She stood, her head cocked as if listening hard. Three shots could be a signal that someone was looking for them.

Jace could see that she was praying for two more. So was he, but the shots didn't come. He watched her eyes widen in alarm. The desperation in her face was so pronounced that he realized they were in more trouble than he'd first thought.

"You know who fired that shot?" he asked.

She nodded, looking sick. "It's his father."

"Raymond Spencer's?"

"He told me his father would be joining us. He heard what sounded like a horn of some kind and said it was his father on his way."

Jace swore under his breath. That must have been the sound he'd heard resembling an elk bugle. They already had one killer tracking them. All they needed was his possibly even more dangerous father. Hadn't he seen on the news that Spencer's father was an ex-military sniper turned antigovernment survivalist? And that the father had brought Spencer up into these mountains to live for long periods?

"And you didn't think to mention this?"

"He made it sound as if his father would be meeting up with us farther back in the mountains. Could you tell how far away that shot was?"

He shook his head. "It's impossible in the mountains to tell where it came from or at what distance." It wasn't nearly far enough away, that much he knew.

She met his gaze, her green eyes wide with fear. "What do you think he shot?"

"Whatever it was, he apparently hit it without having to fire again," Jace said, feeling his stomach roil. He just hoped to hell Buckmaster hadn't sent anyone else up here looking for Bo.

Bo stood trembling and clearly close to tears. "It was his father who always talked about the two of them living back in here, building a cabin, living off the land. Ray . . ." Her voice broke. "He had this insane idea that, with me as his wife, the three of us would live up here. He told me he would protect me from his father even if he had to kill him."

And she thought a man like that wasn't going to follow her? "So we have to assume there's two of them coming after us," he said, wondering how things could get worse. "And that neither of them is on foot." He figured the father would have brought up horses and supplies if the plan had been to live back in the mountains for a long time. "They'll have fresh horses and probably medical supplies. If Ray isn't too badly wounded . . ."

"What are we going to do?"

The way Jace saw it, they had two options, neither of them ideal. They could continue to make a run for it on foot or they could hole up and fight. Given that the older man was bringing up provisions for the two to live indefinitely, he had to assume firepower was part of the supplies. He'd run across a few survivalists. They typically liked guns. Big guns.

"We have no choice. We have to try to outrun them."

"On *foot?*"

He gave her a look. "Unless you have another way of getting out of these mountains."

"I'm sorry I got you into this. But if being angry at me makes it easier for you, please don't let me stop you." Fear had her fired up, ready for a fight.

"Let's not make this personal," Jace said.

"Not make it personal?" she cried. At least her anger had held off her tears. He could be thankful for that, he told himself. He needed her to hold it together so he could get her off this mountain.

"Why did you really come after me?" she demanded. "To rub my face in it? You actually thought I had absconded with the money and had met some . . . man up here, didn't you?"

He couldn't deny it. "Right now all I care about is getting you out of these mountains alive so—"

"So I can go to prison."

He met her gaze. "Bo—"

She shook her head and, turning on her heel, started down the trail as if she wasn't tired, her feet didn't hurt and she hadn't been running on fear for days now.

Jace smiled to himself at the stiff set of her spine, the angry tilt of her head, the agitated swinging of her arms as he followed, leading the horse. It wasn't as though she was ever going to talk to him after this anyway.

Chapter
TWENTY

The storm moved in fast. Dark clouds obliterated the sun, wind whipped the tall pines and the temperature dropped. Frank knew the rain and probably snow weren't far behind.

Once the storm hit, it would be foolhardy to continue. He anticipated the senator putting up a fight. Not that he could blame him. If it was his daughter up here lost in the mountains . . . He thought of Tiffany and quickly pushed the image away.

Tiffany had only pretended to be his daughter as part of a sick plot by his ex-wife to hurt him. Too bad Pam was dead. She would have been glad to know that it had worked. Even when his ex had "programmed" her daughter to not only hate him, but also to come to Beartooth and try to kill him, he'd still wanted to help the girl. It wasn't until he learned all of it had been a lie that he'd felt a moment of intense pain, then a sense of freedom. Neither Tiffany nor her dead mother could hurt him anymore. That was, as long as Tiffany was in the mental institution. If she ever got out—

The first drops of rain splattered in the dust next

to him. He'd already put on his slicker and was debating how much farther they dared go given that they would have a long ride back to the ranch yet to face before this day was over.

He'd heard on his two-way radio that the two helicopters that had been scheduled to fly the area farther to the north had both been grounded because of the fierce winds coming off the peaks. Now, with the storm . . .

Another trail joined the one they were on. Frank noticed horseshoe prints in the dust as the rain began to fall harder. Past the tracks, he saw the body. It lay in a small gully not far off the adjoining trail from the Shields River side of the Crazies.

He reined in, recognizing the red-and-black-plaid wool coat. Outfitter John Cole. John had said he would be riding back in from the Shields River side of the mountains.

"Stay here," Frank ordered the others as he climbed down and moved through the pines to the body. John had been shot once in the head with what appeared to be a high-powered rifle.

Frank had told him to be careful since they both knew that Raymond Spencer could be up here in these mountains. Whoever had shot him must have seen him working his way up the trail, waited and either had taken a lucky shot— or had been a crack-shot sniper in another life. He was reminded that Raymond Jay Spencer Sr., or RayJay as he was known, had served as a sniper in the armed forces. Did that mean he was up here, as well?

The rain began to fall harder. As Frank climbed back up the hillside to his horse, he tried to radio in to his office, but the storm made the call break up.

"Who is it?" the senator asked. "It isn't—"

"No. It's John Cole. He's an outfitter with a camp up here." He didn't mention that John's low camp had been broken into or that John had suspected it might be the younger Raymond Spencer who'd been on the run for three weeks now.

"He's dead?" one of the ranch hands asked.

Frank nodded. "We need to turn back." The senator started to argue. "John was shot. Whoever killed him is probably still up in these mountains. That person could be trying to get a bead on one of us right now."

The ranch hands looked around, suddenly nervous.

"My daughter is up here," Buckmaster said with a curse. "I can't turn back now."

"We have no idea where Bo is except that from what the pilot told us, Jace Calder had been tracking her and she was at least another day's ride back into these mountains. We need to wait and get the choppers in the air. She will hole up somewhere out of the storm, so even if we were close to where she is, we wouldn't be able to find her in this storm."

"You're assuming she is *able* to hole up," the senator said, his voice breaking.

"There is nothing we can do. We have to go back." Frank tried his radio again and got through. "Let the sheriff know over in Park County. John Cole has been murdered, the suspect or suspects still at large. They'll find his body shortly after the Shields River trail connects with the Sweet Grass Creek Trail up from the Hamilton Ranch. We're headed back."

Bo stopped, her heart leaping to her throat. "Do you hear that?"

Jace, suddenly on alert, stopped, as well. "What did you hear?" he whispered, moving up beside her.

She strained to pick up the sound again, but all she could hear was the wind in the tops of the pine boughs. Was that all it had been? She'd been so sure. "I thought I heard a helicopter." She shook her head. It had been her imagination. Just like earlier when she would have sworn she heard one in the distance.

"Come on," he said and motioned for her to get moving again.

She had seen the dark clouds building over the tops of the peaks and felt the temperature dropping only moments before the rain began to fall. Wind whipped the huge drops, stinging her face. She could hardly see where she was going.

Jace had given her his yellow slicker to wear, insisting also that she lead the way. She knew he expected Ray and his father to catch up to them now. It was only a matter of time. She labored through the drowning rain in the too-large coat. Each step took all her strength. She'd never walked so far in her life. Once she got back to the ranch . . .

What if she never saw the ranch or her family again? The thought broke her heart. What if Ray and his father caught up with them? She shuddered, thinking of what they would do to her—not to mention Jace. Jace, the man who had come all the way up here after her.

Not to save her, she reminded herself. Yet he *had* saved her, at least temporarily. Now if Ray and his father caught up to them, they would kill Jace, and it would be her fault. If she hadn't come up here, Jace would be safe on his ranch back down in the valley. She couldn't bear the thought of getting him killed.

She stumbled on an exposed root in the middle of the trail, then slipped. Jace grabbed her before she fell into the mud. She looked at him, surprised. "I thought you would enjoy seeing me floundering in the mud."

"You're wrong. I'm trying to keep anything else from happening to you."

Icy-cold rain poured over her as she stood looking into his handsome face. She'd been in love with this man most of her life, she realized. But the timing had always been wrong. "I really wanted to go to senior prom with you."

He shook his head, rain running off the brim of his hat. "You really want to bring up senior prom *now?*"

"Why not?"

"Because that was fourteen years ago, and we're standing in pouring rain on a mountaintop with two killers after us."

She looked into his blue eyes and felt a sharp pang of hurt. "It isn't just senior prom. It's . . ." She waved a hand through the air. "It's . . ." Tears welled in her eyes.

"Bo, we have to get moving," he said quietly.

She shook her head. "I can't go on." Everything she'd been through suddenly fell on her, crushing her spirit. She dropped to the ground, too discouraged and exhausted to walk any farther, too sick at heart knowing that not only would she never get out of these mountains, but also neither would Jace. "Leave me and go for help."

"Do you really think I would do that?" he demanded as he knelt down beside her.

"Why not? I'm that pampered rich girl who knows nothing about real life. Isn't that what you once told me? A spoiled brat whose biggest problem is how to spend my father's money. So leave me. I deserve whatever happens to me, right? Oh, I forgot, you're determined to take me back and make me face up to my mistakes."

"Bo." The tenderness in his voice was her undoing.

Her chest ached as she began to sob. "I'm serious. Leave me here. Go for help. If you don't . . ." She let out a cry of pain. "I'm going to get you killed."

"Have faith in me," he said as he held out his hand. "Here, let me help you to your feet."

She shook her head, refusing to take his hand. "I can't walk another step."

"All right. We'll rest for a while, but not here. Come on," he said, taking her arm and pulling her up. "You can make it as far as those cliffs."

He led her up into the rocks where one cantilevered out over the mountainside offering them some shelter from the storm. Also, it would allow him to build a fire without any fear of the Spencers seeing the smoke.

After seeing to his horse, he built a small fire under the rock where the ground was dry and so was the kindling. Then he helped her peel off her wet clothing before wrapping her in the sleeping bag and tucking her next to the fire.

She let him, too tired to argue.

"Try to get some sleep."

"What about you?" she asked as she huddled in the bag and fought to stop trembling.

"I'll stand guard."

She looked out toward the darkness and the driving rain. "*You* should get some sleep."

He shook his head. "I'm fine."

"You don't think I can handle it?" she said, turning to look at him.

"No offense, but no." She started to argue, but he cut her off. "Unless you've killed someone lately and I don't know about it?" He nodded. "I didn't think so. If I let you stand guard and the Spencers showed up, you would hesitate, and they would kill you before you could—"

"I get the picture."

"Don't feel bad. Some people think they could kill another person if they had to. Most of them couldn't pull the trigger even against men like these."

She thought about Ray and shuddered. "You might be surprised. Remember? I was with him for two days."

He met her gaze. "I'm sorry."

"I am, too." She sunk deeper into the sleeping bag at the memory. "He had this idea that if he gave me a little time, I'd like him and want to stay with him. That's the only thing that saved me."

Jace looked away for a moment. "I can't imagine what you've been through." She heard the catch in his voice.

She could tell that he wanted to remain angry

with her for taking off, for getting into this mess, for forcing him to become involved, for hurting him five years ago.

"Get some sleep," he said. "We leave again in a few hours."

She looked out past the flames and saw only rain and mist.

"I'm worried about you," Bo said. "I know you have to be exhausted, too."

He reached over to take the pistol from her coat pocket and hand it to her. "In case I fall asleep."

"That's supposed to relieve my mind?"

"Don't worry. I'm not going to let anyone take you without a fight. If that relieves your mind . . ."

She watched him gather more dry twigs from under the rocks and toss them on the fire. The firelight played on his handsome face.

Her eyelids grew heavy. She felt as if she was finally starting to warm up. "Do you think they're both after us now?"

"Yes."

It was too much to hope that the single gunshot they'd heard was one of them killing the other one. "Maybe the father talked some sense into him and they aren't coming after us."

Jace didn't comment. Who was she kidding? Ray was relentless. He'd walk all day and night if that's what it took—even wounded. Add to that a father who not only encouraged his son to live in these mountains off the grid but also was bringing him horses and supplies.

She let her eyes close. "We never got to dance."

He let out a soft chuckle. "I probably would have stepped on your toes."

She smiled to herself as she forced open her eyes to look at him. He sat next to the fire staring out at the falling rain, his rifle cradled in his arms. He was smiling. She closed her eyes, unable to keep them open any longer. She was safe. Jace would keep her that way or die trying.

Chapter
TWENTY-ONE

The rain changed to snow so quickly that Jace didn't realize the temperature had dropped until he felt the first snowflake land on his cheek. He'd retrieved his horse, hating that he had to awaken Bo after a couple of hours, but they had to keep moving. He'd dried out her clothing as much as he could by the fire and then woke her.

They'd covered more ground. He hoped they were putting distance between them and the two men he believed were after them. But then the snow had begun to fall in huge lacy flakes that would soon obliterate everything.

"We need to find shelter," he said to Bo now as snowflakes began to whirl around them.

"But if we don't keep moving—"

"We won't be able to see anything in a few minutes. Come on." He headed for another band of rock towering over them. He could barely make out what appeared to be a cave-like hole in the cliff as snow began to fall harder.

The grass and rocks were already slick from the rain, making climbing difficult. Behind him, he heard Bo struggling to stay on her feet. He reached back and took her hand, pulling her up onto a rock shelf.

"We'll get back in here," he said. The cave was narrow, but as they slipped through the crevice, it opened into a larger space. The ground was dry back in there. He looked up to see a large rock wedged in between two larger rocks high above them. Only a small slice of white sky could be seen. "We should be able to stay dry in here and have a fire."

He opened the pack and pulled out the sleeping bag. It felt cold but not wet. He spread it out along with the rest of their dwindling supplies and tried not to think about what they would do when they ran out. He'd have to kill something and cook it. Which would have been fine if they hadn't had the Spencers after them.

Kneeling, he began to rake up leaves and twigs to build a fire. He wouldn't think the worst. Senator Buckmaster Hamilton would be moving heaven and earth by now to find his daughter. There were people looking for them. The storm was supposed to let up by morning. The searchers would be able to see their tracks in the snow. But so would Ray and his father. If they were both alive. If they were both still trailing them.

The crackling of the flames and the flicker of the golden light on the rock walls almost made it feel warm and cozy inside the small cave. He watched the smoke curl up and disappear through the crack overhead into a sky the same color as the smoke. No one could see it in the storm raging outside.

He turned to look at Bo. She stood hugging herself at the narrow entrance, her back to him. Past her, he could see that a blizzard had blown into the mountains. Late June in Montana, he thought with a sigh.

"Are we ever getting out of these mountains?" she asked without turning to look at him.

He moved up behind her and put his arms around her. She leaned back against him. Her hair glistened with melting snow. She felt small in his arms.

"We're going to get out of here," he whispered as he slowly turned her to face him. "Do you trust me?"

She raised her head to meet his eyes and held his gaze for a long moment. "With my life."

He smiled at that.

"I'm so sor—" Her voice broke.

Jace kissed her as her green eyes swam with tears. She softened against him, melting into his arms, into his kiss. Her arms encircled his neck as he picked her up and carried her deeper into the darkness of the rocks to the outstretched sleeping bag.

He could tell she was exhausted but fighting it. Her strength and determination continued to amaze him. He peeled off her wet clothing. But as he started to lower her onto the sleeping bag, she pulled him down with her.

"Jace."

He heard the plea in her voice and saw a raw need in her gaze. His own need was like a storm inside him. He lay down beside her and stroked her wet hair back from her face. Her green eyes were huge. She was pale in the firelight, her freckles golden. She looked so vulnerable.

"Please, Jace," she whispered as she reached to unzip his coat.

He caught her hand in his. "You've been through an ordeal. I know you aren't thinking clearly. And I would use this situation to be with you, but you have to know that if you and I ever make love again, it has to be for the right reasons."

"We might be dead before daylight."

He put his finger to her lips. "We're going to survive this and then you're going to regret—"

"My only regret is losing you." Emotion made her voice hoarse. "Jace, I was such a fool five years ago. I was . . . scared. I wasn't—"

"You weren't ready for marriage."

"No. I needed to do something with my life, to prove to myself that I had . . . value."

"Value?"

"I didn't want to be that spoiled little rich girl.

I wanted to be my own woman, prove that I could . . ." She shook her head. "That's why I wanted to run the foundation, and look what a mess I've made of that."

"That's not true. Emily's told me about all the businesses you've helped start and others you've helped through hard times."

Bo didn't seem to hear him. "But the worst part is that I messed up things with you. By the time I felt ready, you were gone. You were so hurt and angry and . . ." She locked eyes with him in the firelight. "I knew I'd lost you, and it broke my heart."

He smiled ruefully. He'd never believed in fate, but here they were. As crazy as the circumstances were, they'd been given another chance. He had no idea what tomorrow would bring. All they had was tonight. "I never stopped loving you. I damn sure tried, but, Bo, there is no one like you."

She smiled through her tears as he pulled her to him.

"Promise me that we can put the past behind us when we get off this mountain," she said, drawing back to meet his eyes. "That we can start over, no regrets?"

If they got out of the mountains alive. "I promise."

"And we can make love in a real bed, promise?"

He chuckled. "In a warm, soft bed. I promise."

• • •

Bo had dreamed of being in Jace's arms again, but she'd given up hope of it ever happening. She unzipped his coat and helped him shrug out of his wet clothing. He joined her on the sleeping bag in front of the fire. Wrapping her arms around his hard body, she smiled as he met her gaze.

His kiss sent desire racing through her like flames. She felt his hand cup her breast, the nipple springing up hard as a pebble. He drew back to slide down to take first one hard nipple in his mouth, then the other.

She arched against him, sensations rippling along her skin as hot as the fire blazing next to them. He pressed kisses along her naked flesh, leaving a trail of heat before he reached her center.

"Oh, Jace," she breathed as he kissed the most intimate part of her. His tongue licked at her, making her cry out as she rose higher and higher, quaking with the release that had her clutching at Jace.

He slid his body along hers, coming back to kiss her now achingly hard nipples before reaching her mouth. As he entered her, she felt as if everything in the world had suddenly righted itself.

She clung to him as he made love to her, taking her to places she'd never been, as the fire crackled and the storm raged beyond the rocks. Wrapped in Jace's arms, Bo closed her eyes and prayed for a miracle.

Sarah couldn't sleep. For several hours she had lain awake, listening to the rain. She finally got up and went into the cabin's small kitchen to make herself some warm milk. She used to make warm milk for one of her children who couldn't sleep. Ainsley? Or was it Kat or Bo? That she couldn't remember broke her heart. It felt like a lifetime ago.

She'd missed so much of her daughters' lives. There was no way to catch up. She couldn't blame them, though. She was a stranger. Worse, she was responsible for them now all hiding out from the press. She shouldn't have come back. Why had she?

When she thought about what the sheriff had said—that she was dropped from a plane, parachuted into a spot far from everything and wandered through the woods until she hit the road—and Russell Murdock almost hit her with his pickup, it scared her more than she wanted to admit. How was it that she couldn't remember it, if true? Or had someone just wanted him to believe that's how she'd returned?

Wasn't it possible for someone to set the whole thing up—including putting some of her DNA and blood on the parachute harness?

She let out a laugh. She was starting to sound like Russell with all his conspiracy theories.

But if true, then it made no sense, no matter

how many times she went over it. Why wouldn't she have been able to remember jumping from a plane? That didn't sound like something she would forget—unless she'd done it so many times before . . .

Her milk began to scorch. She quickly pulled it off the burner, no longer interested in warm milk. Instead, she took the nearly empty bottle of wine that Russell had brought to go with dinner and poured the last of it into a glass. Wine in hand, she moved to the couch. The copy of the photo he'd taken of her tattoo was lying on the table next to the couch's armrest.

Picking it up, she stared at the pendulum design. Needless to say, she had no memory of ever getting a tattoo, especially such a strange one. Everything about the past terrified her. Lately, she'd been getting more . . . flashes. She couldn't call them memories. What had happened to her? How had she ended up like this?

Russell was so sure that Buckmaster was behind it—

Her cell phone rang, making her jump. She pulled it out, expecting the call to be from Russell. He often checked on her to make sure she was all right, but usually not this late.

It was Buck. That was even odder at this hour.

"Hello?" she asked tentatively.

"For some reason I thought you might be awake, too," he said. His voice was soft as if he didn't want to awaken anyone in the house. As far as she knew, the only other person in the ranch house was Angelina, his wife.

"Why can't *you* sleep?" she asked.

"Bo is still missing in the Crazies." His voice broke with emotion. "I thought you might have seen it on the news."

"What? Bo is still missing? You were so sure when we talked before that she would be back by now."

"A snowstorm in the mountains stopped search efforts and would have kept her from getting out, as well. As soon as the weather breaks, we're going back up to look for her."

"Oh, Buck, she has to be all right."

"She's smart, and Jace Calder went up looking for her. If he found her . . . I just hope they're together at least. I'm sorry. I shouldn't have called you, but—"

"She's my daughter, too."

They were both silent for a long while.

"I miss you, Sarah."

His words made her heart ache. "I miss you, too."

"I wish there was some way—"

"There isn't. Even if you weren't with Angelina . . ."

More silence.

"I didn't mean to call and upset you. I should let you go."

"Please, call me when you find her."

"I will. We'll find her. I can't lose her. I've already lost so much."

She disconnected and sat holding the phone to her chest. No matter what Russell said, Buck couldn't be the monster he believed him to be. That would mean she was in love with a monster who'd taken away twenty-two years of her life.

The snow in the mountains had changed everything. Frank swore as he listened on the phone to the head of search and rescue describing the conditions they'd run into on the other side of the Crazies.

"The terrain is too dangerous," Jim Martin said. "Even experienced ground crews found many areas too difficult to traverse with the snow."

"What about the searchers in the helicopters?"

"They should be able to see tracks in the snow once the clouds lift." Jim didn't sound optimistic. "The storm isn't moving on as fast as the weather-man predicted."

Helicopters were standing by.

"We had search dogs, horse teams and hikers up there but had to bring them all back when the weather turned," Jim was saying. "All trailheads were monitored overnight in case they tried to come out a different way. The helicopter used thermal imaging technology until almost midnight when the weather got too rough."

Frank knew everyone was doing what they could given the conditions. Improved weather in the next day or so would allow an expanded search, but could Bo and Jace wait that long?

"I've already spoken to the media and told them that, due to the dangerous conditions up there, we can't use any volunteers for the search at this time," Jim said.

Not to mention there was at least one killer up in those mountains, Frank thought. He'd never felt more helpless, but until the weather broke . . .

He'd been fielding calls all evening, ever since the media had picked up the news. Senator Buckmaster Hamilton's daughter missing in the mountains of Montana was hot news—especially since Sarah Hamilton's return from the dead was now becoming old news. Everyone had written her off as a head case. Everyone but Frank.

It had been a long day. He couldn't wait to get home to his wife, already anticipating the beef roast she'd said she was cooking—along with a cold beer. He hadn't realized how late it was, though. The way things were going, he'd never get out of here tonight.

When he looked up from his desk, he was surprised to find Russell Murdock framed in the doorway.

"I saw your rig parked outside. I know it's late and you're busy with trying to find Bo Hamilton . . ."

Frank waved him into the office. Hat in hand, Russell stepped in and closed the door behind him. The sheriff's interest was piqued as Russell nervously took a chair across from his desk and rested a stack of papers on one knee. Sarah Hamilton was still staying with Russell. In fact, Frank was pretty sure Russell had been protecting the woman. Which made him wonder just what the man knew about her that Frank didn't and why exactly Russell was so protective of the senator's wife.

"What's up?" Frank asked.

"We've known each other a long time. Not well, but I know what kind of lawman you are. I trust you." Even after that buildup, Russell still looked hesitant. "I think there's something you should know about Sarah."

There was a lot he should know when it came to Sarah. The mystery of Sarah Hamilton was the real reason he told himself he couldn't even consider retirement. Not yet anyway.

"I hope you know me well enough that you trust I'm not some wacko."

Frank had to smile. Russell Murdock was as far from a wacko as anyone he knew, and he said as much.

The rancher let out a long breath. "Then I hope

300

what I have to tell you won't come as too big a shock."

Frank doubted anything the man would tell him about Sarah Hamilton would come as a shock.

"I think I know why Sarah can't remember the past twenty-two years, and I also believe I know who is behind it. The esteemed Senator Buckmaster Hamilton." He held up a hand as if expecting Frank to object. "I've been doing some research." He spread a stack of papers out on the sheriff's desk. "What do you know about brain wiping?"

Chapter
TWENTY-TWO

Bo woke in Jace's arms to daylight. She opened her eyes but didn't move. His body was warm and solid, and she felt safer than she had in days.

True, it was a false sense of security. Ray and his father were out there, probably looking for them—at least, that's what Jace believed.

She preferred to think that they were smarter than that and had headed back into the mountains to escape being caught. They had to know that someone else would come looking for her and Jace, so why not run?

With that shot they'd heard yesterday, maybe one had killed the other. She suspected Ray was better with a knife than a gun. She doubted even being shot would stop him. But maybe his wound was so bad that his father had put him out of his misery.

Jace stirred and rolled away from her. She instantly felt regret. She turned to see him standing at the edge of the cave opening.

When she saw that he had his rifle in his hands, she sat up in alarm. "What is it?" she whispered.

He motioned for her to stay quiet. Past him, all she could see was white. How much had it snowed? She groaned inwardly at the thought of wading through it to try to get out of the mountains. "Get dressed," Jace said. "The storm has let up. We need to be moving."

Bo heard Jace's horse let out a snort. The trees where the gelding had been tied began to shake viciously. Snow cascaded down from the snow-filled branches an instant before she heard the horse snorting.

She was on her feet, but not before Jace jumped off the ledge, fighting the fallen snow as he rushed toward the trees where he'd left the horse. What had the horse heard that had spooked him?

Wrapped in the sleeping bag, she hurried to the edge of the ledge in time to see the horse come thundering out of the trees, its eyes wide with fear. It reared, striking Jace and knocking him into the rocks an instant before the grizzly bear lumbered out of the pines.

Bo screamed. Jace was still lying in the snow from where he'd been hit by the rearing horse. "Jace!" He had dropped the rifle when he'd fallen, but Bo remembered in a rush that she still had the pistol.

She pulled it out of her jacket pocket and pointed it into the air. She knew better than to try to kill the grizzly. A wounded bear was even more dangerous than a hungry one. She pulled the trigger. Nothing happened. Fumbling off the safety, she fired. At the opening of the cave where she stood, the shot sounded like a cannon going off.

The grizzly, which had been headed for Jace, stopped. She fired again and the bear turned and lumbered back into the trees.

Her heart in her throat, she called down to Jace. "Are you all right?"

"My leg." She could hear the pain in his voice. "I think it's broken."

Buckmaster found Angelina glued to the television.

"The search continues for thirty-year-old Bo Hamilton, the daughter of Senator Buckmaster Hamilton, along with local rancher Jace Calder," the news anchor was saying.

"Hamilton was camping in the Crazy Mountains but failed to return as scheduled on Monday. Calder had gone up to search for her Monday afternoon."

An aerial shot of the Crazies flashed on the screen, making Buckmaster's stomach turn. So much country. Bo could be anywhere. Was she even still alive? He thought of the cold, the snow and shuddered to think what she might be going through. Not to mention there was a killer up there.

The sheriff had tried to play it down, but that outfitter had been *murdered* and as far as they knew, whoever had killed him was still up there.

The news anchor droned on about the large search and rescue team that had been deployed the day before to find the two missing residents.

"Searchers were forced back due to a snowstorm in the mountains. Jim Martin with the local response efforts warned everyone to stay out of the mountains because of the dangerous conditions. The search is set to continue today, weather permitting."

As the news anchor went on to other breaking stories, Buckmaster turned off the television.

"At least there had been no mention of missing funds at the Sarah Hamilton Foundation," his wife said.

Or of the outfitter's murder.

Cussing under his breath, he told himself he couldn't think like that. Bo was alive. She would be found.

Stepping to the rain-streaked window, he looked out at the Crazies. The mountain range was cloaked in clouds. He knew from experience that it was probably still snowing up there at the higher altitude. He hated to think how much snow might fall before this storm moved on.

His poor baby girl. He would have saddled up and taken his men back up the mountain, but he knew there was nothing anyone could do until the storm ended and risking more lives would only make things worse.

He'd looked at his men yesterday when the storm had blown in. Like him, they'd been cold and wet, and the temperature had been dropping fast. Not only that, they were scared after realizing John Cole's killer could still be up there.

"But what about Bo?" he'd asked the sheriff. "She's out in this, maybe hurt, God only knows."

"If Jace is with her, he'll take care of her," Frank had said.

"And if that escaped murderer is with her?"

"There is nothing more we can do until the storm breaks," the sheriff had said. "Go home. I'll keep you posted. As soon as the storm breaks, we'll have choppers in the air, dogs and horse teams on the ground. These people are trained for this. We don't want them to have to look for you and your men as well as your daughter and Jace Calder."

He'd had no choice. Yesterday when the snow hit before they could get out of the mountains, he hadn't been able to see two feet in front of his horse. He knew it was insane to continue looking, but turning back had been one of the hardest things he'd ever done in his life.

But now the waiting was killing him.

He felt as if he was letting down his daughter. Maybe had let her down even before she went up into the mountains. Since Sarah's return, he'd been questioning everything he'd done in the past.

After he'd lost Sarah, he'd thrown himself into

politics. Now he could see that he'd let his family take a backseat to his political career. It broke his heart that his oldest, Ainsley, had recently quit law school. From the time she could talk, she'd wanted to be a lawyer.

Instead, she'd helped him raise her five sisters. Actually, she and a series of nannies had raised the girls while he spent much of his time campaigning for offices that had finally gotten him into the Senate. When she'd grown older, she'd stepped in, taking on most of the responsibility of running the ranch. How had he let that happen?

He felt now as if he'd stolen her childhood as well as too much of her adulthood. When it came to her sisters, he always went to her to find out how they were doing. He still did. Even now, he wanted to call her—as if she could help with what was happening with Bo.

"I don't even know my daughters," he said, voicing his thoughts aloud.

Angelina mugged a face. "That's ridiculous! They adore you."

"I bought them whatever they wanted. I gave them the run of the ranch. I raised them like wild horses that were allowed to run free and do as they pleased."

She shook her head. "Your daughters have all grown into fine young women."

That surprised him, her saying what he'd hoped was true. Angelina had never been a mother to his six girls. If anything, she'd always seemed to resent the way he'd spoiled them.

"Look at the trouble they've gotten into, not to mention this latest with Bo. Maybe if I'd stayed here on the ranch and not—"

Angelina shot up from her chair. "I don't have to ask why you're dredging up the past. *Sarah*." She said his first wife's name with all the venom of an angry rattlesnake. It made him cringe inside.

Not that he hadn't felt bitter about Sarah taking the easy way out and leaving him with six daughters to raise. The girls had needed their mother. Maybe they still did.

"Sarah is to blame for all of this," Angelina said even more sharply.

"I don't blame her."

"Well, you're the only one," she said before stomping off.

He let her go. Bo wasn't her daughter, and Angelina had never had any children of her own. She couldn't understand how he felt right now. Only Sarah could.

As he stared at the mountains cloaked in snow clouds, he thought of what Sarah had said about hating those mountains and being terrified of them.

Right now, he felt the same way.

Nettie studied her husband as he ate his breakfast without tasting it. "How is it?"

308

"Delicious," he said and pushed away his empty plate.

"Liar. I bet you can't even tell me what you just ate." He'd been like this since he'd come home late last night. She knew he was worried about Bo Hamilton and that fool rancher Jace Calder who'd gone up after her, but she could tell it was more than that.

"What is it, Frank?" she asked as she took his plate. "You barely tasted that roast I made last night, either."

"There is just a lot going on right now."

"Pfffft!"

He looked up at her, focusing on her face for the first time since he'd walked in the door last night. She could see him making up his mind about whether or not to tell her. "It's about Sarah Hamilton."

"What's she done now?" When Frank hesitated, she reminded him that this wasn't one of his cases. According to the FBI, there wasn't even an ongoing investigation.

The sheriff sighed. "Russell Murdock shared a theory he has about her memory loss."

"*He* thinks she's lying?"

Frank shook his head. "He thinks her brain was wiped clean of the memories from the past twenty-two years. He thinks Buckmaster is behind it."

Nettie blinked. "That's the craziest—"

"I know. That was my take on it, as well. Apparently, though, scientists have been experimenting with brain wiping for years and are now at a place where they can erase bad memories in rats." Frank got to his feet. "I've got to go," he said, looking toward the Crazies still cloaked in clouds. "The storm is supposed to break. Ideally we'll find the two missing persons today. But we're also looking for an escapee who might be up there. We found John Cole's body. He'd been shot."

"Murdered?"

He nodded.

"You be careful," she said, stepping to him. He put his arms around her and held her close, then leaned down to give her a quick kiss.

"Thanks for breakfast."

She smiled at that and was tempted to quiz him on what he'd eaten. Instead, she said, "I've been doing some research on Sarah Hamilton's tattoo. Did you know that pendulums have been associated with the occult?"

Bo worked quickly, following Jace's instructions. She'd managed to splint his leg and help him back up onto the ledge and into the mouth of the cave. Now he lay breathless from the excursion and pain. He'd lain in the snow for too long. She worried he might be hypothermic.

"You surprise me," he said. She could see that

he was in pain but trying hard not to let her know it.

"Hold still," she ordered as she put first aid cream on his wound where the rock had broken the skin. Was she really worried the wound would get infected? Neither of them would probably live that long.

Forcing that thought away, she asked, "How do I surprise you?"

"You're tougher and more capable than I thought."

She stopped to study his face for a moment. "I'm sorry. Was that a compliment?"

He managed a grin that turned into a grimace. She'd had a first aid class years ago and remembered little of it. But one look at his leg and she knew they had to get out of here as soon as possible.

As she reached for a bandage, he took her hand. "Thank you. I don't know what I would have done without you."

She looked into his blue eyes and fought tears. He wouldn't even be here if it wasn't for her. She pulled her hand free and fussed with his bandage, determined not to cry.

"There, you're going to be just fine," she said as she finished and covered him again with the sleeping bag.

"I'm not going to be able to get out of here under my own steam. I can't walk on this leg."

She almost laughed. They had two killers after them who would probably catch up to them before his leg even became an issue.

"I know. But *I* can. The clouds are lifting. They're going to be looking for us again."

"So are Ray and his father."

She shook her head. "We don't know that. We heard the shot yesterday, but we haven't heard anything since. All I have to do is find a wide-open place and build a fire so the smoke can be seen. In the meantime, you'll be fine here."

Jace grabbed her arm, forcing her to look at him. "Ray and his father will see the smoke. They probably already heard the shots you fired to scare off the grizzly."

She hadn't thought of that. "What do you suggest, then?"

"You get back to the trail and keep heading south toward the ranch as fast as you can."

Bo shook her head. "I'm not leaving you."

"Listen to me—"

"No, Jace. I'm not going to—" She froze. "Do you hear that?"

They both stilled as they listened.

"It's a helicopter." She felt hope rise up in her like helium as she rushed to the cave opening. The storm had passed. She could see patches of blue between the clouds. Soon the clouds would burn off and Montana's big sky would be a canopy of vivid blue. If she could just signal the helicopter . . .

Chapter
TWENTY-THREE

At the senator's insistence, a command center had been set up at the edge of Forest Service property on the Hamilton Ranch. The sheriff hadn't put up a fight when he'd gotten the request from the governor.

"Buckmaster is worried sick about his daughter," the governor had said.

"We all are," Frank had told him, knowing he shouldn't be surprised that Buckmaster had pulled strings to get what he wanted. It did make him wonder how much power the man had—and he wasn't even president yet. He couldn't help but think about Russell's theory.

Frank had always liked and admired Buckmaster, but there was no arguing that he got what he wanted and always had, either through the money or the political power he'd inherited from his father. "I think having the command center there at the trailhead makes sense," the governor had said. "Just between you and me, it might also keep him out of your hair so you can do your job."

"That would be nice," Frank had agreed.

Now he watched as a second National Guard

helicopter set down in the pasture fifty yards away. Earlier one had headed for the mountains to look for the missing Hamilton woman.

Buckmaster was headed for the chopper when Frank caught up to him.

"I'd prefer you stay here, Senator," the sheriff said.

"My daughter's up there. I'm going to look for her. The only way you can stop me is to arrest me. You sure you want to do that, Sheriff?"

Frank sighed. "I got word this morning that Ray Spencer's father might be up the mountains with him. He was last seen taking horses and supplies up a trail on the other side of the Crazies."

"You think he's meeting his son up there," Buckmaster said.

"I suspect that's exactly what he's doing."

The senator looked toward the mountains. "That outfitter was killed on the trail that comes up from the other side."

No one could say that the senator wasn't quick-thinking.

Buckmaster let out a curse. "My daughter might be in those mountains with *two* murderers?"

"I think anyone looking for Bo right now could be in danger," Frank said. "That's why I don't want you to get into that helicopter."

The senator shook his head. "Try to stop me."

• • •

Bo stepped to the front of the cave as the army-green helicopter came into view over the tops of the pines. She began to wave her arms wildly before she realized that dressed as she was, there was no way anyone in the chopper could see her.

She rushed back into the cave, grabbed the yellow slicker and rushed to the rock ledge again. Jace, still covered with the sleeping bag, had braced himself on his elbows so he could see. The helicopter was closer now. She waved the jacket frantically, yelling as she did, even though she knew they wouldn't be able to hear her.

But they had to see her! She couldn't bear the thought of the chopper going on past. A sob rose in her chest as it started to turn away. "No!" she cried.

"It's okay, there'll be more," Jace said.

Now was the moment he picked to try to reassure her?

"No, I have to climb down and build a big fire. Or write 'Help' with sticks in a clear spot. I can't let—" She faltered as she heard the helicopter. It had turned back toward her. "He's coming back," she cried and began to wave the yellow slicker again. *He sees us!*

Tears burned her eyes. "He sees us!" She started to turn to smile back at Jace when she caught something out of the corner of her eye.

A flash. It happened so fast, for a moment she couldn't make sense of it. The chopper was headed in their direction. One of the crew members had seen her waving to them. The next second there was another flash and noise like a whistle as some-thing streaked across the sky.

"What—" Bo didn't get to finish. Smoke suddenly billowed from the helicopter. Like a wounded bird, the chopper rolled to one side and, as if unable to fight gravity, began to fall toward earth.

It disappeared from sight beyond the pines and the slope of the mountain. Bo held her breath, her heart in her throat. For just a moment before that, she'd been so happy. She'd thought they were going to be saved. She'd thought this whole ordeal was almost over.

Then she heard the horrible sound of the chopper as it crashed and exploded.

At the sound of the explosion, everyone at the search command center turned to stare up at the mountains. Smoke curled up from the pines into the clearing blue sky.

"Tell me someone didn't just shoot down that chopper," the senator said to Frank, his eyes wide with fear. Only moments before, they'd been arguing about the senator getting into a helicopter.

"What the hell is going on?" Buckmaster demanded.

Frank had no idea.

"What was that we saw before the helicopter went down?" one of the search and rescue men asked.

"It looked like an RPG, a rocket-propelled grenade," a National Guard man said. The officer in command was already on his radio. "Who up there would have shot it down?" he demanded of Frank.

"I can't say for sure, but I suspect Ray Spencer Sr. is up there. He's an ex-military sniper turned antigovernment survivalist. His son, Ray Jr., is the escapee we believe is also up there. Ray Jr. is wanted on a murder charge."

"We have to get up there," Buckmaster said and stepped toward the National Guard helicopter.

"Sorry, Senator, but I have my orders. No civilians," the commander said. "This is now a military operation."

Bo stood for a long moment, too shocked to move. "Someone shot down the helicopter." Even as she said it, she still couldn't believe it.

"Whoever fired on it is close by," Jace said. "And that wasn't a rifle shot."

She swallowed as she looked down the mountainside. The sun had come out, making the snow sparkle like something out of a fairy tale. It seemed so incongruous since she and Jace were in a nightmare that she suspected

317

was never going to end. Or would end too soon.

His words finally registered. She'd seen the streak of light before the chopper took the hit. She had a pretty good idea where the shot had originated. Help wasn't going to be coming. Not quick enough.

"Ray's father was in the military," she said. "He told me that his father was a crack shot."

Jace looked as worried as she was. "But to shoot down a National Guard helicopter?" He shook his head, clearly shocked. She figured he'd also come to the same conclusion she had.

Ray and his father weren't planning to be taken alive. Since Ray blamed her, that meant they would be coming for her and Jace, and soon.

Pushing to her feet, she pulled the handgun from her pocket to reload it. She found more ammunition in Ray's pack.

"What are you doing?"

"The only thing I can do. You saw what they did to that helicopter. Clearly they're planning to go out in a blaze of glory. As you said, if Ray is alive, he isn't going to let me get away. I'm not going to let them kill you. If I can help it."

"Hold on, Annie Oakley. We already talked about this. If you go down there, do you really think you can kill one of them?" She hesitated just a little too long. "That's what I thought. Forget it, Bo. You aren't going down there."

She understood what he was saying. But she

318

also knew that if she stayed here, they would be sitting ducks. Whoever had shot down that chopper could just as easily turn one of those rockets on them.

Bo had to do something, and Jace wasn't going anywhere. "You keep the rifle. If I fail and they find you . . ."

"Bo, don't do this," Jace said as he tried to get up, grimacing in pain.

She gently pushed him back down. "Thank you," she said, leaning down to brush a kiss across his lips.

"For what?" he demanded, clearly both frustrated and upset.

"For being my hero."

He looked at her, fear in his expression. "I'm no hero, and if that kiss was supposed to be goodbye . . . you promised me a whole lot more than that last night. I'm planning to collect in full once we're off this mountain."

She smiled. "I'm counting on it, too."

Rising, she put the loaded gun into her coat pocket and stepped off the ledge into the snow. Fortunately it had snowed only about half a foot overnight. She slogged through it, taking a longer route so she didn't leave a trail right back to Jace if she failed.

Could she kill Ray or his father? The thought made her shudder, but the alternative was so much worse . . .

She didn't worry about making too much noise as she approached the spot from which she believed the men had fired to take down the helicopter. Remembering the gunshot they'd heard the day before, she wondered what she would find when she reached their camp.

Before she saw anything, she heard the whinny of one of the horses.

"Hello?" she called out. She knew there was no way she could sneak up on them, fearing her attempt *would* get her killed.

"Hello?" she called again as she kept walking. She had to be close. But who was out there, and could she pull the trigger when she came face-to-face with one or both of them?

Jace had never felt so helpless. Bo was going to get herself killed. Or worse. He tried to get up again, but it was useless. He couldn't walk let alone climb off this mountainside in the snow with a broken leg.

He could barely breathe as he listened for the sound of a gunshot.

Damn that woman. He had to do something. He knew what she planned and why. She thought she could save him by giving Ray Spencer what he wanted—*her!*

Jace couldn't bear the thought. If there had been any way to stop her—

The days of pretending he didn't care about Bo

Hamilton were long gone. Hell, if he was honest with himself, he'd been in love with her since junior high. He'd screwed things up with the senior prom, but they'd been given a second chance. Then five years ago, Bo had broken it off. Now he understood why, but now this. He feared they might have run out of chances.

The one thing he knew was that he couldn't just lie here and let the woman he loved get killed or become a mountain bride to a psychopath. He had to do something and quickly. He'd always been so capable, so sure of his abilities.

But he'd never been trapped on a snowy mountain with a broken leg before. It was a humbling experience to be this helpless. He wasn't about to let it beat him, though.

Her breath coming out in puffs of white frosty clouds, Bo tried to still her trembling from the cold and her fear. She'd told herself that she would do whatever she had to. She couldn't let them kill Jace. All she had to do was stall for time. The Spencers had to know that this mountain would soon be crawling with armed men determined to stop them.

But the rescuers wouldn't be coming quickly enough. She had to do this if she hoped to save Jace, save both of them.

And yet she feared what would happen when

Ray saw her. He and his father had just shot down a National Guard helicopter, sealing their fates. That's if Ray was still alive. Even if his wound hadn't killed him, his father might have.

But either way, she figured Ray's father knew about her. She'd heard enough about RayJay and seen what he'd done to his son to know he would blame her for all of this.

As strange as it seemed, she hoped Ray was alive. Even though he'd told her what would happen if she ran, she thought she could convince him that she would go with him. If she could talk him into trying to get away rather than dying up here on this mountain . . .

Bo knew how foolhardy this was. But she'd had to do something. Otherwise, they would find Jace and . . .

She heard a sound ahead, something alive, and it wasn't a horse. She thought about last night in Jace's arms and knew she would do whatever she had to. Her love for Jace pushed her on. If she had to kill one or both of the Spencers . . . As if she would get that chance.

Still, the thought made her tremble harder. Where was the Bo Hamilton who used to be so deter-mined? That old Bo was definitely not the woman who'd packed up and headed for the hills when she'd realized money was missing from the foundation. Or the woman who'd been drinking too much at her sister Livie's engagement party.

Ahead, she saw several horses, but not hers. A weathered older man sat bundled up against the cold as he huddled over a small fire. She looked around for Ray but didn't see him. Standing there, stone still, she wondered if there had been a mistake. This man didn't look like someone who'd just shot down a helicopter.

Thinking he hadn't heard her approach, she stepped closer. She had to assume this was Ray's father, RayJay.

Where was her horse? More to the point, where was Ray?

The older man looked up slowly as if sensing her standing there. But the moment she looked into his blue eyes, she knew he'd heard her coming all the while. He gave her a once-over and then, his gaze going to the gun in her hand, began to laugh. "Ya plannin' to shoot me?"

"Where is Ray?" she asked.

The man rose. He'd looked small, even frail, hunkered over the fire. But as he straightened to his full height, she saw that he was almost as big as his son. And like Ray, he looked fit for his age. "He said ya were a looker. Explains why he done somethin' so stupid." The man took a step toward her.

She glanced around, listening for Ray, but hearing nothing. "Don't come any closer."

"What ya goin' a do? Shoot me in cold blood? Ya already kilt my son. Might as well kill me, too."

Ray was dead?

He took another step toward her. "We coulda lived up here just fine, me an my boy. Now look at the mess ya made."

I made! Bo thought. She took a step back. She didn't want to shoot this man. And she doubted that one shot would stop him. The thought of emptying the gun into him turned her stomach.

But she could tell by the look on his face that she would have no choice but to kill him. If he reached her, he'd wrench away the gun and—

He took another step. If she didn't fire now . . . She aimed the pistol at his heart and pulled the trigger.

It clicked.

The safety! She hurriedly flipped the safety off as the man launched himself at her.

Ray had heard the voices. He couldn't believe his ears. His daddy had Bo? He dropped the halter rope of the lead horse he'd been moving back to camp. Grabbing the gun his old man had brought him, he rushed toward the fire as he heard the first shot.

When he cleared the trees, he saw his father knock the gun from Bo's hand and send her sprawling in the snow. He rushed to her, helping her up and shielding her as his father pulled his own weapon and pointed it at Bo.

"Git outta the way!" his father ordered.

"Ya ain't gonna to kill her." Ray hadn't stood up to his old man since he was twelve. That beating had left scars worse than all the other beatings. "I'm keepin' her."

"Keepin' her?" his father crowed. "Yer grabbin' her in the first place is why we're goin' to die up here."

"We kin get away. Take her to Mexico."

RayJay shook his head. "Ya've lost yer mind. Ya think she's goin' anywhere with the likes a ya, yer crazy. She don't want ya."

Ray rubbed a hand over his face. "Tell him it ain't true," he said without looking at Bo. When she didn't answer, he faced her, praying to see something other than disgust in her green eyes.

Jace heard the gunshot, then the sound of raised voices. Looking off the mountain, he thought he knew where the voices were coming from. It was too steep and the snow too deep for him to try to walk down there even if he could put weight on his broken leg.

But he recalled something he and his brothers had done as boys. The pain in his leg took his breath away, but he managed to pull himself, the rifle and the sleeping bag to the edge of the rock face. It took some maneuvering, but he got his legs into the sleeping bag and zipped it up. He held the rifle. He hoped to hell this was going to work. The mountain was steep enough. The snow slick enough. If he could use the stock of the rifle to steer, he could ride the sleeping bag like a sled down the mountain. The June snow was wet and would hold him up, although it would also be fast. With luck, he could get close to where the voices were coming from without nailing a tree.

Saying a prayer, he pushed himself off feet-first and went sledding down the mountainside on the slick fabric of the sleeping bag.

"I will go with you," Bo said as Ray turned to look at her. She nodded, meeting his gaze, hoping he believed it. Anything to get him away from Jace. More searchers would be coming, only this time armed. She didn't want to speculate on her odds of getting out of this alive, but she had to try.

"Yer ain't goin' nowhere," RayJay spat.

"Look out!" Bo cried as, past Ray, she saw his father take a long stride, gun raised.

He struck his son in the side of the head with the butt of the weapon. Ray's gaze locked with Bo's for one heart-stopping moment. Then his eyes rolled back into his head, and he went down hard at her feet in the snow.

RayJay let out a curse as he looked at his son

and then lifted the gun in his hand. "I shoulda shot 'im the other day instead of tryin' to scare some sense into 'im. My son's a damned fool," he said as he took aim. "I ain't so gullible."

Bo heard the boom of the shot, felt the sound rumble through her and then blinked in surprise when she felt nothing. She hadn't realized that she'd closed her eyes until she opened them to find RayJay standing in front her. He had a surprised look on his face. His free hand had gone to his chest. Blood flowed out over his fingers as he lowered the gun in his hand to look down at his son as if he'd assumed it had been Ray who'd shot him.

Ray hadn't moved. His eyes were wide-open, but blood pooled in the right one, and the snow was dark where blood had leaked from his ear.

Bo had assumed the same thing as RayJay. But with a shock, she realized that Ray couldn't have shot his father, because the blow to his head had killed him.

RayJay seemed to come to that conclusion even slower than she had. Like her, he glanced around for a second before he started to raise his gun again, defeat and regret in his expression, none of it for Bo.

Everything had happened within seconds. She'd frozen at RayJay's attack but now forced herself to move. She grabbed for the older man's gun, trying to wrestle it out of his hand.

Even with him wounded, he was strong and fierce. He broke her grasp and shoved her away, raising the gun again to fire.

Bo fell into the snow just inches from where RayJay had knocked the gun from her hand earlier. She snatched it up and rolled over, the weapon clutched in both hands as she pulled the trigger.

The air around her exploded with the sound of two shots. She blinked sure she'd only fired once. RayJay had stopped a few feet from her. Now he dropped his gun, his eyes glassy with shock. His legs gave out under him. He slumped to his knees. As he fell face-first into the snow, Bo looked past his body to see Jace propped up against a tree, most of his body cocooned in a sleeping bag, the rifle in his hands.

Tears burned her eyes as he smiled at her. At the sound of more helicopters, she dropped the gun and stepped out in the clearing to wave her arms.

Chapter
TWENTY-FOUR

Jace remembered little of the helicopter ride to the hospital except for Bo holding his hand. Once he was wheeled into the emergency room, the doctor gave him something for the pain. When he came to, his leg was in a cast and his sister was sitting next to his bed.

She leaped up when she saw that he was awake. "You could have been killed, and it would have been all my fault."

He laughed. It felt good. "How many times have I said those same words to you? A little different having the shoe on the other foot, huh."

She nodded and hugged him. "I was so worried about you. I'm just so relieved that you're all right."

He looked toward the door of his room. "Bo was by earlier. I thought she might have come with you."

"When I saw her, she was headed for the foundation to meet with the auditor."

Jace lay back against his pillow. He'd actually forgotten about the auditor and the missing money. "She'll figure it out."

Emily looked worried. "I sure hope so. I'd hate to see the foundation close."

"I'm sure it won't," he said although he wasn't sure of that at all.

"I have a date Friday night," his sister said and quickly added, "Don't give me that look. I think you'd actually like him. He's nothing like any man I've ever dated. He's really . . . geeky. He works at a coffee shop." She laughed. "But he's . . . nice."

Jace figured the poor guy wouldn't last past tonight, but he said, "I'm glad you found someone nice."

Bo felt as if she was facing a firing squad as she stepped through the door of the Sarah Hamilton Foundation. But she'd faced much worse up on the mountain, she told herself. She'd checked to make sure Jace was in good hands before her father had picked her up at the hospital and taken her back to the ranch.

"I know you're anxious to hear all about what happened on the mountain," she'd said when she saw the worry lines in Buckmaster's face. "Jace Calder saved me. I'm all right. Really. You can stop worrying."

"Can I?" he had asked as he glanced at her freshly bandaged wrists.

"Yes. I need to get back to town, get ready for my appointment with the auditor at the foundation office. I called from the hospital. He's concluded his investigation of the books." At her father's raised brow, she shook her head. "He said we would talk about it today."

"Why don't I come with you?" her father had suggested.

She'd placed a hand on his arm. "I appreciate that, Dad, but I need to do this alone."

Now she lifted her head, chin up, spine straight, and reminded herself that she was Bo Hamilton, the woman who'd survived a violent criminal. She would survive this, too.

The auditor was waiting for her in the conference room. A stern-looking older man in a black suit, he looked like the perfect executioner.

She apologized for the delay in seeing him, but he waved it off and tapped at the myriad of papers spread across the huge table.

"I found out what happened to your money," Mr. Alderson said and adjusted his wire-frame glasses to focus dark eyes on her.

Bo silently gulped and dropped into a chair across from him. All the while, she was repeating a mantra in her head: *don't let it be one of my employees.*

"The account was hacked in March," he said without preamble.

"Hacked?" she echoed.

"From what I can tell, it was done from various

locations abroad, which was probably why you didn't catch it sooner."

She sat back, too relieved to speak. Hacked. By someone in another country. Not one of her employees.

"Did anything unusual happen around that time at the foundation?" he asked.

"*March?* My mother came back."

"Your *mother?* Sarah Hamilton, the person the foundation is named for. Is she on the board?"

Bo shook her head. "Sorry, I was just thinking out loud. She's not involved in any way. I thought of her because you mentioned March."

"Has your mother been living abroad?" he asked, studying her over the top of his glasses.

"I . . . I don't know. But like I said, I'm sure that the hacking of the account has nothing to do with my mother. My father started the foundation in her name after she was believed drowned in the Yellowstone River. As it turns out, she survived." She waved a hand through the air as if to say *end of story.* "I'm sure this has nothing to do with her."

The auditor didn't look as convinced. "She isn't involved with the foundation?"

"Not at all. I'm sorry, but I can't think of anything that happened in March that might be relevant to this."

"No new employee?"

She shook her head. "Nothing." It was just a coincidence that they'd gotten hacked about the time her mother had returned. Unless her mother had been a computer hacker the past twenty-two years. The thought almost made her laugh.

But she reminded herself that her mother could have lived abroad for the past twenty-two years. Who knew? No one but her mother.

"So how do we catch this hacker and get the money back?" she asked him.

"That will prove difficult at best. The first thing we need to do is try to keep him or her from taking any more funds. We'll change all the passwords and set up more security, but even then it will be hard to keep a really good hacker out."

"I'm just so glad it wasn't one of my employees." She was still shaking inside with the remains of her fear as well as her relief.

The auditor looked up at her. "We don't know for a fact it wasn't one of your employees, but our investigators will begin tracking the money and running background checks on your people and anyone else associated with the foundation." He met her gaze. "You will be included in the investigation. I'm sure you realize that."

"Of course."

"Often the trail is long, the job arduous, but we have a very good success rate at catching the culprits. It will take time, though." He rose and began gathering up the papers and putting them into his briefcase.

"I appreciate you staying until I could get back," she said, also getting to her feet.

"Not at all. I was so sorry to hear what you went through. It sounds like you are lucky to be alive."

"Yes. Very lucky."

"And the man who went looking for you? How is he?"

"Jace Calder. He's recovering from a broken leg and a few contusions." She hadn't seen him other than to stop by his room at the hospital. "He saved my life."

The auditor shook his head. "I can't imagine what you went through."

After he left, Bo walked around the office. Up on the mountain, she'd told herself that she should step down from her position at the foundation. She'd been so sure it was her fault the money was missing. Even if one of her employees had been behind the theft, she'd felt responsible. She was the one who'd hired this ragtag bunch.

Relieved that it didn't appear to be anything any of them had done, she realized how much she loved this job. Her stepmother, Angelina, had always said that the foundation was too much responsibility for her. Truthfully, she hadn't felt qualified for the job. But she'd wanted desperately to prove herself.

For a while up on the mountain, she would have agreed that she had no business running the foundation. But not now. Now she was thankful that this was a part of her life as well as the people she worked with. It appeared even with the loss, they were still in business. They would raise more money.

If what had happened up on the mountain had taught her anything, it was that she was stronger than she realized—just as Jace had said.

The thought of him filled her with warmth. She wanted to call him and tell him how the audit had gone, but hesitated. She would talk to him later, when she went by to take him home from the hospital.

At a tap on her office door, she turned to see Jace's sister. Bo had to laugh at the young woman's concerned expression. Emily must have been waiting for the auditor to leave—or the sheriff to come.

She motioned Emily and her daughter, Jodie, in.

"Is everything all right?" Emily asked, looking scared.

"We were hacked by someone thousands of miles from Montana."

"Do they know who?"

"Not yet. But the auditor is turning it over to the investigators—and putting in more safeguards to keep the hacker from taking any more of our money. How are you and Jodie doing?" She took in Emily, trying to see what was different about her. "Did you do something to your hair while I was gone?"

She shook her head. "I met someone."

"It's a boy," Jodie said before taking off to go dig toys out of the toy box Bo had brought in for visiting children.

"A *boy?*" Bo asked with a laugh.

"A man I met." Emily changed the subject. "I just saw Jace. He'll be off his feet for a while." She met Bo's gaze. "How did it go up there on the mountain, the two of you?"

Bo raised a brow and laughed. "Don't tell me you were worried we wouldn't get along?"

Earlier at the hospital, Jace had said that now that they were back to civilization, they might both change their minds about what they'd restarted in the mountains. She'd told him unless he changed his mind, she would be picking him up to take him to his ranch later when the doctor released him.

"You and my brother have never had much luck getting together," Emily said with obvious regret. "I still feel so bad about the two of you missing the senior prom because of me."

"Because of *you?*"

"He never told you what happened that night?" Emily looked as if she might cry. "Oh, Bo, I'm so sorry. Jace was so excited about his date. He got a second job after school so he could rent a tuxedo."

"He did?" Even when they'd gotten back together before, they had agreed not to discuss prom night. All Jace had told her was that something important had come up. More important than her, Bo had thought.

"He was so handsome in his tux." Now Emily did cry. "It was all my fault. I did something really stupid. I snuck out and was hitchhiking into town when this older man stopped for me. He gave me some beer and . . ."

"Oh, Emily, you were only, what? Twelve?"

She looked ashamed. "I was so stupid, so sure I could handle myself, so sick of Jace telling me what to do. He was just trying to keep the ranch after our parents died. I was such a brat."

Bo stepped to her to give her a hug. "You were just a kid."

She nodded, tears in her eyes. "When the man tried something, I jumped out of the car and ran. I called Jace from a pay phone, but the man came back . . . Oh, Bo, I'm so sorry. But if he hadn't shown up when he did . . . We had to go to the sheriff's department after that. I ruined his date like I ruined a lot of other nights for him. I don't know why he's put up with me."

Bo shook her head. "He loves you. He's your brother. Now you have your own little girl to raise."

337

"She'll probably pay me back for how terrible I was, huh." She wiped at her eyes. "I can't believe Jace didn't tell you what happened."

"He tried," Bo said with a sigh, remembering how awful she was to him. "But, Emily, that was years ago. In the grand scheme of things . . . your brother just saved my life."

"I know, but if he'd made it for his date with you to the prom . . . Don't you ever wonder if you two might have stayed together? You could be married by now with a couple of kids."

Bo laughed and shook her head. "I certainly wasn't ready for that. Things happen in their own time. Surely you have realized that."

"I'm starting to," Emily said as she turned at the sound of a tap on the front window. Alex Ross passed and waved.

"Alex Ross is the perfect example of why we have to keep the foundation going," Bo said. "You probably don't know this because you're involved only in the media part of the foundation, but Alex applied for one of the first small business loans I approved. He started with one coffee shop and now has six across the state. He is still one of my favorite success stories." She noticed that Emily had gone pale. "Is something wrong?"

The younger woman shook her head. "I thought he worked part-time at this one. I'm so embarrassed."

Bo was studying her. "Alex? You and Alex?" She laughed. "Is it . . . serious?"

Emily shrugged. "I think it could be."

"Good for you. I hope it works out. I like Alex a lot."

"Alex makes Mommy smile," Jodie said, joining them.

It was late afternoon before the sheriff returned to his office. Bo Hamilton was safe, and Jace Calder's leg would heal. The helicopter pilot and crew member had managed to get out of the chopper before it exploded, and were both expected to pull through. The Spencers' bodies had been brought down out of the mountains. Frank suspected one of their rifles was the murder weapon used on John Cole, and ballistics would prove it. He had statements from both Bo and Jace. His work was done for the moment.

Relieved everything had turned out so well, he sat down at his desk and picked up the reading materials Russell Murdock had left behind.

Brain wiping. He'd never heard of such a thing—let alone a Dr. Ralph Venable.

He didn't know what to make of this information. At first it had sounded like something out of a sci-fi movie, but the more he looked at the articles, the more he understood why Russell believed it.

If possible, it could certainly explain Sarah's

missing twenty-two years—if she had crossed paths with this Dr. Venable.

Undersheriff Dillon Lawson stuck his head in the door. "You were looking for me?"

Frank motioned for him to come in and close the door. "Russell Murdock brought me an interesting theory about Sarah Hamilton's missing years. Take a look at this and tell me what you think," he said, gathering up the papers and handing them over. "Then see what we can find out about this Dr. Venable. I'm curious where he was doing his research back then."

Dillon glanced down at the papers in his hand and then up at Frank. *"Brain wiping?"*

"I know it sounds crazy, but I think Russell might have stumbled onto something. We know that after Lester Halverson pulled Sarah from the river, she made a call and someone picked her up. She wasn't seen again until a few months ago. Russell believes it was Buckmaster who picked her up that night and whisked her away to some mad scientist's clinic."

His undersheriff frowned. "Why would he do that?"

"Russell's theory is that something happened between Sarah and her husband that would make her leave six children, including her recently born twins, and drive into the Yellowstone River in the middle of winter."

"That has definitely been bothering both of us,

as well. But we also know that suicide victims don't always have a clear reason for what they do."

Frank nodded. "The press has been blaming postpartum depression and has written her off a a bad mother and possible lunatic. Six kids that close together . . . But it still doesn't answer the question of who picked her up and why she disappeared. Or why she came back now."

Dillon looked down at the papers again. "If this was possible twenty-two years ago . . . I'll see what I can find."

Frank nodded, glad Dillon was taking it seriously. "All this time, I've been worried about the senator," he said. "Maybe I should be more worried about Sarah's safety."

Angelina had been expecting the call.

"Time to pay up," journalist Chuck Barrow said with obvious impatience. "You've put me off long enough. Unless you want me to air—"

"I told you, I don't know where Sarah is. Russell Murdock is hiding her."

"Right. But your husband knows where she is."

She gritted her teeth, hating the reminder that her husband had been meeting Sarah, often behind her back.

"Check out his navigation system in his car. It will show the past few places he's gone."

She hadn't thought of that. "He goes for his daily horseback ride soon. I'll do what I can while he's gone." She disconnected and went to the window to look out at the mountains. It was always something, she thought. At least Bo was back. So far it appeared that she'd had nothing to do with the missing money at the foundation, since she hadn't been arrested yet.

All was peaceful on the Hamilton Ranch front for the moment. Soon she and Buckmaster would be back in Washington or on the campaign trail. She loved every minute of campaigning. All the different cities, all the people who came to see him, Angelina right at his side. The loving sane wife. She'd bought a whole new wardrobe befitting a first lady. It would be so nice to leave the ranch, the children and Sarah in the dust. To have all the attention on Buckmaster and herself for a change. She couldn't wait.

If the journalist was right, Buckmaster knew where his former wife was staying. It would be in his navigation system. That alone sent her blood to the boiling point. Why couldn't he just let Sarah go? For such an intelligent man, he could be so stupid.

She smothered her aggravation and thought instead about what would happen if she turned the information over to Chuck. He would go to wherever Russell Murdock had hidden the woman. Then what? Would Sarah panic and run far away? Angelina let out a bitter laugh at the thought. Not likely.

Would she talk to the journalist? Also not likely. She would slam the door in the man's face, call Russell and he would again hide her away so that not even Buckmaster could find her. Wouldn't they both assume that Buckmaster was to blame for her being found?

Angelina smiled at the thought. Maybe this would work in her favor. Whatever it took, she had to get Sarah out of their lives.

From the window, she watched her husband gallop off across the pasture. He would be gone for a couple of hours. Ideally it wouldn't take her that long. She pulled out her phone and called up a video online that told her how to access informa-tion on her husband's navigation system in his SUV.

He'd left the vehicle parked in the garage. All the better. She didn't want one of his daughters stopping by and catching her. They didn't come and go as often now with the press camped out by the gate, so in a way that was a blessing. Try living with six young girls who couldn't stand the sight of you.

She told herself that those days were behind her. Buckmaster's daughters were finally old enough that none of them would be moving in with them at the White House. An occasional visit for a few sentimental photos of the happy, well-adjusted family would be perfect. Maybe the girls could stay out of trouble and keep the focus on their father, she thought as she went down to the garage.

Once behind the wheel, she turned on the navigation system. It didn't take long to find what she was looking for. She took out her cell phone. "All right, I'm in his vehicle," she said when Chuck answered.

"See if you recognize the last place he went."

"The last place he went was to see her."

"You're sure?"

"Yes."

"Give me the information."

"Not until I know that you'll continue to portray Sarah Hamilton as the lunatic she is," she said.

"After I get an exclusive with Sarah, everyone will get on board with whatever I write. It will go viral. No one is going to start printing that she is mother of the year, trust me."

"Whenever a man says 'trust me,' I break out in hives."

"You want this woman out of your life? Well, I'm the man to do it. Give me the information. I'll take care of Sarah Hamilton."

Angelina sucked in a deep breath and let it out slowly. "If you betray me—"

He chuckled. "Would I betray the soon-to-be first lady? I'm no fool."

She'd warned Buckmaster about never making bargains with the kind of people who would one

344

day call in an IOU that he couldn't afford to pay.

But she would give anything to be rid of Sarah. Even by making a deal with Chuck Barrow, a journalist who would sell his own mother for a story.

She read off the information from the navigation system.

The tap on the side window made her jump.

"Is anything wrong?" Kat Hamilton mouthed.

Angelina ended her call, removed Buckmaster's key from the ignition, and shoved open the SUV door, forcing her stepdaughter back. She'd seen Kat's expression. The most suspicious of Buckmaster's six daughters, Kat was the one she often found watching her. It was no secret Kat didn't like or trust her.

"I thought I'd left my scarf in your father's car," she said, trying hard not to be flustered. Kat would have seen the navigation system on since it was the only light within the SUV when she'd walked up. She would tell her father, but he wasn't suspicious by nature like his daughter, so he would believe anything Angelina told him.

"Did you find it?" Kat inquired, her tone calling Angelina a liar as if she'd said the actual words.

"No, I must have left it elsewhere."

"Apparently." One look into Kat's gray eyes,

eyes so intent like her father's, and Angelina knew that the young woman couldn't wait to tell.

"If you're looking for your father—"

"No," she said. "He just left on his daily ride, didn't he?"

Kat had always been the problem child. "I've been so busy packing for our trip that I hadn't noticed," Angelina said.

Later, when it came out that Sarah had been found hiding out in a cabin in the mountains, would Kat put it together?

Angelina told herself she would cross that minefield when she had to. Ideally, Buckmaster would be too busy campaigning to give credence to Kat's accusations.

Brody McTavish stuck his head through the hospital room doorway. "I heard you were causing trouble and they wanted to kick you out."

Jace smiled at his friend. "I can't get into too much trouble," he said, pointing at the cast. "I'll be on crutches for weeks."

"Well, don't worry about your animals. I'll see to them until you're on your feet again." Brody turned serious as he approached the bed. "I'm just glad you're alive. I tried to join the search, but they turned us back. Half the county was ready to come look for you. But I knew if anyone could save the fair damsel and get both of you out of those mountains, it was you."

"I have to admit I had my doubts a few times before we got out of there. I suppose you heard about the Spencers."

Brody nodded. "How's Bo?"

"I don't think it's really hit her yet. A violent criminal had her for days up there. When I found her—" he shook his head "—she was tied to a tree. She was in rough shape."

"I heard the bastard's dead?"

Jace nodded. "Bo was amazing. Where she found the strength to do what she did at the end . . ."

Brody was grinning at him. "So the two of you made up. About time."

"It's not that simple. Thinking you're going to die in that kind of situation . . . you say and do things."

"Did you say or do anything you didn't mean?" his friend asked.

"No, but Bo—"

"You still don't trust her?" Brody asked with a curse. "What is it going to take?"

Jace shook his head. "Time."

"Well, you're going to have that, laid up the way you're going to be."

"Aren't you curious why she went to jail?" his cousin asked when Alex stopped by Big Timber Java before his date later that evening.

"Her boyfriend set her up. That's why he's in

prison and she only got a little jail time. How do I look?"

Jeff considered him for a moment before he laughed. "Geeky. Don't you own a pair of jeans?"

He'd taken great pains to look his best. "Of course I do, but it's a *date*."

His cousin shrugged. "You look like you always do."

"And that's bad?"

Jeff laughed again. "Hey, she agreed to go out with you, didn't she? Go with that. Maybe she likes uptight guys."

When he showed up at Emily's front door, he'd been nervous. Maybe he should have played down the date and worn jeans, but with a nice shirt. Her house was cute, brightly painted and sitting among some tall pines.

He took a mint from his pocket and quickly popped it into his mouth as he waited, then knocked again. His palms were sweating. He'd never been like this before a first date.

It was Jodie who opened the door. "Hi."

"Hi." She had her mother's big blue eyes. Hard to say if she had her mother's hair since Jodie's was blond, and clearly Emily had dyed whatever her original hair color had been a raven's-wing black.

"Mommy bought a dress, but now she isn't sure she likes it," the child said.

"Jodie." Emily's voice from back in the house

had a nervous plea to it that made him relax a little.

He laughed. "I'm sure she looks beautiful in whatever she wears," he told the precocious three-year-old.

"Invite him in," Emily called. She appeared a few moments later wearing a green paisley print dress and heels. The dress fit her perfectly, accentuating curves he'd never seen on her before. "Is it too much?"

He shook his head. "You look . . . beautiful." She'd replaced the row of earrings she usually wore in each ear with only one set of silver hoops. A single silver chain necklace gleamed at her throat. He could see that she felt uncomfortable in clothing she normally didn't wear. She'd dressed as she'd thought he would want her to dress.

"I think you're beautiful no matter what you're wearing, though," he added. "You didn't have to change your usual style for me."

She smiled. "The truth? I feel like I sold out."

"Then change, please. I don't want to change anything about you. If you feel uncomfortable in the dress—"

"No," she said, running both palms down her hips. "I feel . . . almost ladylike. It's okay once in a while," she added with a laugh.

He truly did love that laugh. The babysitter, Emily's landlady, Ruby, arrived, and they left. The ice broken, they talked about growing up in

Montana and people's misconceptions about the state, about their favorite movies, about what food they would pick if they got only one choice while stranded on a desert island.

They had fun, something Alex hadn't done in a long time. Eventually he'd have to ask her about the man he'd seen in the car. But he didn't want to spoil this evening.

When Bo called the hospital, she learned that Jace had been released. His friend Brody had given him a ride home. She'd hoped he would have called her.

Up on the mountain, she'd thought that they'd been given another chance. She loved Jace. He was a good man. But she could understand why he wouldn't trust her love. She'd hurt him too badly five years ago.

When she'd visited him in his hospital room, Jace had been distant.

"You need time to heal," he'd said. "I know you're strong and that you think the ordeal you've been through is over. But give it some time."

"Don't you mean, give us some time?" she'd asked.

He'd smiled. "I love you, Bo. That won't change."

"But you think I'll change my mind again."

"A little time won't hurt anything, will it?" he'd asked.

She couldn't bear the thought of them going

back to the way they'd been the past five years. She thought about their lovemaking on the mountain, the promises they'd made. True, they both needed time to heal. But fate had brought them together again, and she wasn't going to let Jace go without a fight.

He could have all the time he wanted. But that didn't mean she was walking away. She picked up his favorite pizza and beer and bought a movie she knew he would like. Her car smelled like sausage, pepperoni and mushroom pizza as she drove out to Jace's ranch. She hadn't been out here for five years. The house, though old, was freshly painted white with pale green shutters. The barn looked new and so did the corrals.

She thought about what Emily had told her. How had Jace, just a teenager, saved the ranch after his parents' deaths? He'd even gotten good grades while working two jobs. She thought of the tuxedo he'd rented with money he'd saved and how excited Emily said he'd been.

It made her heart ache to think what he'd been through at such a young age. She considered what had happened to her up on the mountain. Jace's hardship had turned him into the man he was now. It would take time to know how much her capture on the mountain had affected her.

But she'd survived it. She had awakened

grateful and filled with new hope. She felt stronger, more confident, more sure of what she wanted in life. What she wanted was Jace. Now all she had to do was prove it to him.

Balancing the pizza, a six-pack of cold beers and the DVD she'd bought in town, she knocked at the door. She could hear voices inside the house and felt a moment of panic.

What if there was another woman here?

Of course he might have a girlfriend. But wouldn't Emily have mentioned that? Wouldn't Bo have heard he was dating?

The door opened. For a moment, she didn't recognize Brody McTavish, a neighboring rancher. Brody was dark-haired like Jace and equally as handsome.

"Well, look who's here!" Brody said over his shoulder, then gave Bo a wink.

"Who is it?" Jace called from somewhere deep in the house.

"Dinner, I believe." Brody grinned. Taking the bag with the beer and movie, motioned her inside. "How do you feel about pizza?" he called to Jace.

"You ordered pizza?"

"I couldn't have ordered something you needed more," he said more quietly to Bo as he led her back to the large living room.

A fire crackled from a stone fireplace, bathing the nicely furnished room in warmth. Jace sat in an overstuffed leather chair, his casted leg resting on an ottoman. Surprise registered on his face, then curiosity. "Bo?"

"I heard somewhere that you were a fan of pizza," she said.

"And beer," Brody said as he pulled two bottles from the bag. "Let me get an opener for these." He disappeared down the hall.

"If this is a bad time . . ."

"Your timing couldn't be better," Jace said as Brody returned with the beer and opener. "I was getting to the point where I couldn't take another of this man's jokes."

Brody laughed. "He loves my jokes. Don't let him kid you. Oh, look at the time," he said glancing at his watch. "Call if you need me." He grinned, picked up his cowboy hat from where he'd apparently tossed it earlier and, tipping the brim, turned to leave.

"Please don't go on my account. I should have called."

"Later," Brody said.

"Thanks for saving me," Jace said, then turned serious. "Really."

Bo stood in the middle of the suddenly much too quiet room after Brody left.

It was Jace who broke the ice. "Did I hear him say you brought pizza?"

They ate in front of the fire and talked about everything but their ordeal on the mountain, senior prom or the foundation's missing money. Bo figured Emily had already told him about the overseas hacker.

The time passed so quickly that they didn't get around to watching the movie before she had to leave.

"Thanks," Jace said as she pulled on her jacket. "Dinner was delicious."

"Do you like barbecued short ribs?" she asked impulsively. "I was thinking I might put some on tomorrow. I could maybe—"

"That movie you bought?" he asked. "Maybe we could watch it tomorrow."

It wasn't until after dinner and the movie that Emily told Alex about Harrison Ames and how he had controlled her.

"There's something I need to tell *you,* then," he said.

When he told her about the man who'd been watching her, Emily's throat closed, strangling any speech.

"He's been there the past few times when you've taken your coffee break," Alex said. "Big guy, lots of tattoos, longish dark brown hair, driving one of those large older-model American cars."

She nodded numbly.

"You know who he is?"

"No." But if he'd been watching her, she had

an idea why. Just as she had a pretty good idea who had probably sent him. "You're sure he's—"

"I'm sure. As soon as you leave, he watches you, then he drives away."

She clasped her hands together to keep them from trembling as she thought about the break-in at her house.

"I didn't mean to upset you," Alex said. "I thought you might know him."

Emily shook her head, but the description could fit any number of Harrison's friends.

"Emily?" Alex reached over and placed his hand over hers. "I took down his license plate number. If you really don't know him, maybe I should take it to the sheriff."

She flinched at the thought. If it was one of Harrison's friends . . . "I can't believe you did that," Emily said.

"I hope you aren't angry."

"Angry? No, it's just that Harrison is dangerous, and if this guy is a friend of his . . ."

Alex laughed. "I'm tougher than I look."

She tried to smile, suddenly scared. "He could have been sent by my ex."

"Why would he send . . . Sorry, it's none of my business."

"I'm sure it's nothing," she said.

He nodded. They'd been sitting out in front of her house. Now he killed the engine and opened his door. She was already part way out of his car when she realized he was coming around to her side to open her door for her.

She felt like crying as he held the door open and she slowly climbed out. Her eyes burned, and her throat contracted with disappointment. She'd felt the change in him the minute she'd said she was sure it was nothing.

They both knew that wasn't the case, but she didn't want him seeing that side of her old life. And now he had.

"I had a nice time," she said as he walked her to the door.

"I'm glad," he said, stopping on the bottom step. "I did, too. Emily, I'm here if you need me." He held up a hand. "I know. You can take care of your-self, but we all need someone sometime, okay?"

She nodded.

He reached to draw out his wallet. "Does your babysitter need a ride home?"

Always the gentleman, she thought.

"No, my landlady lives next door."

He held out a twenty.

"That's too much," she said, not taking it.

He dug out a ten and looked at her.

"It really isn't necessary." He pushed it into her hand. An awkward few moments passed.

"Alex—" His gaze met hers, and she felt a warm rush of strong emotion.

"I guess I'll see you Monday," he said.

She nodded, even though she wasn't sure the foundation's doors wouldn't be closed forever by Monday.

He turned and walked back toward his car. She wanted to call after him, but she didn't know what more she could have said. She'd hoped that she'd put that old life behind her. More than anything, she hadn't wanted that life to touch this new one she was building.

But hearing about the man who'd been watching her, Emily knew she hadn't escaped. Her old life had found her and at the worst possible time, just when she was starting to feel good about herself. Harrison might be locked up in prison, but she would bet that he'd sent someone to see what she was up to.

As Alex drove away, she looked around, scared. Not for herself. But for Alex. It would be just like Harrison to have someone hurt Alex if he thought she cared about the man. She was just thankful that Jodie wasn't Harrison's child.

She didn't see anyone parked down the dark street, but she couldn't be sure that the man hadn't been watching her both at work—and at home.

Which meant he knew about Jodie.

She grabbed the end of the porch railing as her knees threatened to give way. For a moment, she couldn't catch her breath, couldn't think or move. Of course that had been the man who'd broken into her house and taken the photo of her and Jodie. Harrison must think that Jodie was his.

What was she going to do? Maybe more to the point, what was the man watching her going to do?

When Emily entered the house, she found her landlady snoring on the couch. She went straight to her daughter's bedroom. Jodie was curled up in her bed, fast asleep.

As she looked at her baby's angelic face, her emotions bubbled up. She wanted more than anything to be a good mother. She'd made so many mistakes and feared she would make more. But above all else, she had to protect her daughter.

Finding her wouldn't have been a problem because she'd come home to the area where she'd grown up. So why bother watching her?

She wiped at her tears, realizing she was crying, and thought of Alex and their date. She'd had fun. That surprised her more than she would ever admit to anyone.

Alex was smart and funny. She liked him. She hoped she would see him again. He didn't seem like the other men in her life who'd let her down. She hoped that would prove true. As Jace always said, she had a real trust issue.

Jace. She'd been so worried about him, and for

a good reason, as it turned out. At least he was safe now.

She'd heard there was another storm coming in. Earlier she'd seen the clouds over the Crazies. Now she heard the plink of rain at the window and glanced up.

Through the grate her landlady had put on Jodie's window, Emily saw a face looking in at her.

She screamed.

Jace couldn't have been more surprised to see Bo at his door. Since they'd gotten off the mountain, he'd told himself that they didn't know each other anymore. That the five years they'd been apart this last time had felt like a lifetime and too much water had run under the bridge.

Also, he'd worried that once safe, Bo would realize the same thing.

Then she'd shown up with pizza, beer and a movie. "You remembered my favorite pizza," he'd said earlier as they sat in front of the fire.

"I remember everything," she'd said without looking at him.

He'd nodded to himself.

The evening had been pleasant. He'd forgotten that they used to be friends. Or that she probably knew him better than he knew himself.

Take things slow, he warned himself now, then

laughed. With his leg in this huge cast, the only way he would be taking things was slow. He had weeks laid up. Way too much time to think.

But Bo was coming back tomorrow with short ribs, another of his favorites. He smiled to himself.

"So how did it go?" Brody asked when he called not ten minutes after Bo had left.

"Are you hiding outside my house?" Jace joked.

"I just happened to see her SUV go by. Mere coincidence. Well?"

"It was . . . nice."

"Nice?" Brody laughed. "Let me ask you this. What is Bo's favorite pizza?"

"Pineapple and Canadian bacon."

"Uh-huh. The woman loves you."

"What if it is too late for us?"

"How can you even say that?"

"Because what happened up on the mountain happened because she thought we were both going to die the next day. Now that she's back home—"

"Wait. Did what I think happened on the mountain happen?" Brody laughed, knowing he wasn't going to get an answer. "You overthink life. This isn't like running a ranch, buying and selling cattle. It's *love*. It doesn't take a lot of thinking. It just is."

"Spoken by the man who has avoided love for thirty-some years."

"I just know it when I see it. Holler if you need me, but I'm assuming Bo will be back tomorrow." There was a smile in his voice. "Did you happen to leave me any pizza?"

Alex got Emily's call before he reached his house outside of town.

"I think it was the man you saw," she cried. "He was standing outside Jodie's window. He . . ." Her voice broke. "I think he was the one who broke in a few days ago. I thought nothing was missing, but then I realized that a photo I had by my bed of me and Jodie was gone."

"Did you call the sheriff's office?"

"Yes, they were just here. I told them you might have the man's license plate number. He fit the description of the man you told me about. The deputy wanted us both to come down there. I know it's late—"

"I'll pick you up. Do you have someone to watch Jodie?"

"My landlady. I scared ten years off her life when I screamed. Woke Jodie up, but she's fine now. My landlady is making her hot cocoa."

"I'll be right there."

When he arrived at the house, Jodie was curled up on the couch with Emily's landlady.

"Are you all right?" he asked as he and Emily drove to the sheriff's office.

"I'm fine. I was just startled."

He glanced over at her. She seemed calm, in control. She wasn't the kind to get hysterical. Instead, she seemed even more protective of her daughter. He liked that about her.

The deputy was waiting for them. After taking down the information, he asked Alex more about the times he'd seen the man.

"You're sure he was watching Miss Calder?"

"Definitely. That's what made me notice him. He seemed so intent on her comings and goings."

The deputy turned to Emily. "You say he might have some connection to your former boy-friend, Harrison Ames?"

"I don't know that for sure. It just seems likely."

The deputy studied his notes for a moment. "You say entry into your house was through your daughter's window and that the photo taken was of the two of you." He glanced at Alex, then back to Emily. "Where is the baby's father?"

"He's out of the picture."

"Is it possible this man has a connection to the baby's father?"

Alex found himself waiting for the answer, as well. The man's interest in Jodie worried him.

"There's no connection," she said with a shake of her head. "Jodie's father didn't travel in the same circles as my ex-boyfriend."

The deputy seemed to think about that for a moment. "This man seems interested in your daughter. If he is a friend of your ex-boyfriend, who I understand is serving time in prison, then . . . is there any chance that Harrison Ames thinks Jodie is his?"

When Emily didn't answer, Alex looked over at her. Her face had crumpled, and he could see that she was fighting tears. He reached over and took her hand.

"If it would be easier, I can leave," he whispered to her.

She squeezed his hand and shook her head. Lifting her face, she met the deputy's gaze. "I became pregnant shortly after Harrison's arrest. Her father is married, an upstanding member of society in Billings, a decent man. He and I . . . it was a moment of weakness for him. I asked for a paternity test after Jodie was born, not because I wanted anything from the man, but so I knew who my daughter's father was. It wasn't Harrison."

Alex squeezed her hand back.

The deputy nodded. "It seems Harrison might be thinking otherwise. Would you be willing to have another paternity test done to assure him he is wrong?"

She nodded.

"We'll talk to this man. I doubt we can get him on breaking and entering, but we'll try. Mostly we just want to make sure he doesn't continue shadowing you," the deputy said and got to his feet.

As they left, Emily said to Alex, "You didn't know what you were getting into, did you? I would understand if—"

"I told you, I want to get to know you."

"Well, you're getting to know me. I'm so sorry."

He shook his head. "Hey, we all come with a past. Someday maybe I'll tell you about mine."

She looked over him as they walked out of the sheriff's department, into the beautiful summer night. She saw a sadness in his expression as if he was thinking about that past. Maybe he, too, had regrets. "I can't wait to hear about it."

Alex caught her hand and brought her to a stop. Cupping her face in his hands, he kissed her. As he drew back, he smiled. "I had a wonderful time tonight."

She laughed and shook her head. "Even a visit to the sheriff's department?"

"Next date I think we should go to a movie that Jodie can see."

Emily smiled through her tears. "That sounds wonderful."

When Russell drove up to the cabin the next day, he didn't see Sarah. Normally she would have come out on the deck. He felt a jolt of worry. What if the press had found her? Reporters had been clamoring to get her story. It was why he'd hidden her out here. What if she'd fallen and—

When she appeared at the side of the cabin, he was confused to see that she was dressed in jeans and a flannel shirt. He hadn't purchased either for her. Even stranger, she had a long-handled shovel in one hand and he could see even from a distance that her hands were muddy, as were the knees of the jeans.

"Sarah?" he called, feeling slightly off balance by this image of the woman.

Not only that, she had seemed both surprised and upset by his unexpected appearance. Normally he would have called on his way to let her know he was coming. Today he'd come on the spur of the moment. He'd been thinking about her and had just driven toward the mountains to check on her.

Now he felt as if he'd caught her doing something she shouldn't have.

"Is everything all right?" he asked as he got out and walked up the slope to her.

She gave him an embarrassed shake of her head. "You're going to think me so foolish. I found a dead cat this morning on the deck. The poor thing. I couldn't tell if it starved to death or died of some illness. I found these clothes in the closet and a shovel in the shed out back."

"You should have called me. I would have been happy to do it for you," he said, noting that she looked winded as if the exertion had worn her out. He reminded himself that she probably wasn't used to the altitude compared with where she'd spent the past twenty-two years.

"I put the cat in a plastic garbage bag and took it back into the woods to bury it. I didn't realize what a job it was going to be." She sighed.

Even dirty and tired, her cheek smeared with soil, she looked beautiful. The physical work had put color in her cheeks, and her blue eyes shone with something close to excitement. He realized she must have been going crazy up here for some-thing to do.

"Let me get cleaned up," she said. "I need to wash these clothes before your daughter finds out I borrowed them."

"She said to use whatever you found up here," he assured her as he took the shovel from her. "I'll put this away for you. I picked up some groceries for you, a couple of steaks I could throw on the grill and a huckleberry pie I bought at the Branding Iron café. I hope you're hungry."

"Ravenous," she said as she trotted up the steps like a woman half her age.

Later, Russell noticed that Sarah's energy level had dropped. He could see that something was bothering her and guessed it was the fact that the senator was leaving again. He'd seen on the news last night that Senator Buckmaster Hamilton was scheduled for a debate in Iowa in a few days. That meant he and his wife would be leaving Montana for an unspecified amount of time.

He decided to address the elephant in the room head-on. "I heard that Buckmaster is leaving for the campaign trail," he said and took a bite of the meal he'd brought.

"Yes, he called to tell me earlier," she said without looking up from her plate. "Now that Bo is safe, there's nothing keeping him here."

"Then Angelina is going with him?"

Sarah looked up. "She's his wife."

"Are you going to be all right?" he asked and reached across the table to take her hand. She'd seemed more than a little distressed earlier when he'd found her coming back from burying the dead cat. There was still something jittery about her. He feared she was thinking about taking off for only God knew where.

"If you're unhappy staying here . . ."

"No. That is, I love spending time with you. The rest of my day . . ." She looked away.

He felt his heart do a little loop-de-loop. "So you're considering moving onto the ranch as the senator suggested?"

She laughed. "Not as long as Angelina is alive!" She shook her head and squeezed his hand, then let it go. "That isn't what I meant. It's taken me a while, but I've come to realize that I no longer have a place in Buck's life. So," she said, trying to look more cheerful, "I need to get a life of my own."

That sounded good to him, unless getting a life of her own meant leaving. He asked her as much.

"You've been wonderful, but I can't keep doing this." She held up her hand to kill his protests. "For all of our sakes, I need to move on."

He threw down his napkin and rose from the table. Reaching for her hand, he pulled her to her feet.

Russell had never been impulsive. He thought out everything before making a decision. He told himself he'd been thinking about this for months. Even as he drew Sarah into his arms, he knew this was still out of character for him.

But he couldn't let her leave. Over these months, he'd fallen in love with her. He was tired of pretending otherwise, and he said as much.

"Marry me," he said. "Sarah—" He was ready to list all the reasons they should be together, but she didn't give him a chance.

"You're right. I need to find my own happiness. That's what Buck did. He's got his political career and a wife by his side." She met his gaze. "But I can't destroy your life in an attempt to make mine better."

"You won't destroy my life."

She let out a laugh and stepped away. "You don't know how close I was to saying yes."

"Then do."

She shook her head. "Even not knowing where I've been, what I've been, you'd marry me?"

"I love you."

She took a breath and let it out slowly. "You know me better than anyone. At least what there is to know."

"Once you move on, the press will lose interest in you. You can have a normal life."

She stared at him for a long moment. "Normal?"

"Wouldn't you like a normal life, Sarah, out of the public eye?"

She nodded, a tear coursing down one cheek. "What about my past?"

"It hasn't come after you. It's been months. Photos from your time with Buckmaster have been plastered all over the internet and newspapers around the world. If there is a past that you have to fear, then you should have heard from it by now, don't you think?"

She wiped at the tear with her free hand. "I don't want to hurt you."

"You won't. And should this past that you fear come looking for you, I'll take care of it."

"Buck will be—"

"Off campaigning for president with his wife at his side," he interrupted, knowing what she was going to say. Of course, Buck would be furious. If he'd had his way, he would have Sarah living on the ranch, locked away so he wouldn't have to give up either wife.

"Your former husband has had months to make a change if he was so inclined," Russell said not unkindly. "He chose the presidency and the wife who could best get him there."

Sarah heard the truth in Russell's words, but it didn't make it any easier. Maybe Buckmaster had kept her in prison for the missing years she couldn't remember. Maybe not. But there was no doubt that she was a prisoner now.

Russell was right. Her options were limited. She could take off, try to disappear again, but with her photo—even one from years ago—everywhere, she wouldn't be able to run from the publicity. Even with the money that Buck had given her to live on, she would be a recluse, hidden away out of sight while he followed his dream.

"You have no idea what you're proposing."

"Don't I? The press will quit hounding you once you break your ties with Buckmaster."

"I'll still be the mother of his children."

"His *grown* children. There's no story there. Right now, it's a love triangle. You're the odd woman out. As Mrs. Russell Murdock, you'll be a forgotten footnote in history."

She stared at him. He was offering her anonymity.

"Let Buckmaster go. He's let you go."

She felt herself weaken. He was right. She and Buck could never be together again. Even if something happened to Angelina and there was a chance for her and Buck to find each other again, the press would crucify him. He could never get elected with her at his side. Buck deserved to be president. He'd worked hard for it. No matter what he might have done after she tried to kill herself, she believed he would be a good president.

"Well, Sarah?" Russell asked. "Will you marry me? I'll get down on one knee if—"

"That isn't necessary. The media is convinced I'm a flake, a lunatic, a bad mother and a mental case. Can we do this right by starting with an engagement? Not a long one. Just long enough that this doesn't come off as something I've done that is even crazier."

He smiled. "I'll get you a ring tomorrow."

"I will need to talk to Buck first." She saw him grit his teeth.

"Whatever you need to do."

Sarah studied his handsome face, thinking about the grave she'd dug earlier today. Now she felt as if she was digging Russell's. He knew how she still felt about Buck. He really seemed to believe that his love could conquer all. She almost felt sorry for him. She tried to tell herself she wasn't using this kind, loving man, but she knew she was.

"You might want to prepare your daughter."

His expression said he doubted anything could prepare his daughter for this. "I don't care what anyone else thinks."

That was good, because she suspected the county would think he'd lost his mind. Love did that to a person, she thought.

"I should call Buck."

Senator Buckmaster Hamilton stared at his open suitcase. In Washington, he had a staff. But here at the ranch, he preferred doing things himself. He liked his life to be as down-to-earth as possible. It's why he rode his horse every afternoon he was home. He didn't want to forget his roots.

It was also why he didn't own a jet, even though Angelina had never understood it. He was a man of the people. It was why he thought he would be a good president.

He realized he'd been standing there staring at his open suitcase ever since Sarah's call.

"You can't be serious!" he'd cried when she'd told him she was going to marry Russell Murdock.

"Buck, I need to move on with my life. You have. Give me that same chance."

Phone to his ear, he'd paced the room, too worked up to think of what to say, let alone what to do. "I don't know what to say."

"Say best wishes."

"When is the wedding?"

"Not right away."

"Good. Promise me you won't announce your engagement until I get back."

"Buck—"

"You know I have these fund-raisers and debates coming up. I should have a break at the end of September. If marrying Russell is the right thing, then waiting a couple months isn't asking too much, is it?"

"What would be the point?"

"I need time to get used to this. You've hit me with so much . . . Promise me you'll wait. Also, I'd like these debates and press conferences to be about what needs to be done in this country— not about my personal life."

"All right."

He began to pack, each step weighted with the impact of Sarah's news. Now that Bo was safe and things were taken care of at the foundation, it was time to get on the campaign trail. His constituents were clamoring for him at fund-raisers. He was scheduled for several debates along the way as he made a sweep through the Midwest this coming week.

He would be starting with the early caucus states. Iowa, New Hampshire and South Carolina. He needed that early lead if he hoped to lock in the party nomination by next summer.

Feeling light-headed, he sat down a moment on the bed and rubbed a hand over his face. Hadn't he seen this coming? Only a fool couldn't see how Russell Murdock felt about her. But Sarah . . . He shook his head and got to his feet again. He had to get packed. He had to keep putting one foot in front of the other. He was going to be the next president.

But there was no elation, no sense of adventure, no joy at the prospect. It felt more like a duty that had been handed down to him from his father. He couldn't let anyone see how much pain he was in, especially Angelina.

He'd always traveled a lot, usually with her at his side. While they hadn't discussed it, he knew she was planning to go with him. He thought of Sarah and quickly pushed the image of her away. His earliest dreams had been of Sarah standing next to him when he became president of the United States.

A news anchor's voice droned from the television in the corner of the bedroom. "Our lead story this morning is the disappearance of journalist Chuck Barrow. Barrow, a correspondent for a news media organization, had been covering Senator Buckmaster Hamilton's election. His SUV was found last night in a ravine at the edge of the Crazy Mountains in Montana, but there was no sign of the journalist. A bloody coat found in the car would indicate that he was injured and might have wandered off into the mountains in a confused state. Local search and rescue teams only recently found—"

He snapped off the TV at the sound of footsteps in the hallway. "Are you packed?" Angelina asked from the bedroom doorway.

"Just about." He turned. "How about you?"

She smiled her campaign trail smile. "All packed. I thought we might go over some of the debate questions on the way to the airport."

He nodded although he thought he had the issues down cold. Nor was public speaking a problem for him, especially when he was talking about something he felt so strongly about. For a while, he'd forgotten what was important. Doing what he could to help his country at this critical juncture—that was where he needed to turn his attention.

Thanks to Angelina, he had a good support system in place. With her brother, Lane, gone, she'd taken over, hiring the people who would make his campaign run like a well-oiled machine. That was her strong point—that and standing by her man.

"What was that on the news just then?" She frowned toward the television.

Buckmaster shook his head. "I wasn't listening," he said, realizing it was true. He'd been lost in his own thoughts.

She studied him for a moment. "We're going

to do this. We've come too far to let anything or anyone stop us," she said as she moved to him. She kissed his cheek and stepped back to meet his gaze. "Everything we've been through, it's all going to be worth it. You'll go down in history as one of the great presidents."

He tried to smile. "I hope you're right," he said, thinking of Sarah, his daughters and the choices he'd made to reach this point. The price had been high, but he suspected it would get higher before the election next year.

EPILOGUE

Jace found himself almost sorry when it was time for the cast to come off his leg. He'd loved Bo's visits. They'd gotten to know each other again, could joke or not have to talk at all. Some nights Brody would join them. Jace could tell that he liked Bo and approved.

"Well?" Emily demanded now as she drove him to the doctor to get the cast taken off.

"Well, what?" he asked even though he knew exactly what she was asking.

"You and Bo. Well?"

"Not sure what you want me to say, little sister."

"You know darned well. I've seen the way you light up when she's around, and I've never seen Bo this happy. She's always smiling at work. I actually heard her singing to herself the other day as she was sending a fax."

"That must have been terrifying. I've heard her sing." He mugged a face.

"Bo sings nice," Jodie said from her car seat behind him.

He laughed and smiled back at his niece. "I was just kidding. She has a beautiful voice."

"Don't blow this," Emily said. "You have to . . . do something."

He rubbed a hand over his jaw as he looked out at the mountains in the distance and remembered how close he'd come to losing Bo. The Crazies were beautiful this morning in the sun, the peaks still snowcapped, the sky above them a breathtaking cloudless blue. And yet he felt a chill at the memory of what she'd been through up there. He'd wanted to give her some time to get over the ordeal. He had also wanted to give her time to change her mind, he realized.

"I've been doing some thinking about it," he admitted.

Emily pulled into the doctor's office parking lot. "I couldn't believe you never told her why you stood her up that night. I wish she could have seen you in your tux. I know the two of you would have a houseful of kids by now."

"Now there is a frightening thought."

Emily turned to him. He saw the girl she'd been and the woman she'd become since having her daughter. "I've never thanked you or told you how sorry I am for all the grief I've put you through over the years, Jace."

He looked at his sister and realized she really was growing up. He hugged her, thinking about the struggles they'd been through. Maybe it was time to look toward the future instead of back.

"How are things with Alex?" he asked as he reached for his crutches.

His sister beamed. "Good. Really good."

"Jace, what's going on?" Bo asked as Jace tied the blindfold into place and then took her hand and led her out the back door of his house. She'd come out to his house at his request. It had been weeks since he'd gotten his cast off, but they had made a tradition of pizza night and a movie at his house.

What she hadn't expected was to find him waiting with a blindfold.

"I know we promised to look to the future and have no regrets about the past, but there is one thing I wish I could change in the past."

"Okay, you're scaring me."

He laughed. "No, I'm not," he said close to her ear. "I've seen your courage, remember? Nothing scares you."

"Right." She put her free hand out as he led her through the summer night. When he stopped, she felt the rough side of a building. His barn. "Jace?"

A door creaked. He pulled her in, and the door closed behind her. She caught the faint smell of hay and something sweeter.

"Stand right here. Don't move and don't peek."

She stood perfectly still. She heard a rustle, then soft music. Smiling, she recognized the song. It was the one the committee had chosen as the theme song for their senior prom. Her eyes burned with tears.

Jace touched her arm. "Ready?"

She nodded, her heart lodged in her throat as he untied the blindfold. Bo blinked. The barn was decorated with tiny lights, crepe paper streamers and silver cardboard stars—just as she had helped decorate the school gym the day before the senior prom she never attended.

"Oh, Jace." He'd built a small dance floor at the center of it all. She turned to him. "You didn't have to do this."

"I've hated it all these years that I took away your senior prom," Jace said. "I know it's not the same—"

"It's perfect."

"Not yet." He motioned to the tack room. "I believe there is something in there for you. I'll be waiting here for you."

Bo crossed to the tack room. The dress was exactly like the one she'd chosen for their senior prom. She couldn't believe it since she'd discarded that dress after her disappointment. Her sisters, bless them, must have told him about the dress so he could find one like it. Now she fingered the silken fabric, eager to put it on. He'd thought of everything. There were shoes to go with it, a small table with a brush and her makeup along with a mirror.

Her fingers trembled as she slipped out of her shirt and jeans. She was actually breathless, her face flushed as she swooped her long hair up and pinned it into place. How had Jace done all this? He must have gotten her sisters to help, and Brody and of course Emily.

She smiled and fought tears as she realized just what it had taken to do this for her. As she slipped the dress on and let it drop over her body, she felt like Cinderella going to the ball. She slid her feet into the heels and then glanced at herself in the mirror. Her cheeks were flushed, her eyes bright as emeralds. She almost didn't recognize herself in the happiness on her face.

Pushing open the door, she stepped out and saw Jace standing on the small dance floor, dressed in a tuxedo. Wow. The sight of him took her breath away. Just when she thought he couldn't look any more handsome . . .

He let out a low whistle. "Bo, you're . . . so beautiful."

"So are you."

She stepped to him, thinking of all those nights they'd sat around watching movies and eating pizza. They'd found their way back to each other. Maybe the third time was the charm. She sure hoped so.

"You said up on the mountain that your only regret was not dancing with me," he said shyly as he held out his arms.

She felt as if she'd been waiting years for this moment. Her heart soaring, she stepped into Jace's arms.

•••

Jace didn't believe in fairy tales, but this night felt like one. They'd danced as if dancing under real stars. He finally pulled her close and kissed her. Desire and something even stronger coursed through him. *Love.* He'd never wanted anyone the way he wanted her.

But he wanted her for more than just tonight. He wanted her for always. He'd asked her once before to marry him, but she hadn't been ready.

"Jace, this was wonderful," she said, a little breathless as the kiss ended.

"Yeah?" He brushed his fingers over her cheek and met her gaze. "I made you one other promise up there in the mountains."

Her green eyes sparkled. "I thought you might have forgotten."

"Not likely." He cocked his head at her. "Have you changed your mind?"

She grinned. "Not likely."

He took her hand. "Then come with me."

The night air felt warm as a summer rain shower as they walked from the barn back to his house. Once inside, he led her to the bedroom.

"A real bed," she said, smiling up at him.

"But like I told you up in the Crazies, I don't want to make love with you unless it is for the right reasons," he said.

"Like the fact that I'm in love with you and you're crazy about me?" she asked.

He chuckled. "That's a good place to start. I *am* crazy about you. I love you, Bo. See that bed, though? I want you in it, but not just tonight. I'm a long-term commitment kind of cowboy."

"Is that right? Good thing you found the right cowgirl, then, wouldn't you say?"

Jace swung her up into his arms, carried her into the bedroom and kicked the door shut.

Center Point Large Print
600 Brooks Road / PO Box 1
Thorndike, ME 04986-0001 USA

(207) 568-3717

US & Canada:
1 800 929-9108
www.centerpointlargeprint.com